ELIZABETH TAYLOR

(1912–1975) was born Elizabeth Coles in Reading, Berkshire. The daughter of an insurance inspector, she was educated at the Abbey School, Reading, and after leaving school worked as a governess and, later, in a library. At the age of twenty-four she married John William Kendall Taylor, a businessman, with whom she had a son and a daughter. She lived much of her married life in the village of Penn in Buckinghamshire.

Elizabeth Taylor wrote her first novel, *At Mrs Lippincote's* (1945), during the war while her husband was in the Royal Air Force. This was followed by *Palladian* (1946), *A View of the Harbour* (1947), *A Wreath of Roses* (1949), *A Game of Hide-and-Seek* (1951), *The Sleeping Beauty* (1953), *Angel* (1957), *In a Summer Season* (1961), *The Soul of Kindness* (1964), *The Wedding Group* (1968), *Mrs Palfrey at the Claremont* (1971) and *Blaming*, published posthumously in 1976. She has also published four volumes of short stories: *Hester Lilly and Other Stories* (1954), *The Blush and Other Stories* (1958), *A Dedicated Man and Other Stories* (1965) and *The Devastating Boys* (1972). Elizabeth Taylor has written a book for children, *Mossy Trotter* (1967); her short stories have been published in the *New Yorker*, *Harper's Bazaar*, *Harper's* magazine, *Vogue* and the *Saturday Evening Post*, and she is included in *Penguin Modern Stories 6*.

Critically Elizabeth Taylor is one of the most acclaimed British novelists of this century, and in 1984 *Angel* was selected as one of the Book Marketing Council's "Best Novels of Our Time". Virago publishes nine of her sixteen works of fiction.

A GAME OF
HIDE-AND-SEEK

ELIZABETH TAYLOR

With a New Introduction by
ELIZABETH JANE HOWARD

PENGUIN BOOKS – VIRAGO PRESS

PENGUIN BOOKS
Viking Penguin Inc., 40 West 23rd Street,
New York, New York 10010, U.S.A.
Penguin Books Ltd, Harmondsworth,
Middlesex, England
Penguin Books Australia Ltd, Ringwood,
Victoria, Australia
Penguin Books Canada Limited, 2801 John Street,
Markham, Ontario, Canada L3R 1B4
Penguin Books (N.Z.) Ltd, 182–190 Wairau Road,
Auckland 10, New Zealand.

First published in the United States of America by Alfred A. Knopf Inc. 1951
First published in Great Britain by Peter Davies 1951
This edition first published in Great Britain by Virago Press Limited 1986
Published in Penguin Books 1986

Printed in Great Britain by
Cox and Wyman Ltd, Reading, Berkshire.

INTRODUCTION

Elizabeth Taylor did not receive very much attention from the public during her lifetime, although she was much appreciated by her peers—notably Elizabeth Bowen and Ivy Compton-Burnett. Reviewers never tired of comparing Taylor with Bowen and here is a letter from Miss Compton-Burnett to Elizabeth Taylor that must have pleased her.

Dear Elizabeth, I have just read the last word of *A Game of Hide-and-Seek*. I never see books in terms of other books, or writers in terms of other writers, and I want simply to congratulate you on your achievement, and thank you for the admiration that it is so good to feel, and for the pleasure you have given me.

Elizabeth Bowen, in the best and most interesting review that was written of the novel when it came out calls it "a story whose theme is love". She goes on to say that

Two masterpiece love stories in our language, *Persuasion* and *Wuthering Heights*, have been written by women, but long ago: they await successors in our day. Still more, they await *a* successor; a single book which shall merge the elements in those two. To suggest that *A Game of Hide-and-Seek* fills this gap might both embarrass the author and, by making an exaggerated claim for it, injure the novel. Soberly speaking, however, it is not too much to say that *A Game of Hide-and-Seek* has something of the lucid delicacies of *Persuasion*, together with, at moments, more than a touch of the fiery-icy strangeness of *Wuthering Heights*. The characters are of less high voltage than Emily Brontë's; on the other hand, they dare and envisage much that Jane Austen's could not.

In spite of such professional acclaim, Elizabeth Taylor did suffer from lack of general notice. Her subject matter—the middle classes in the country—was just beginning to be unfashionable about the time when she began publishing in the forties; she had little—almost nothing—to do with the literary world; her nature was fastidious and reserved; in public, with people whom she did not know, she was definitively shy. I remember that the first time I met her was when I had to interview her on a television book programme when her novel *In a Summer Season* was published. The interview was supposed to last about eight minutes; of course I had read the book and very much admired it, and I had prepared some thirty questions to ask her about her writing—to be on the safe side. It wasn't: we got through those questions in about a minute and a half, since Mrs Taylor, looking like a trapped and rather beautiful owl, answered everything with two of the shortest words in the English language. It was years later that I met her again and gradually got to know and to love her, but a—mutual, I suppose it must have been—reserve meant that we never talked about writing. Her life was a very quiet one, centred upon her marriage and her children and grandchildren: her work—like Miss Austen's—quietly put aside for family or household requirements. This is not to say that her work was incidental to her life; I think it was central, but she was a very private person and guarded what was most precious to her with sensitive and successful care. She had great stamina and no arrogance.

A Game of Hide-and-Seek is her fifth novel, and in many ways I think it one of her best. Certainly, by then, she had found her voice, and this book displays the full spectrum of her gifts—the economy with which she can present a character, the skill with which she builds the environment and daily lives of her people so that you feel you know exactly what they might be doing even when they are not on the scene, her delicious funniness which is born of her own unique blend of humanity and razor-sharp observation that enables her to be sardonic, devastating, wry and sly, but mysteriously without malice, and—notably in this book—her capacity for romantic feeling and situation that never spills over into sentiment.

This is the love story of Harriet and Vesey, beginning when they are still children and enduring through long separation and other vicissitudes into middle age. Both are only children: Harriet's mother was one of the early feminists and it is a source of not quite covert enough disappointment to her that her daughter is without professional ambition—is apparently content to be the mother's help to her mother's friend Caroline. Vesey is also an only child: his mother works in a beauty clinic, so that in holidays he is left in a pale, satiny flat in London with nothing to do but frighten the housekeeper:

His way of beginning always with "For instance" or "However", as if some sort of conversation had gone on before, trapped her again and again.

"Nevertheless, should you find yourself passing Madame Tussaud's the woman with the hook through her stomach is quite an unusual little tableau ..."

Before she could shut the door, he would manage to add, flicking over the pages of a magazine "For those, of course, who like that sort of thing" as if he merely catered to her own sick fancies or love of the bizarre.

Vesey goes regularly to stay with his Aunt Caroline in the country, and it is there that he and Harriet have met since they were young. The novel begins when they are both eighteen. Here they are on their first walk together.

For the first ten minutes they were explaining to one another why they had chosen to go for this walk together. Boredom had driven them to it, they decided; a fear, on Vesey's part, lest he should be asked by Hugo to mow the lawn—a wish, on Harriet's part, to collect wild flowers for the children to draw. If the walk turned out badly, it could be the fault of neither, for neither had desired it nor attached importance to it . . . They had not yet learned to gush. Their protestations were of an oafish kind.

The walk, however, sets the scene—their pioneering with worldliness moves into a nervous, gentle exploration of love. Harriet is entirely absorbed in him: "in her diary, she walked right round Vesey and viewed him from every angle and in every light". Vesey

needed Harriet for his own reasons, to give him confidence and peace. In the shelter of her love, he hoped to have a second chance, to turn his personality away from what he most hated in himself, to try to find dignity before it was too late. Playing the fool bored him. With the failure of school behind him, he hoped to shake off the tedious habit.

In one sense, there is nothing particularly unusual about Harriet or Vesey, but as Mrs Taylor presents them, there are no two people exactly like them either. The subtle and seldom dealt with paradox of the ordinary and the original, the universal and the unique is something that this novelist really understands; it could indeed be said to be her hallmark. So many writers strain for original characters, or pose them in the dull and awkward stance of the ordinary man or woman, achieving in either case no more than a series of prototypes that illuminate nothing. We read those books and forget them, much as we forget the innumerable people we encounter in life with whom we have had no communication beyond the exchange of opinions, or facts, or of our habitual emotional responses. Mrs Taylor presents the reader with the opportunity of suspending judgement, of altering responses, of discovering more than they knew before: reality, after all,—at least in this context—is no more than each of us can believe. One reason that I re-read Elizabeth Taylor's novels is because she increases my sense of reality.

Harriet and Vesey take the two much younger children to the neighbouring Market Town for the day, which includes lunch in a Tudor café. In spite of the fact that the children have been brought up as vegetarian, Vesey orders chops.

[Joseph] became very loud and swaggering and took up the too-large knife and fork and began to cut his meat, which was on a level with his shoulders. Vesey took off his own jacket and folded it neatly for a cushion. Perched on this, Joseph wobbled insecurely. "Blood comes out", he said, looking uncertainly at his plate . . . "We can get bread any day," Joseph explained to the waitress who handed him a basket of rolls. His elbows stuck up like wings as he tried to cut his meat. When Vesey leant over to do this for him, Harriet whitened—she felt her face blanching—with an extreme tension of love, with a momentary awareness of his personality so sharp that her own seemed to be nothing. She was only eyes looking at Vesey and heart recording her confusion.

But back at Caroline's, the deceit creates tensions; Vesey feels Harriet's disapproval—unbearable to him—and he lashes out at her and at the children.

"When you are hurt, you lay waste all around you," Harriet said quietly. "No one is safe."
She was dismayed at loving someone imperfect. She tried to think of Vesey that day at lunch cutting Joseph's meat for him. She could not believe that anyone so loved could be flawed by spitefulness, the quality above all others that distressed her, or that tenderness and cruelty could inhabit the same person, dwell side by side, one sometimes intensifying the other.
"Hurt?" Vesey repeated. It was the one charge he would not have brought. "Bored you mean, perhaps?"
"Yes, I expect you are bored as well," Harriet said sadly.
All through the long winter and the spring, she would not have him near her; yet, now, standing so close beside him, the moment which should have been so precious was worse than useless—it shrank, and

stopped and curdled. The blue flowers that she carried in her hand she would surely hate for the rest of her life.

Vesey is sent home in disgrace to London. Having shaken hands with him formally in Caroline's hall, Harriet walks on the common.

Deep in the bitter smell of bracken, she lay down and closed her eyes ... with her face in her hands, her body hidden in the bracken, she began to weep. She did not so much indulge herself in this great torrent of weeping as become passive while the weight of tears cleared from her. A year is a long time to wait for someone beloved. In the morning, she would set about living that year, comforting herself across the great waste of days.

Vesey drops completely out of her life, and unable to bear the same routine without him, Harriet gets herself a job in a gown shop (one of the funniest sequences in the book). She meets Charles, a lawyer "an elderly man of about thirty-five", who comes to live in the neighbourhood. Vesey puts in one or two brief appearances—once while he is at Oxford when Harriet asks him to join her at a local dance she is going to with Charles—but he does not turn up. Then there is a memorial service for Caroline during the war and he appears, looking clumsy and desolate in his battledress—by now Harriet has married Charles and has a daughter. And then one night he turns up—many years later—at the same dance place—by now he is an actor in a small touring company—he and Harriet have their dance, watched by Charles for whom Vesey—even from the beginning of the marriage—has always been a shadowy, unacknowledged threat. Here are the married couple at home later that night.

When Charles came back, she took the hot-water bottle gratefully, for her teeth were chattering. She went over to her side in a ball, curled round it for warmth. When Charles got into bed he tried to unclench her as if she were a hedgehog rolled up for protection. She went tighter and tighter.

"My darling Harriet," he said, lying on his back away from her, resigned. "No one there to-night was as beautiful as you. I always know that, wherever I go, no other woman will be as lovely." But he could not uncurl her with flattery either.

He put out his hand for hers. She grasped it hurriedly as if to stave him off. Tears ran silently out of her eyes, slanting across her face into the pillows. He knew by her quietness that she was weeping. "Habit teaches me nothing," he said. "All these years can't prove to me that you are mine. The disbelief dies hard." He ran his arm along under her shoulder and kissed her, careful to avoid her tears.

The disbelief never does die. Harriet has carried Vesey in her heart for so long, and Charles has known so little and imagined so much about Vesey that the marriage has always been undermined, and now, with Vesey's reappearance, it is covertly in danger. Charles, like many angry and frightened people, cannot prevent himself from making matters worse . . .

The novel has an ending which manages to be enigmatic and very moving, but indeed much of it is moving and this is partly because Elizabeth Taylor is wonderfully good at *implying* love. Harriet and Vesey do not protest or declare their feelings: the love is chiefly implicit—their constant need to be with each other permeates the book. I can think of very few love stories that have this quality in a form so pure and so credible.

Elizabeth Jane Howard, London, 1985

I

SOMETIMES in the long summer's evenings, which are so marked a part of our youth, Harriet and Vesey played hide-and-seek with the younger children, running across the tufted meadows, their shoes yellow with the pollen of butter-cups. They could not run fast across those uneven fields; nor did they wish to, since to find the hiding children was to lose their time together, to run faster was to run away from one another. The jog-trot was a game devised from shyness and uncertainty. Neither dared to assume that the other wished to pause and inexperience barred them both from testing this.

At first, the younger children were pleased to foil them, but soon grew bored, sitting up in the branches of oak-trees, or crouching among bales of scratchy hay. Their whispers and giggles would grow into talk and laughter; they would examine their gnat-bites, pick at their scratches and soon begin to sing taunting songs and cry out in mockery. Though they did not care to be caught, they were vexed when after so long nothing happened. Sometimes they would see Harriet and Vesey coming across the fields, their long shadows going before them. Then they would quicken with excitement and call out in disguised voices or imitate a cuckoo. But mostly they were silent. They watched the shadows thinning and lengthening and the cows moving indifferently through the grasses.

"One should go one way and one the other," Joseph would say, but Deirdre knew that they would never part.

At the beginning of the holidays Harriet played with the

children to humour them, hiding always in the loft as though it would please them to have the game made easier. Vesey would not play at all. He sat on his bed writing a story. Then one evening he decided to join in. He became robust, avuncular, patronising. He and Harriet would lead them a fine dance, he said. As usual, Harriet hid in the loft and Vesey squeezed down behind the old swede-mincer in the barn. But more recently, Deirdre noted, they had both been hiding in the loft. She wondered why she continued the game, which had become, for her, so unexciting. She, at ten, was not so innocent as Harriet and Vesey at eighteen. She imagined a guilty but simple intimacy up there in the loft; her childish mind could not envisage the confusions of shyness, pride, self-consciousness, fear of rebuff or mis-understanding, which between childhood and maturity cloud and complicate that once so simply-imagined act. So Vesey and Harriet sat in that dusty stuffiness, among old pots of paint, boxes of bulbs, stacks of cobwebbed deck-chairs, rather far apart and in silence. Harriet would peep from the smeared window; Vesey would sit, hunched up, his hands round his knees, staring at a leaning tower of flower-pots. The only interruption was when one of them timidly swallowed an accumulation of saliva. The ticking of each heart, which they believed the other must hear, was like a pendulum rocking in a hollow case. What they thought was heaven, would seem like hell to them in later life.

Harriet, seeing Deirdre cross the yard below, would whisper "They are coming," her face quite strained as it could not have been, at her age, over a game. Vesey would move his eyes towards her, as if to move his head, too, would betray them. Without breathing almost, they would await the appearance of Joseph's head above the ladder; (for, though Deirdre knew where to find them, she sent little Joseph up to do the hauling in).

A different hiding-place would have prolonged the search and their exquisite stay in heaven or hell; but neither could suggest what might mean their betrayal to one another. Both upheld the pretence that they played the game for the children; they could not reveal what they had scarcely acknowledged in secret, their real reasons or their need.

Vesey's aunt, the mother of Joseph and Deirdre, was Harriet's mother's closest friend. As young women (a smudged photograph recorded this) they had once been hustled, gripped above the elbows by policemen, up the steps of a police-station. In the background, shop-windows showed great holes like black stars. Harriet, not able to bear this picture nor to ignore it, heedless of former sacrifice, as history makes all of us, saw only that her mother had exposed herself to mockery and ridicule, that she looked ugly, wild, a little mad, her mouth darkly open, her hat sideways. And Vesey's Aunt Caroline the same. She had no inkling of what had flowered there in that police-station, the hating eyes of the women outside, the laughter of the men, at last excluded. The doors swinging shut obliterated the street. Harriet's mother began to cry softly. She had not slept for two nights, contemplating her first, dreaded act of violence. Caroline's look of compassion and encouragement across that dingy room steadied and emboldened her. It was a look which went from one to the other many times in the years which followed: years during which history gave in. They wondered sometimes if their courage had been wasted; if time would not despite them have floated down to them casually what they had almost drowned in struggling to reach. Soon feminism became a weird abnormality; laughter was easily evoked at the strange figures of suffragettes with their umbrellas raised, their faces contorted and, one supposed, their voices made shrill with fury and frustration.

Lilian, Harriet's mother, married early and was soon widowed. Harriet herself fulfilled none of the ambitious desires of the older women. An only child, she spent much of her energy in filling in the gaps of her life with

3

imaginary characters. She showed no inclination to become a doctor or a lawyer, still less to storm some still masculine stronghold, the Stock-Exchange or holy orders. Through inattention, she lagged behind at school; facts she only feebly retained; loneliness, and the imagination needed to combat it, tired her. She could not pass an examination. 'What brilliant career to choose for her' became 'what to do with her at all', when she left school. The famous look passed from Caroline to Lilian. Although they never mentioned that room at the police-station, it was not forgotten and they were always closer because of it.

Until they could think of something better, Harriet would go to Caroline each day, to help with her committee work and give lessons to the children. Only a couple of miles lay between the two houses and bicycling to and fro Harriet felt sometimes like a shuttle being passed from one to the other; felt, as she had often been made to feel, that she was nothing very definite herself. She worried about her future, for she knew that she was only marking time, teaching Joseph to read, mending Deirdre's clothes, brushing the dogs, clacking out on the old typewriter with two fingers badly-spaced letters (the carbon round the wrong way so that at the end the letter would be on both sides of the paper), waiting for Vesey to pass the window.

She took refuge even more in day-dreaming, in flamboyant situations which she mastered. Her inclination at this time was only to lie and think of Vesey at night before sleep, but day-dreaming of an exhausting and routine kind must set to some sort of rights the world from which she might approach him. Until she had (although only imaginarily) made a place for herself in which she was no longer alien, useless, she could not go to meet him even in her dreams, and before she had solved that first problem she would fall asleep. So Vesey was seldom reached. She did not come to the point of enhancing those still scenes in the loft, nor did she put any words to them.

4

Vesey was an only child, too. His mother was not widowed, as Harriet's was. She was merely too busy to have more children. She did much more like to go out to work and, sitting at her lacquered desk beside perfectly arranged flowers and two white telephones, received, although without rising, clients at a salon for beauty treatment.

Vesey meanwhile slid about London, swung on to buses, hung about railway-stations, trying to stave off boredom. He found a way of passing time by frightening the housekeeper, would lie on the sofa in the pale, satiny flat trying to detain her while he described anything horrid he could remember or invent. "For instance, when people are *flayed*," he would begin, as she stood with a tray at the door. . . . "Ah, yes, flayed" . . . dreamily he lengthened the vowel of this word . . . "a small incision at the roots of the hair, say . . ."

"How dare you think up such wickedness!"

His way of beginning always with 'For instance' or 'However', as if some sort of conversation had gone before, trapped her again and again.

"Nevertheless, should you find yourself passing Madame Tussaud's the woman with a hook through her stomach is quite an unusual little tableau. . . ."

Before she could shut the door, he would manage to add, flicking over the pages of a magazine: "For those, of course, who like that sort of thing," as if he merely catered to her own sick fancies or love of the bizarre.

But when she had gone, the clock began to tick again. The light through the organdie curtains seemed stifled. The blond furniture and carpet (for rooms of that kind were all off-white in those days) could, when viewed through half-closed eyes, suggest dust-sheets and drugget and everyone gone away. If a petal fell from a flower, he was startled, as if he had seen something which, like the progress of the clock's hands, should be accomplished when no one is looking.

5

He read a great deal. He wrote stories in the styles of Wells and Tchehov, Kipling and Edgar Allan Poe. He was bored at school, bored at home, bored on his country-holidays with Aunt Caroline and Uncle Hugo. His stories of flaying, of stomach-hooks, were here suppressed. Joseph and Deirdre may not be told stories of buryings-alive: ghosts, Caroline said, were not frightening, only silly; in the way that some words were not clever, but silly; and some anecdotes not funny, not in the least rude, only silly. Vesey and the children did notice that 'silliness' was what made Caroline's neck redden most of all; more perhaps than rudeness or obscenity; but that they could never prove, for nothing *was* obscene or rude. 'Sensible' was Caroline's favourite word. "There's a sensible girl" was the highest praise Deirdre received. To be silly was to be not sensible. As time went on, Deirdre began to wonder if her mother had been altogether sensible on all occasions, to suspect that she herself had come into the world because of silliness. Try as she would, Deirdre could not regard the sexual act, with which she was at this time rather taken up, as sensible. As she had observed it in animals, it seemed at best ridiculous, at worst daunting and frantic. She could regard it in either light. Relating it to her own parents, as children must and will, she did not retract in horror; but laughed. Strictly utilitarian as she believed the act to be, she limited Caroline's occasions of being not sensible (in fact, of being utterly and frivolously and fantastically silly) to twice—herself and Joseph. It was strange that the very thing her mother hated most—not being sensible—had given her what she loved the best; her two children. Deirdre did not doubt that she and Joseph were loved most. She had a happy childhood and when she grew up she had many a happy surprise.

Caroline was rather torn in two about Vesey's mother's attitude to her son. That women should be emancipated she had fatigued herself in her youth and endured mockery; but Vesey had not grown up a robust or happy child and she

6

could not but lay blame for his paleness on the London flat, or his boredom and restlessness, upon lack of attention. "If it were for something worth while . . .!" she hedged. As far as she could imagine, nothing could be less worthwhile than pandering to the vanity of rich London women, the idle, the predatory (who had once cut her, or laughed at her as she marched in processions). Picturing the smooth flattery of Vesey's mother, she could only think the child (even her own ideals) sacrificed for nothing. But, white-skinned, even in the country he never tanned or coloured. Early in September he would return to London like a ghost, faintly mauve across his brow and his sharp shoulders; (for, stripped to the waist, as Caroline would have him, he would only, week after week, become more and more gnat-bitten: his chest remained white; the bones showed in rows). She never managed to send him back looking like a reproach.

In the flat, while the housekeeper was out shopping, he made one or two experiments at his leisure. Every opened bottle in the cupboard he had tried from time to time. He would smoke with his head out of the bedroom window. In his mother's room one day he put on her jewellery, sniffed at her scent, varnished his nails, read a book on birth-control, took six aspirins, then lay down like Chatterton on the window-seat, his hand drooping to the floor.

When the housekeeper returned, he had half-opened his eyes. "I am doing away with myself," he had said. "I have supped my full of horrors." When she had rushed out for salt-and-water, he had turned his head to the pillow to stifle his giggles; but, strangely, some tears had fallen upon the oyster satin.

His love of teasing and sensationalism was thwarted somewhat in the country. Caroline and Hugo scorned such nonsense themselves and were vigilant over their children. Harriet alone was susceptible, but only to more literary or romantic horrors. The stomach-hook made her laugh, but

7

the story of Mrs Rossetti's exhumation she listened to chin in hand.

They—she and Vesey—had known one another since early childhood; but his return this summer of their eighteenth year brought to her own knowledge her love for him. His personality had for long influenced hers, as the moon influences the sea, with an unremitting and inescapable control. Her mother had seen that influence and thought it not always for the good. *She* found motives for Vesey's exuberances and, threaded through these motives, disquieting traces of cruelty and cynicism.

Caroline's house was Victorian and nondescript, surrounded by worn lawns, ramshackle outbuildings, lurching rose-arches. Inside, although threadbare rugs lay crooked on rather dusty floorboards and curtains were bleached by sun and rain, the first impression was of comfort and friendliness, that people mattered more than houses, that children were more important than the covers of the chairs, that dogs were, too. Spaniels flopped up and down the stairs; lay on beds and turned bloodshot and reproachful eyes as doors were opened; stretched out and suckled their young across the hearthrug.

Hugo Macmillan had still much of that poetic ebullience which distinguished so many young men just before the 1914 war. He suggested in middle-age, a type of masculinity now perhaps vanished to the world; the walking-tours in perfect spring weather, Theocritus in pocket: an æsthetic virility. He had gone on being Rupert Brooke all through the war—a tremendous achievement—and was only now, much later, finding his enthusiasms hardening into prejudices and, sometimes, especially with Vesey, into a tetchy disapproval of what he did not understand. His old-fashioned liberalism now contained elements of class-hatred; his patriotism had become the most arrogant nationalism. His love and sympathy for the women of his youth, his support in their fight for a wider kind of life, made him unsympathetic to the

8

younger women who had come after. Every feminality these young girls (he even called them Flappers) felt free enough to adopt (and they were fewer than usual at that time) he openly despised.

The time before the war had been so idyllic to him that he measured everything against those days; he could not feel at home among so much that seemed spurious. If we do not alter with the times, the times yet alter us. We may stand perfectly still, but our surroundings shift round and we are not in the same relationship to them for long; just as a chameleon, matching perfectly the greenness of a leaf, should know that the leaf will one day fade.

Hugo saw little change in himself, could beat Vesey at tennis and swim faster, took his cold bath each morning, loved his wife as dearly now as at the beginning of their marriage, on their honeymoon in the Forest of Fontainebleau after that First World War. (He had taken her to see some battlefields.)

Vesey constantly irritated and surprised him: his lack of gallantry towards Harriet, his laziness, his cynicism, the gaps in his knowledge. "Who in the world is Edward Carpenter?" he had asked, lolling as usual on the sofa with the wireless on too loud, and had not seemed impressed by Hugo's exasperated answer.

On the other hand, Hugo did not know that to Vesey he seemed more old-fashioned than his grandfather. His grandfather would certainly not have spoken of taking a glass of ale at an inn, and those Chestertonian phrases had, to Vesey, such a period flavour as to seem deliberately affected.

The antagonism Hugo felt for his nephew, although it was in reality impatience with another person's youth heightened by nostalgia for his own, was fogged by nobody's having a good word for Vesey. Caroline, Lilian, Vesey's own father all combined to disapprove. Even Harriet, Hugo noticed, turned her head when he came in and affected to read her book.

9

Hugo was fond of Harriet. Although not clever, she was not meretricious. Her silky brown hair was tucked back with childish artlessness behind her ears, her face was innocent of make-up, her clothes were boyish and practical. When she walked, as she sometimes did, with him and the children, she knew the old English names of the wild flowers; she shut gates; carried waste paper home from picnics. Vesey, on the other hand, had been seen walking across a field of winter wheat and was always careless of other people's property; had left a copy of *The Roadmender* (moss-green suede) out on the lawn in a thunderstorm, had found the book, he explained, too little worth reading to warrant carrying it indoors.

Sometimes Hugo was so annoyed that he was fearful of losing his composure and took up the bellows and began blowing steadily at the wood fire. This was a sign that he was on edge and did not wish to hear what was being said; but it was unfortunately a sign which only Caroline heeded. Vesey was not interested: Harriet thought what a nuisance wood fires were.

When she arrived in the mornings, Vesey was still in bed. She would listen for sounds of his rising, watch for him to pass the window. Once, leaving Joseph and Deirdre while she went to fetch painting water, she met him in the hall. He was reading a newspaper and was still in his dressing-gown. The dressing-gown flurried her dreadfully. She had never seen him with so many clothes on. He seemed muffled up; his black hair was unbrushed. Going back through the hall, slopping the cups of water, she would not glance in his direction.

"Harriet!" He left it till she got to the door, till she was nearly away, as if he were a cat with a mouse.

"Yes? Yes, Vesey?"

Still reading the *Manchester Guardian* with close interest, in a vague voice he said: "Shall we go for a walk this evening?"

With her back to him, she answered, joy unsteadying her voice: "Yes. I think that would be all right."

"Oh, if you don't care to, you need only say."

"No, I think it will be quite all right."

She pushed the door open with her foot, as her hands were full. He did not attempt to help her. Joseph and Deirdre looked up from the table inquisitively, as if it were not only painting water she was bringing in. She sat down in her chair, her arms through the bars at the back of it, braced stiff, her fingers locking her hands together, excitement broken loose in her.

"The sign of a good painter," Deirdre said, "is not going over the edges." She drove yellow to the very edge of a petal and no farther. "Or letting it run," she added. But Joseph had let it run badly. Bluebells ran into celandines and the sky into the grass. His page was so wet, so rucked up, that he pushed it all aside. Vision or nothing, he seemed to declare, kicking at the table-leg. Harriet could not coax him back to work. Neat Deirdre looked up in smug surprise.

For the first ten minutes they were explaining to one another why they had chosen to go for this walk together. Boredom had driven them to it, they decided; a fear, on Vesey's part, lest he should be asked by Hugo to mow and mark the tennis-lawn; a wish, on Harriet's part, to collect wild-flowers for the children to draw. If the walk turned out badly, it could be the fault of neither, for neither had desired it nor attached importance to it. In a few years' time, they would be dissembling the other way; professing pleasure they did not feel, undreamed of eagerness. They had not yet learned to gush. Their protestations were of an oafish kind.

When they had established their lack of interest in being together, they became silent. Harriet gathered a large bunch of quaking-grass from under a hedge. Vesey kicked a stone down the middle of the road.

'If only,' Harriet thought, 'there were no *women* at

universities! If only they still were not allowed!' (Her mother once had taken tea at Girton with Miss Emily Davies. It had seemed to her well worth going to prison to have been so rewarded.)

But Harriet saw Vesey lying in a punt, his fingers trailing in the water as he watched through lids half-closed against the sun a young woman who was reading Ernest Dowson to him. Her imagination excused Vesey from any exertion, as probability did also. The boat drifted as if by magic past Bablock-Hythe and under Godstow Bridge towards the Aegean Isles. And all this time, Harriet herself sat at the schoolroom-table typing Caroline's letters; for pocket money.

Vesey, whose next steps would take him over the threshold of a new and promising world, wished to go without any backward glances or entanglements. He was not one to keep up friendships, never threw out fastening tendrils such as letters or presents or remembrances; was quite unencumbered by all the things which Harriet valued and kept: drawers full of photographs, brochures, programmes, postcards, diaries. He never remembered birthdays or any other anniversary.

Although he was ambitious at this time to become a great writer, he saw himself rather as a literary figure than as a man at work. At school, he had often turned to the index of a History of Literature and in his mind inserted his own name—Vesey Patrick Macmillan—between Machiavelli and Sir Thomas Malory.

"Everything seems so certain for you," Harriet said, as they toiled up the side of a hill towards a wood. "So uncertain for me."

"In what way?"

He stopped with a hand against his lower ribs, out of condition as his Uncle Hugo never had been in his life.

"That you are going to Oxford, and can pass exams."

"Exams are nothing," he said. ('They do not seem

12

to be,' Harriet thought, 'to those who pass them.')

Both wanted to sit down in the shade at the edge of the woods: neither would suggest it.

"And then you'll be a schoolmaster and have a great deal of money," Harriet said without irony, her mind on her own pittance.

"A schoolmaster?"

Vesey stopped dead, holding back a long springing branch so that she could go by. "Why do you say that?"

"It is what I heard Caroline say."

He had not held the branch quite long enough and Harriet now disentangled it from her hair.

"She would! These old-time suffragettes!" Vesey said tactlessly. "They are only happy if they can see men in a subservient position."

Harriet could not see that it was in the least a subservient position. She could scarcely imagine more authority or scope.

"Then what will you do?" she asked.

"I have never told anybody, but I mean to be a writer."

Harriet flushed; both at the confidence and at the nature of it. She bent down hastily and began to tug at some bracken to add to her bunch.

"To write novels?" she asked.

He preferred the more oblong shapes of books on literary criticism, belles lettres. To become a man of letters, he would make special to himself one smallish aspect of literature, read all the books about it, add another of his own. Anything later encroaching on his territory, he would himself review.

"The novel is practically finished as an art form," he replied.

"I suppose it is," said Harriet.

"Virginia Woolf has brought it to the edge of ruin."

"Yes," said Harriet.

"But it was inevitable," he added, laying no blame.

13

"I suppose it was," Harriet said, in a slow, considering way. The novel—headstrong parvenu—seemed headed for destruction. No one could stay its downward course and, obviously, it did not deserve that Vesey should try. Virginia Woolf with one graceful touch after another (the latest was *Mrs Dalloway*) was sending it trundling downhill. She had been doing this unbeknown to Harriet who had never even heard of her.

She had wished to include her own future in their discussion and he had not given it a glance. She sighed theatrically, but he failed to ask her why. Plunging through dead leaves, they were obliged to walk in single file, twigs snapped under their feet, briars tripped them. Cool and vast, the wood seemed a whole world; the light was aqueous; when a cuckoo gave its broken, explosive cry it echoed like a shout in a closed swimming-bath—for some reason, chilling and hysterical as those sounds are.

Vesey now had a blister on his heel. He sat down on the fine, transparent grass that grows beneath trees and took off his sandal. His foot was white and veined and rather dirty. He rested it in the cool grass and leaned back against the trunk of a tree. Harriet stood awkwardly before him, feeling too tall.

"Have you a handkerchief?" she asked.

"No." He smiled. He looked rather fagged, as if this evening stroll had been too much for him.

If only her own handkerchief were of the finest cambric, smelling of flowers! She took out a crumpled cotton one left over from schooldays, with 'Harriet Claridge' printed clumsily along the hem.

"Why 'Harriet', I wonder," Vesey asked, reading it. "Though it is quite a pretty name."

"It was after Harriet Martineau."

"Ah, yes, of course." He smiled again.

"I could tie it for you."

"I cannot bear anyone to touch my feet."

14

She rearranged her bunch of flowers and held them out at arm's length to consider them.

"None the less, sit down beside me," he presently said.

Surprised, she hesitated, then sat down rather round the tree from him so that they must talk slightly over their shoulders. Her hands, at her side, pressed into dry twigs, the empty cases of last year's beech-nuts.

"I hope you will be very happy, very famous," she said. To say this more easily she laid an edge of mockery to her voice.

Her brown, ink-smudged hand pressed down into the dead leaves drew his attention. Looking sideways, he examined it carefully.

"Thank you," he said, and his voice, too, sank into mockery. She could not allow to him the same motive as her own and, imagining he had wished to rebuke her, pointed out that it was time to go home. "Or you will be late for supper," she said, as if he were intolerably preoccupied with meals.

Nervously, tenderly, he put his own hand over hers.

"*You* will be late too," he said, as if nothing had happened.

"My mother . . ." she began; but she could not continue. She seemed to have stepped over into another world; confused, as though the demarcation had been between life and death, she imagined herself swimming, floating, in a strange element where hearing and sight no longer existed.

"Your mother what . . .?" he asked. He slid his hand up her arm and into her sleeve.

She could not remember what she had been about to say. Watching a velvety grey spider crossing her ankle, she was surprised that she did not experience her usual fear and disgust.

Vesey had turned to face her and the tree. She had never seen his face so close to her own, nor dared to look at him as she looked now. He drew her away from the tree into his arms and rested his head against her, and still she could not move but was locked up in amazement and disbelief. Only when he loosened her, as he soon did, sensing her constraint,

15

did she begin to relax, to tremble. She raised her hands stiffly. Pieces of twig, small stones, were pressed into the creased and reddened palms. She brushed them on her skirt and stared about her. Then a great silence, of despair, ennui, disappointment with herself, widened in her, like a yawn. The trees seemed to march away from her into the darkness; the wood was a chilly vault, the birds had stopped calling. Vesey sat beside her still, prising bits of white flint out of the mossy earth with a stick which kept snapping. Absorbed, he did this. Fatally, she covered her face with her hands.

"What is wrong?" he asked gently.

He drew her hands away and kissed her cheek. In spite of his seeming assurance, he was not really sure.

"Harriet?"

"Yes, Vesey?"

"Have I done wrong?"

"No."

The yawn, the disappointment was contagious. Touching her again, his excitement undiminished, he was at the same time reminded of the dullness of consequences. The tears which she had not let fall cautioned him. He began to wonder if violent embraces are not often induced by not knowing what to do next, of losing one's nerve as much as losing one's control. He put his sandal on again, easing it with elaborate care over the bandage, frowning, as he buckled it.

"It is only . . ." she began unpromisingly (that daunting opening to long complaints, long confessions) "only that sometimes I worry about the future. And hearing you to-night . . . so sure . . . there is nothing for *me* to do, as there is for you. I wonder what will happen to me . . ."

Relief made him robust.

"Someone will marry you," he cruelly said. He stood up and brushed leaves away, then he put out his hand to help her to her feet.

·   ·   ·   ·   ·

16

"I do think," Caroline was saying in her most reasonable voice, "that another time . . . of course, it doesn't matter in the least while we are alone . . . obviously, it's of no importance to me that you take the last rissole . . . I'm not the faintest bit hungry, and, if I were, could have had more cooked . . . but perhaps it would be a bad example to the children if they were here for you just to—without offering it, I mean—to take it as a matter of course. I *hate* having to say this, but it is a question, I suppose, of principle . . . after all, we were always agreed that this isn't one of those houses where the man is lord and master and boss and bread-winner, taking everything for granted . . ."

"He could certainly not do that," Hugo said, tipping the nut-rissole on to Caroline's plate.

She flushed. "My dear Hugo, surely you have not taken offence because I spoke frankly?"

"It is what people do take offence at."

"You know I couldn't eat another thing."

She returned the rissole to his plate.

"And now I could not either," he said, abandoning some spinach as well and putting his knife and fork together. The rissole was back on the dish where it had begun, among the shapes of the other rissoles which had been outlined by cold fat.

As the meal continued with rhubarb-pie Caroline's explanation also continued. What she simply hated saying she always said for a long time.

Hugo said little. He knew that she was a good wife, though a bore. But even her moral code had its less tiresome side.

When at last she had finished, "Vesey is late," he said.

"I have put some cold food on one side for him."

"I should have thought that he need not put you to such trouble."

"But meals are made for people, not people for meals," Caroline said with smooth serenity.

.   .   .   .   .

17

Harriet strove to measure, to assess, Vesey's consciousness of her: not so much to find out what was his attitude towards her; but if he had an attitude. Her diary, once full of blank pages, became cramped and congested on the days when she saw him. Reading it later, when she was lonely, it did not seem that she had quite told the truth. She stored up all his sayings against the long winter when she would not see him; but the very ink she wrote them in seemed to lay emphasis which did not belong. Some days had only one line: "I went to Caroline's. I did not see V." But the next day might spill back upon that page. ("Vesey mowed the lawn. Vesey looked tired. Vesey is reading Walter Pater." Vesey's opinions of Walter Pater would then appear. Two days later, Harriet was reading Walter Pater. She did so agree with Vesey and, should he ask her, would say so, but he did not ask her.) In her diary, she walked right round Vesey and viewed him from every angle and in every light.

On the days when she did not see him, she was sometimes tempted back after supper and would bicycle slowly along the tarred road and past Caroline's house, suddenly staring ahead when she drew level, as if hateful scenes were being enacted on those smooth lawns. Relieved, she would bicycle on in the darkening evening, the air cool against her, her tyres swerving on the gravelly road. Before she reached home, lights would be on in the cottages she passed and she would duck her head seeing the bats slanting, darting between the hedges. Insects would strike her: she feared especially the flying beetles. All anticipation gone, she would be glad to be back. She could not think why she had set out in the first place.

Her mother worked in the garden until late, and the cottage had a deserted stuffy air with no lamps lit. The fires had been laid so long that the paper was sooty and the twigs covered with cigarette-ends and bits of cotton.

The cottage, like most of them in this small hamlet, which house-agents called an artists' paradise, was a labourer's

18

cottage neatly prettified, with diamond panes and new thatch. Geraniums were planted trustingly outside the hedge. The stones in the front path had been cracked to accommodate clumps of thrift. All of these cottages showed their past usefulness by the names painted in Gothic script on little swinging boards—The Old Bakehouse, The Old Malthouse, Cobbler's, Shepherd's Cottage. Lilian and Harriet were at Forge Cottage: across the road at The Old Vicarage, Elizabeth Garrett Anderson had once stayed for a fortnight.

Lilian Claridge had, in middle-age, a soft prettiness and transparency. Her fine, thin skin was like crumpled tussore, darker than her prematurely white hair and deeply shadowed under her eyes. If she were brave, she was brave with a tautness she could not for long sustain: if she were angry, she was angrier than she intended. She, not Caroline, had wept at the police-station; but she had dealt the first blow: nervousness hastened her. At Harriet's age, she had kept a diary, too; but more evenly and consistently. It had been a five years' diary, thick as a Bible, with brass corners to the covers and a little key. Turning the pages now, she could not see that the key had been necessary. In the years when it might have been, she was too busy for diary-writing. But then, the days had gone innocently by: Miss Brown had scolded, had exhorted, had kissed her good-bye when she left school. She went to tea with old ladies; she pasted scraps on to a screen: she trimmed her hats and sewed insertion round her camisoles. Once, it was recorded, she had tried to make a great fruit cake with eight eggs and crystallised cherries; but when she took it from its tin the middle had fallen out and she had shut herself in her room in tears. Always in tears. Tears with the family when she threw in her lot with Mrs Henry Fawcett, tears with Mrs Henry Fawcett when she left her for the Pankhursts and prison, tears every night in prison. Her face had not stood up to so much crying: crumpled and bruised, it begged her friends to beware, betrayed her to her enemies.

She and Harriet lived uneasily together: they were more intimately placed than suited either. Harriet's failures at school had been a matter of agonised embarrassment for both. Success is always less awkward. It does not make claims upon pity or tact: congratulations are easier to give than condolences. Her mother's timid smile, her way of saying "It doesn't matter" had the opposite effect to what had been intended. 'I have failed as a daughter, too,' Harriet would think.

In her last term at school, she had concentrated all her hopeless confusion upon the examination papers. The clock ticked, the time went and the confusion grew tighter, denser. Waiting after school on the day the results were pinned to the notice-board, she could not run to see, as the other girls did; eagerly and excitedly. Numbly, she approached the edge of the semi-circle. Under a thick ruled line her name was isolated. "Oh, *bad* luck!" the smiling girls paused to say, pushing out of the crush to hurry home. She dreaded her own moment of entering the house. Her mother, drawn time after time to the window, was caught there looking out as Harriet opened the gate. She tried, having seen her daughter's face, to fade back into the room. She put on a careless look, her embarrassed smile, and went with a quick light tread and a dismayed heart into the hall.

"Oh, mother!"

"But it doesn't *matter*. We didn't truly expect, and we truly don't care. You are so late home that I must make fresh tea."

With her quick and casual manner, she thrust back Harriet's tears which would have been much better shed.

Now, later, she was paying for her mistakes. Harriet was sealed off completely; not only by good manners, self-control, reserve; but also by lies. She told lies about meeting Vesey and her habit of staying late at Caroline's. She made excuses and gave wrong reasons.

20

Lilian did talk to Caroline. Both disapproved of Vesey. They thought him callous and affected. His lazy cynicism was an irritation to them. He had been badly brought up and was not to be trusted.

"But I think she doesn't much *like* him," Caroline said. "We see no sign of it here: rather the reverse."

Although Lilian was not confided in, she could not ignore the evidence of Harriet's excitement and all the bicycling about. She felt a desperation in the girl's behaviour and as fast as she tried to comfort herself, could only see that she knew nothing about her: neither how far she would commit herself; nor what she would be likely to feel. Unlocking her old diary, Lilian found no clue there. She found only floods of tears, and there was no proof that Harriet ever cried.

Harriet's own diary, which had no lock and key, would have told her mother all she did not want to know; but a woman who has been to prison for her principles does not discard them so easily, and the thought, which did go so far as to enter her head, retreated immediately in shame. Harriet had not described her love in writing; but Vesey's most trivial doing or saying, crammed up and down the margins, obliterating headings about Pheasant Shooting and the Phases of the Moon, would have plainly revealed to her mother the pitiful and one-sided truth.

After their walk in the woods, Harriet faced the day's page uncertainly. There was either far too much space or only one-hundredth part enough. Time had expanded and contracted abnormally. That morning and all her childhood seemed the same distance away. "I cannot put down what happened this evening," she wrote mysteriously. "Nor is there any need, for I shall remember all my life." And, although she was so mysterious, she was right. Much in those diaries would puzzle her when she turned their pages in middle-age, old age; many allusions would be meaningless; week after week would seem to have been wiped away: but that one entry, so proudly cryptic, would always evoke the

21

evening in the woods, the shadows, the layers of leaves shutting out the sky, the bronze mosses at the foot of the trees, the floating sound their voices had, and that explosive, echoing cry of the cuckoo. She would remember writing the words in the little candlelit bedroom. Outside, her mother trundled the wheelbarrow laden with weeds down the gravelled path. Harriet closed the diary and shut the window against the moths. Later, when she was in bed she tried to return to the wood where Vesey had kissed her, but doubt and disappointment overtook her again. She could not believe that caution and uncertainty could have so wickedly crippled her happiness at such a time. She longed for a second chance, to have the moment at her disposal again. The story began to be how she imagined having behaved. But the recollection of that walk back in single file through the trees, shuffling in the dead leaves, stiff, self-conscious, hinted that they had reached some stubbornness in one another, that they had broken the past in such a way that nothing could repair it. In despair she lay awake wondering about the morrow. With one of her few flashes of perception she imagined Vesey peacefully asleep.

Another day is another world. The difference between foreign countries is never so great as the difference between night and day. Not only are the landscape and the light changed, but people are different, relationships which the night before had progressed at a sudden pace, appear to be back where they were. Some hopes are renewed, but others dwindle: the state of the world looks rosier and death further off; but the state of ourselves and our loves and ambitions seems more prosaic. We begin to regret promises, as if the influence of darkness were like the influence of drink. We do not love our friends so warmly: or ourselves. Children feel less need of their parents: writers tear up the masterpiece they wrote the night before.

So Harriet met Vesey bravely in a more sober world.

22

While she was propping her bicycle against the wall of the house, he called to her from an upstairs window. She waved with what she thought was a beautiful negligence and disappeared into the house.

Because he realised how Harriet tumbled the same thoughts about and about in her head, Vesey had regretted his experiment of the evening before. He had lost no sleep over it, though. He could not make a fuss in his mind about such triviality. He had his life before him, he assured himself. 'After all,' he thought this morning, watching himself in a mirror as he combed his hair, 'we are children: no more.' He did not know that at his age most youths believe that they are men.

The streak of cruelty which Lilian had perceived in him was real enough, but used defensively. He would not have wished to be cruel to Harriet, who had not threatened him. Indeed it had begun to seem to him that only she was set against the great weight of disapproval he felt upon him. His mother treated him, at best, with an amused kindliness. Among her friends she drew attention to him as if he were a beloved marmoset on a chain, somehow enhancing her own originality, decorating her. After her day's work, while she bathed, he brought her drinks, carried messages to and from the telephone. In later years, the word 'mother' brought to his mind the steamy bathroom, the picture of her creamy-yellow body with its almost navy-blue hair, the hands and feet with their darkly varnished nails. This was his only time alone with her. As soon as she was dressed, she belonged to other people. He was the quaint little monkey handing round olives and cigarettes, sipping gin to amuse them. His father always went straight to his study when he arrived home. His appearance in the drawing-room was a signal for his wife's friends to scatter. With his own especial remote geniality, he would drink his one sherry and speed them all on their way: large and formidable, he underlined their flimsiness, and "Poor Barbara!" they would laugh, bundling into their little cars, sitting on one another's knees. "What a bloody old bore he is!" In search of a gayer host, they would drive away.

When Vesey went to school, he realised at once that this background was better not mentioned, but he felt—for he was quick to atmosphere—that its influence upon him was not un-noted: certainly not by masters who seemed to be waiting for him to commit some outrage, to manifest some unwholesomeness; and not even by the boys, who were dubious and suspicious. He suffered very much at school occasions when his mother came looking like an elder sister, and still more when, which was more often, she did not come at all.

He did not make any close friends, for he had too much to hide. Since he could not have affection, he thought he would have admiration. His laziness was assumed, to hide his dislike of small failures. What he could not have, he did not care to have. Disruptive, cheeky, he provoked tired sarcasm from masters. The best he ever had from anyone was callous applause, laughter at his antics, and he became the same sort of little monkey that he had been at home.

Caroline and Hugo, so sound, so moral and so earnest, tried to do something for him, but he reacted to their charity with rudeness. Only Harriet showed approval. She had always shown it and now, at a time when he most needed some success with personal relationships, her approval had grown warmer and more positive. What Caroline could not see and Harriet tried to hide, he had begun to perceive. He needed Harriet for his own reasons, to give him confidence and peace. In the shelter of her love, he hoped to have a second chance, to turn his personality away from what he most hated in himself, to try to find dignity before it was too late. Playing the fool bored him. With the failure of school behind him, he hoped to shake off the tedious habit.

Against this need he had for her were set the feelings he had about Harriet herself. He knew her almost too well to

24

be able to realise her clearly; but he began to see that she was
brave and candid, oppressed by the ideals of an older
generation, enduring boredom and an enforced childishness
and loneliness. She would have been surprised that he
should find her beautiful, and it was a colourless and
wavering beauty that he observed: fleeting, from day to day.
Every sign of fatigue showed under her thin skin, in her
rather lank pale hair. Set against the smartness of his
mother's friends, he found her clothes (still school ones,
improvised, altered), her untidy eyebrows, her rough little
hands, very touching and delightful; and her voice, too,
which was clear and light with, in moments of agitation, a
hurried stammer.

Cruelty had, in him, its other side of appalled tenderness.
When his nature betrayed him into this tenderness, he
would violently retract and cover up in cruelty. Knowing his
weakness, he had meant to shield Harriet from both.
Having failed once, he was determined not to fail again, was
set on helping her out with gaiety and friendliness. Full of a
jauntiness he did not feel, he went downstairs this morning
to meet her.

Caroline was sitting among a litter of fruit-peelings and
letters, dictating. Harriet, with a cup of coffee beside her,
scribbled madly on a pad, for she did not know shorthand.
She wore a faded blue shirt tucked into a tweed skirt; her
bare feet with rather broken nails looked narrow and frail in
clumsy, handmade sandals. Her straight hair fell in separate
strands over her shoulders. On both wrists thin silver
bracelets hung loosely.

Vesey sat at the table and began to shake cornflakes out of
a packet, but Harriet did not look up. Only when Caroline
had finished dictating did Harriet reach for her coffee, and
then, as she began to drink, her eyes turned towards Vesey: he
saw her timid glance above the rim of the cup—and smiled.
She went on drinking: but her eyes narrowed in response.

Against his mother's knees Joseph lolled, eating an apple.

25

His dry, light-brown hair looked almost grey: it stuck out like feathers all over his large head.

"Do take him to have his hair cut," Caroline said to Harriet.

Joseph began to whimper into his apple.

"Be sensible," Caroline bade him. "And Harriet shall take you for lunch in Market Swanford afterwards." In her own mind she did not mean this to be a bribe, but Joseph took it to be one.

"Vesey, your mother writes to say you are to buy new shoes," Caroline said. "I will give you the money. She says you are to spend at least a guinea on them." Harriet looked with respect at Vesey, but Caroline with doubt, considering this strange extravagance. "Well, it will be a little expedition for you," Caroline went on, "and when Harriet has done the letters, you can all be off."

Harriet began to wonder if she could bear the strain of a whole day-out with Vesey. Anxieties mingled with her delight: anxieties about ordering food, controlling the children, expense, and how to find the ladies' lavatory.

Vesey walked up and down the shop in the grey suède shoes. Harriet and the children sat in a row watching. The shop with its shelves of white boxes was cool and dark. Beyond the open door the street was another world, but that panel of shifting colours in the sunlight emphasised the sombre interior.

Harriet, not much used to shopping, still experienced a feeling of crisis when she stepped off the busy pavement into a shop, where she seemed awaited and was to be judged. Her stammer increased. Shop-assistants looked blankly patient listening to her, waiting for her to be done. Just now, at the grocer's, with Vesey standing by, she had been in a panic to know how to seem off-hand enough; had rehearsed in her mind the giving of the order, but they still had to say 'pardon?', they still brought Bisto instead of Rinso, and when she had asked for petit-beurre biscuits in French, as she thought she should, they had not known what she had meant. Almost showing the list, as if she were a child, she had blushed, dreading to try again; but Vesey had laughed very much. He had said "Petty burr, dearie" in a loud voice. It had saved her; but she had not wanted to be saved by him. Her shame in the eyes of the shop-assistant was not so painful as Vesey's having witnessed it.

She was glad now to be only a spectator. No more was demanded of her than to take Vesey's side against the shop-assistant and this she did spontaneously and whole-heartedly. All three of them were united in their praise of Vesey's choice and as the shoes were only eighteen and elevenpence there would be two shillings left which Vesey said he could quite justifiably spend on ice-cream.

Harriet admired the way in which he took his time, discussed his plans, and had shoes lying about all over the floor. The assistant, who had begun with tan Oxfords, now withdrew from the discussion, wearing the look of aloof distaste Vesey had grown so used to seeing on the faces of schoolmasters.

At the confectioners', Deirdre suddenly remembered that she would get infantile-paralysis if she ate ice-cream that had not been made in her own home. She pushed the dish stubbornly on one side and was only appeased when it was shared out among the others. Smug and relieved, she nibbled at a limp wafer and watched them taking their great risk.

Joseph, with his bony temples now bared, the tendons of his neck shaved close, looked a different child. What hair was left showed the furrows of a comb drawn through the thick brilliantine.

Carrying the box of shoes and the basket of groceries, Vesey led them round the market-place, in one entrance of Woolworths (where they were told not to touch) and out of the other, examining the graves in the churchyard, reading the menus outside cafés and public-houses. The pavement

27

burnt through their thin sandals; they felt the warmth of brick walls as they went lingeringly down the street. Deirdre tagged along behind Vesey; Joseph held Harriet's hand. They felt the complete identity with their surroundings which children know, especially in summertime when, relaxed and opened out like flowers, they drink the sun. They drift, tack across pavements, trailing hands along railings; stare; bemused, idle; given up to growing; they string out along the roads, separate, humming to themselves; heedless of time passing.

Only hunger jolted them. Like middle-aged parents, Vesey and Harriet settled the children to their lunch at a window overlooking the High Street. The Tudor Café had beams of stained deal tacked across the ceiling and diagonally across walls. Bottle-glass windows of a greenish shade obscured the light, coats-of-arms and wicker furniture looked wonderful to the children.

When the waitress came, Harriet decided quickly. Indeed, for vegetarians there was no choice. She was lucky in liking macaroni-cheese.

"A chop," said Vesey, and if he had ordered a magnum of champagne Harriet could not have been more alarmed. "Have a chop, Deirdre," he added.

"I don't know what is a chop," Joseph wailed.

"A chop is meat," Deirdre said, glancing at the waitress as if for confirmation.

"Please, Vesey!" Harriet whispered timidly.

"Old stick-in-the-mud Harriet!" he laughed.

The waitress took the weight off one leg and stared out of the window above their heads, yawning.

"I don't know what is a chop," Joseph said again.

"A chop is a little piece of meat with a bone and some fat and it is grilled," Vesey said, so distinctly that people at other tables could hear him.

"I don't know what is grilled," Joseph said, enjoying himself.

28

"Three chops, one macaroni-cheese," the waitress said, beginning to write.

"They have never eaten meat," Harriet told Vesey.

Deirdre turned accusing eyes on him, but said nothing. She gave him a steady assurance of blaming him later. Innocent party, her face said.

"Four chops," Vesey said suddenly. He nodded mockingly at Harriet.

"Vegetarians live cheaper," Deirdre said, reading aloud from the menu. "Macaroni-cheese is only eightpence."

"Hush!" Harriet implored. "You must lower your voice, Deirdre. You are not at home."

"We certainly aren't *there*," Joseph said, as the chops were put in front of them. He became very loud and swaggering and took up the too-large knife and fork and began to cut his meat, which was on a level with his shoulders. Vesey took off his own jacket and folded it neatly for a cushion. Perched on this, Joseph wobbled insecurely. "Blood comes out," he said looking uncertainly at his plate.

Across the table, Vesey and Harriet smiled at one another, Harriet catching in her lower lip with her teeth. "Caroline will be angry," she said.

Vesey touched his tie and cleared his throat. "My children!" he began. "It is clearly understood, I hope, that this repellent orgy of corpse-eating will not be mentioned to either of your parents . . ." Deirdre smiled to herself as she chewed . . "and, in fact, will be obliterated from your minds the moment we leave the precincts of this more-or-less baronial hall . . ."

"We cannot teach them to tell lies," Harriet said in a low voice.

"We cannot do that," Vesey agreed. "We should have come to the task too late. We can only prevent them from telling the truth."

"Meat is nice," Joseph said.

"We do not often get the chance," said Deirdre.

29

Harriet thought that she and Vesey threw out a beautiful protection over the children. Everything she shared with him seemed hallowed, even this guilt of eating chops.

"We can get bread any day," Joseph explained to the waitress who handed him a basket of rolls. His elbows stuck up like wings as he tried to cut his meat. When Vesey leant over to do this for him, Harriet whitened—she felt her face blanching—with an extreme tension of love, with a momentary awareness of his personality so sharp that her own seemed to be nothing. She was only eyes looking at Vesey and heart recording her confusion.

"It has been an experience," said Deirdre at last, putting her knife and fork together.

Going back in the bus, Vesey seemed abstracted. He sat in the seat next to Harriet with his arms round the basket of shopping, his fingers fringing his bus-ticket, his eyes narrowed at the tunnel of branches through which they wound their way. In those days, trees laced together above many a road; buses took perilous journeys, with twigs scratching at either side; cars, meeting them, backed up into gateways. The bus-conductor was like the conductor of an orchestra. He guided the conversation, drew out the shy or bored or tired, linked the passengers together, strangers spoke to one another through him; on the last bus of the day it was he who controlled the badinage, helped the drunks up and down the steps, chose his butt and his allies, and made a whole thing out of an assortment. This afternoon, heat and the dullness of the hour discouraged him. A few words about Joseph's haircut and he subsided disconsolately, whistling through his teeth. When a woman began to shell the peas which she had bought in the market into her straw hat, he sat down beside her to help.

Harriet watched the woman's plump hands deftly cracking open the pods, stripping the peas into her upturned hat, the calm accuracy of her wrist and fingers, the unhurried pace;

30

and, beside her, the man's clumsiness, the sudden bursting open of the pods, his groping on the slatted floor for the peas which bounced about the bus like bullets. Each empty shuck went over the woman's shoulder and out of the window.

"It is like *Hansel and Gretel*," Harriet whispered.

Vesey looked slowly, uncomprehendingly at her, as if he were returning from some remote place, surprised to find her at his side.

"The trail of pea-shucks," she tried to explain.

He turned his head to look. "The birds will devour them," he said. "Nothing will ever be known of our whereabouts."

The long tunnel of leaves began to look impenetrable; each turn of the road revealed only greenness. His face reflected a greenish pallor.

Joseph knelt at the window looking out, humming tunelessly. Deirdre slumped back, watching, as if she were hypnotised, the woman shelling the peas.

"It has been lovely . . ." Harriet began, but her stammer caught at the words and she looked away, out of the window, her throat moving—he could see—with embarrassment, so that she was unable to continue.

"What has been lovely, my dear girl?" he asked.

She pressed the palms of her hands close together between her knees. "It will be so dull when you go back," she said with sudden bravery, and resolve.

Considering the changes, the promise, of his own near future, he did not know how to answer what seemed the obvious truth without condescension or discouragement.

"You will be all right," he said, smiling, denying her any comfort.

"If Mother asks us," Deirdre suddenly turned round to enquire, "what do we say we had for lunch?"

"That you had tomatoes and potatoes and peas. And bread."

"Suppose she says why only that?"

"You will say 'We thought you wouldn't like us to have meat'."

Deirdre rehearsed this under her breath.

"Then you will be telling the truth," Vesey said, with his careless smile.

"I didn't have any bread," Joseph said, coming away from the window which was all steamed over with his breath.

Caroline was back from her meeting in time for high tea.

"My poor little boy!" she said to Joseph, smoothing his cropped head. "Harriet, don't run away."

"I ought to go," Harriet said, sitting down.

"This is prison fare," said Deirdre casually, looking at her salad.

"I said I could have bread any day," Joseph reminded them.

"I wonder," said Vesey, staring at the children, yet at the same time spreading butter with a cynical deliberation, "I wonder if Harriet and I will be playing hide-and-seek with you to-night."

'The meat has over-excited them,' Harriet thought. She had always heard that it inflamed the baser instincts.

"I liked you-know-what," said Joseph.

"We had ice-cream. I hope that was all right," Harriet said quickly.

"There was money over from the shoes," Vesey explained.

"But there could not have been," Caroline said. "The money was your mother's. You should not exceed what you are allowed."

"The ice-cream was not the best part of the day," said Joseph.

"He was a good boy having his hair cut," Harriet said hurriedly.

"I was a good boy eating my din-din," Joseph said in a baby voice.

"Mother," said Deirdre, "we save a lot of money being

32

vegetarians, don't we?"

"Only in doctors' bills," Caroline replied. "Why do you ask?"

"I noticed macaroni-cheese was only eightpence."

"And here was I feeling sorry for you that they had no vegetarian dish," Caroline said, and laughed.

"Vesey bought some nice shoes," Harriet interposed.

"Yes, we must look at them after tea."

"They are grey," Deirdre said.

Caroline frowned. "How do you mean—grey?"

"They are grey suède," Vesey said quietly. He looked down sideways at the tablecloth, leaning back in his chair as if fatigued.

"Grey suède," said Caroline.

"Yes."

A little silence fell; or rather, was drawn down. Caroline picked up her cup and drank tea steadily. Her cheekbones were scarlet.

"Aren't grey shoes nice?" Joseph asked.

Caroline smiled as she replaced the cup very quietly in its saucer.

"Nice?" she repeated in her amused, indulgent voice. "I don't think 'nice' or 'nasty' enter into it."

Vesey flicked a crumb across the table, then another.

"More salad, Joseph?" Caroline asked.

"I'm not hungry."

"What did you say?"

"I'm not hungry."

"No, *thank* you."

"Only a little bit then," he said. He lifted up his plate innocently.

Vesey, his eyes half-closed, nodded, as if at some private thought, which pleased him.

"That was touch and go," said Deirdre as they strolled through the fields.

33

"Only because you made it so," Harriet said coldly.

"You want to have your cake and then blame others that you have eaten it," Vesey added.

"Only it was meat," Joseph said.

"And you find the danger of blaming more exciting than the other part," said Vesey.

"As if I care," Deirdre said, wiping tears away with her fingers.

"You are not to be out of our sight until you go to bed," Vesey said. "Since you are not to be trusted. If you go off on your own without a responsible person—either Harriet or me—the consequences will be such that I could not answer for."

"You can't be with us for the rest of our lives," Joseph muttered.

"Speak up, Joseph," Vesey said. "I am afraid that we didn't have the pleasure of hearing what you said."

"I said you can't be with us for ever," Joseph said bravely, staring ahead as he walked across the field.

"Ah, correct! Time will part us; other commitments will engage me. Yet no matter where you are, you will be continually reminded of me, feel my presence as strongly beside you as you feel it now. Strange, that! Very, very strange! Remember, my dear Joseph."

"I don't believe you."

Deirdre put her arm across her brother's shoulders. They walked unevenly over the bumpy stubble, awkwardly entwined.

"Don't tease them," Harriet implored him; for the sight of the two children plodding on together touched her painfully; but what touched her more painfully was Vesey's mood from which the teasing sprang. His face was whiter than ever; his words fell like the strokes of a whip. For Caroline had shown distaste; now Harriet disapproval.

"Every time you go for a walk you pick flowers," he said. "Like a bloody little cockney."

34

Harriet stared at her bunch of bleached chickory as if she could not believe her eyes, or her ears.

"I shall tell mother you said 'bloody'," Deirdre said, turning round.

"*That* wasn't very sensible of him, was it?" Vesey said lightly, in Caroline's voice.

"When you are hurt, you lay waste all around you," Harriet said quietly. "No one is safe."

She was dismayed at loving someone imperfect. She tried to think of Vesey that day at lunch cutting Joseph's meat for him. She could not believe that anyone so loved could be flawed by spitefulness, the quality above all others which distressed her, or that tenderness and cruelty could inhabit the same person, dwell side by side, one sometimes intensifying the other.

"Hurt?" Vesey repeated. It was the one charge he would not have brought. "Bored you mean, perhaps?"

"Yes, I expect you are bored as well," said Harriet sadly.

All through the long winter and the spring, she would not have him near her; yet, now, standing so close beside him, the moment which should have been so precious was worse than useless: it shrank, and stopped and curdled. These blue flowers she carried in her hand she would surely hate for the rest of her life.

The children, feeling themselves no more the chief butt of Vesey's bad humour, loosened and drifted apart, hopped in and out of the furrows, singing, and when Joseph turned again it was seen that all was forgotten, or forgiven.

"We could go in to Hardy's Farm," he said to Vesey, and he smiled hopefully, as if their relationship had always been amiable, and might be more so.

"I doubt if Harriet here would care to," Vesey said.

"Could we, Harriet?"

"It is trespassing," Vesey said, glancing at her, then at the sky.

"How can we trespass on someone who is dead?" Deirdre asked.

"Harriet would jib even at that."

The farmyard to which they came had the derelict look of after an auction-sale; bills were stuck to the walls and littered the ground; there was a smell of dried cow-dung and trampled grass, and going in through a creaking gate they disturbed pigeons who seemed not to have been disturbed for a long time. Empty barns and stalls enclosed the yard. Along one side, the house with its blank windows faced them.

It was easy to climb in through the pantry window. Then the cold and silence of the empty house lay before them, the carvernous dark kitchen with its broken stone floor and cobwebbed plate-racks and mossy sink.

"It smells like the tomb," said Deirdre.

"I don't like it," Joseph whimpered.

"Harriet and I are going upstairs to the haunted room," said Vesey.

"Rooms can't be haunted," Deirdre said in a terrified voice.

"There's my sensible girl," said Vesey.

"Harriet is afraid," Joseph observed.

"Harriet is a ninny," Vesey told him. He spoke as if Harriet herself were no longer there. "She lets words break her bones. She hides her face at the slightest thing. She picks all these flowers to comfort herself because her hands are trembling."

The children, not understanding, opened a cupboard and looked in. A mouse ran out and they drew back into one another's arms. Now that Vesey's voice had stopped echoing round the walls, they could hear a tap dripping dismally into the sink.

Harriet walked out of the kitchen and down a brick passage into the hall. She tried to steady herself by breathing slowly and deeply, hoping her tears would recede. It was a physical struggle, for her mind seemed empty. At the crest of each breath, weeping threatened her. Far away now the

36

voices of the children sounded, as if at the bottom of a well. When she thought she heard footsteps coming after her, she sped silently up the stairs, for though she had kept back her tears, she felt she would not if she were made to speak.

Doors stood ajar on the landing, and on this floor sunlight streamed in. From the window, she could see the blond stubble and the dark elm-trees, gnats in the golden light and, below, a tangled garden with purplish roses upon sagging arches.

In the largest room a carved canopy jutted out where once a bed had stood, torn hangings still drooped from it. On the window-sill was a broken wine-glass and a box of pills. 'I suppose the old man died in here,' she thought, but it was the living she feared and the footsteps of the living pursuing her. She was cornered in this room and had nowhere to hide.

"Harriet!" said Vesey, but she would not turn away from the window. "Don't go on being silly, there's a good girl! My God, what a funny room. I suppose he died here." He opened the box of pills and offered them to her. "I dare you to take these and see what happens. Ah, come, Harriet! Don't sulk. If you don't speak to me, I shall cut my artery." He held the jagged wine-glass to his wrist. "You see, I mean it." A little bead of blood grew larger on his white skin.

"Don't be absurd, Vesey!"

"That's better. I don't mind what you say as long as you speak to me. Only the *looks* I get I can't abide." He threw the wine-glass into a corner, where it splintered with a frail sound against the wall.

"Where are the children?" Harriet asked.

"They went out again. The mice frightened them. Do mice frighten you, Harriet?"

"No."

"What does frighten you?"

She turned away from him and put out her hand to the carved canopy-post, steadying herself.

"I think you are at the end of your tether," he said.

37

She leant her head against the post, her arm crooked above it.

"Sometimes I feel that I am, too," he added.

He put his hand out and touched her hair, but she only buried her head deeper against her arm. The moment he began to caress her, she felt weakness besetting her. It transgressed her stubborn intention; like a slow stain it spread across her self-defence; visible, she feared, as it gathered and overtook her.

When she looked at him, he could see the mark of the carved wood dented quite deeply across her brow: at first it was white, then slowly reddened. He gathered her up close to him and kissed her. He felt her warm hands in his hair and saw himself very tiny in her eyes. This time, she returned his kiss. Their hearts knocked and raced. Rigidly together, flesh against bone, they stood without moving, undergoing a sense of being not in their right element.

At the back of her extreme tension was a feeling of disbelief and unreality, for she had never reached this limit in all her dreams about him, and all her vague yearnings, dissatisfactions, disturbances, were resolved so suddenly that she felt goaded and overthrown.

And now they seemed no longer alone. A third presence was sensed—their own passion, to which they were answerable. He laid his hand against her beating throat, smoothed her polished shoulder.

She became passive, but conscious of waiting, of being only delightfully checked.

"Darling, did anyone do this to you before?"

"Of course not, Vesey."

"Promise?"

"But I can't promise the past."

She had no coquetry; his was merely an absurd question.

"Did *you?*" she asked suddenly and fearfully. She dreaded the answer, as if he were some old roué.

"Did I what?"

38

"This."

"Hundred of times."

"No. Truthfully."

He took her close to him again. "No, I never did," he said in a hurried voice. He swayed with her in his arms and shut his eyes. The weakness of their legs seemed a sly trap of nature. But there was nowhere in this empty room; only the dusty floor.

"If only," said Vesey, "the bed was still here. We could lie down together and draw the curtains round."

Feeling he should not have said that, she was none the less elated that he had. She imagined them lying there side by side; secret, blissful, entranced.

When Joseph's voice was heard calling, both started with the shock. They remembered the children. Harriet put one hand to her blouse, the other to her hair; the gesture of a much older, much guiltier woman. She had never looked so grown-up.

"Where are you?" Joseph wailed from the garden.

When Vesey looked out, he saw him standing below with a bunch of roses in his hand.

"So you have stolen as well as trespassed?" Vesey called down, his voice still wavering and hurried.

"Coo-ee! Vesey!" shouted Deirdre, coming out from some trees and wandering across the lawn towards the house.

Vesey turned back from the window and looked at Harriet. She was picking up her flowers which were scattered on the floor.

"Are you all right, Harriet?"

"Yes." She smiled.

"We had better go."

"Yes."

He hesitated a moment longer, watching her; then he turned back to the window and leaned out.

"Coming!" he yelled, his hands cupped to his mouth, for the children were drifting away. The sound flew back into the room and echoed round the walls. "Coming! Coming!"

Later, Vesey went back some of the way with Harriet towards her home. He pushed her bicycle and she walked beside him, carrying her bunch of flowers. A woolly mist had risen and cows moved knee-deep in it, vague shapes against the gathering darkness. The rasping sound of their breath broke the silence, and, far away, the cry of owls. They walked along the footpath without speaking, trod on the colourless flowers in the bearded grasses.

Time's wingèd chariot was not a thing that they could hear.

When Joseph cried out in his sleep, Caroline put down her sewing and ran to him. Still strange from his hair-cut, he lay in bed gabbling fast in a worried way as if he had no time to explain before disaster would overcome him.

Caroline smoothed the damp feathers of hair away from his hot forehead.

"No, Vesey! No, Vesey!" Joseph shouted.

"What is it, my pet?"

Then incoherence followed. She strained to listen; but the sounds only resembled, were not really words. She woke him gently, settled him again in his bed and when he seemed peaceful at last she went downstairs to Hugo.

"I shall be glad when Vesey goes," she said at once. "He works these children up to fever-pitch with his sensational stories and his teasing. Only to-night, Deirdre said that he told her Hardy's Farm is haunted. Something fantastic, unwholesome about the boy, and Lilian feels it too. Grey suède shoes! What will his mother think?"

"Send him back," said Hugo.

"How can I? We always have him in the summer."

"Say your mother's coming and there's no room."

Caroline walked round and round considering this. "I should like mother to have a holiday," she said at last.

.   .   .   .   .

40

Harriet's diary had spilled back over yesterday, but she could not cram in all that had happened. She heard her mother coming up to bed and curved her hand secretively across the top of the page, but still her pen raced on. "Vesey takes size 8 in shoes," she wrote.

'How unbearably pathetic people's rooms are when there is no one there!' Harriet thought. It was the next afternoon and she was left alone to type letters.

The landing was quiet. All through the house, the hall clock could be heard ticking. Caroline had taken the children out to tea. Vesey had not been seen all day.

As long as she could hear the clinking of crockery far off in the kitchen, Harriet knew that she was safe. She stood half on the landing, half in Vesey's room, looking in at the neat bed, the book beside it, the white shoe-box on a chair, the blank mirror.

Her ears still attentive to the sounds in the kitchen, she tip-toed across the creaking floor-boards and stood looking down at the dressing-table. A little clock rustled anxiously, a comb was stuck in an up-turned hair brush. Vesey's school dressing-gown hung at the back of the door; his sponge dried on the window-sill. The room was poignantly impersonal, as if it rebuked Harriet. The curtains suddenly rattling along their rod, bellying out in a gust of wind, made her start dreadfully. When she was calm again, she took Vesey's hand-towel from its rail and holding it to her face as if it were some sacred relic, breathed in its beautiful fragrance of Royal Vinolia soap.

"So Vesey is leaving?" Lilian said at supper-time.

Enormous calm and fortitude the young have when they are first in love and hiding it.

"Is he?" Harriet asked.

"So Caroline told me when we were out to tea."

"I thought he was staying until September," Harriet said

vaguely. To give her hands something to do, she took more potatoes.

"Caroline wants his room for her mother, so that she can come for a holiday. She has been rather out-of-sorts."

This phrase sounded odd to both of them, but Caroline had used it and now Lilian handed it on. It hedged: meant nothing.

There is a game which children play in which they creep up to one who is hiding his eyes; step by step, frozen still with innocence at each quick glance they go tentatively forward, until at last they grow close, close to the point of touching. This evening, Lilian, stealthily, step by step, tried to draw near to Harriet, knowing that one false move would set her back where she began. They gave one another alternate glances across the table. So carefully, each careless-sounding remark was passed. But Lilian was conscious only of check. Fatigue and shock had had the effect upon Harriet of making her warier. Her fit of nervousness sustained her. It did not deceive Lilian, but it baulked her. She was the one who tired first. Back at base, defeated, she felt a great exhaustion of disappointment and misunderstanding. Her daughter, however, was not (which some widows say) all that she had. She had, in fact, Caroline. Caroline would comfort her. She had not wanted to break down her child's resistance, but she did want to feel reassured that it was right for Vesey to go away, that Harriet's pain now would save her from worse ones in the future. She hoped that she was right in wanting this, and to-morrow Caroline would tell her that she was.

With beautiful indifference, Harriet asked: "And when is he to go?" She put her knife and fork neatly together and looked boldly and cruelly at her mother.

Stunned and depressed, she wrote in her diary before she got into bed: "I did not see V. In two days he will be gone."

.   .   .   .   .

42

Harriet laid her plans with pathetic cunning. If Vesey must go, her only possible comfort would be if he were to write to her. She could not see any way for him to begin to do this. Even if he should care to—and he had said he was no letter-writer—she thought that some excuse would help him, if she could find one.

"I am being sent down," he told her, looking in as he passed the window.

"Vesey dear!" Caroline called from the middle of her herbaceous border. "I shouldn't interrupt Joseph's lesson if I were you."

Vesey bowed to Harriet and slouched away.

" 'Ned and Fan sat on the log,' " Joseph droned loudly from the old-fashioned primer Caroline had found. Harriet shut her eyes to hide her impatience.

For the rest of the day she did not see Vesey. When she left in the early evening, he was out on the tennis-court pushing the old mower. The blades whirred noisily; he did not, in all that clatter, hear her approaching and she came right up to him holding out a book. He turned in surprise and pushed his hair from his glistening forehead with a trembling hand.

"It is too hot for you to be doing this," Harriet said.

"I know, but I must curry favour. Though I can curry it until I am blue in the face as far as Caroline is concerned."

"What have you done?"

"I have contaminated everyone within my orbit. Given meat to innocent children and encouraged in them sickly ideas about the supernatural . . ."

"Who said this?"

". . . I have given Joseph nightmares. I am decadent and affected. I have interrupted you at your work and tried to seduce you in an empty house."

"You say bad things about yourself to stop other people from saying them. You hurt yourself by saying them and that last bit hurt me too."

43

"Don't stammer.

"Has Caroline said all that?"

"I can read Caroline like a book."

"How could she guess things which only you and I know?"

"About trying to seduce you?"

"You know I . . . you know that I didn't take your remark seriously."

"Don't *stammer*. Perhaps you told her," he suggested.

She did not answer. She looked down the length of the tennis-court, half of it covered with daisies, the other half shaved in irregular lines.

"Or perhaps," he went on, watching her closely, "I mentioned it myself and it has slipped my memory. What is this?"

"A book of mine, I thought you might like to read."

He took it from her and turned its leaves.

"I have very little time left to me, and a lot of favour-currying to do. I don't want a bad report from here as I had from school."

"When are you going?"

"To-morrow after lunch."

"I hope I see you again."

"I hope so too I'm sure," he said promptly.

He put the book down on the grass and turned to the lawn-mower. He smiled at her and nodded and then at a tremendous pace and with a deafening sound went off down the tennis-court away from her.

In the morning, he was about the house, wearing his London clothes. His suitcase stood ready in the hall. Now that he was going, Caroline relented, enough to pick a basket of apples for him and roses for his mother. At lunch, he seemed excited. The children, Caroline noticed, would not meet his eye. At the sight of Harriet's controlled smile, her over-alertness at passing plates, her over-vivacity,

44

Caroline for the first time began to doubt what she was doing. "I have my children to consider," she begged herself to remember; but she was not a callous woman, nor insensitive, and if there was any misery of her own creation, her own precipitating, for whatsoever good reasons it was done, she did regret it.

"You may as well go home after lunch," she told Harriet, trying to find some way to make amends. "Joseph can have his rest and all the letters are done."

"If you are sure?" Harriet replied with her polite smile. She bent over Joseph and made a border of plum-stones round his plate. "This year, next year . . ." she began to count. Joseph looked surprised at this sudden attention.

Vesey came into the hall as she was leaving. In his dark suit he was no longer part of the holidays, nor of anything that had gone before. He seemed strange to her.

She felt no pain, no wish to hasten or prolong this moment in the sunshine at the foot of the stairs.

"Good-bye, Vesey."

She only hoped that he would not mention the book which she had lent to him; that, at best, he was keeping it for an excuse to write; or that he would remember later and be obliged to write, and be jogged occasionally by the thought of her.

"Good-bye, Harriet."

He smiled kindly and looked into her eyes. They hesitated, and then shook hands formally. As she stepped over the dogs which lay sleeping at the open door and began to walk down the garden, he leaned back against the chimney-piece, his hands in his pockets, and watched her go.

Departure in the afternoon is depressing to those who are left. The day is so dominated by the one who has gone and, although only half-done, must be got through with that particular shadow lying over it. She could not return to her mother at that hour. To-morrow, she would begin the desolate task of ticking off the days of her life until Vesey

45

should come again; to-day her despair was too dreary. She walked on the common which lay near to her home. The glades, dark, with their bracken smell, offered her a shelter which her home denied her. Deep in the bitter smell of the bracken she lay down and closed her eyes. She thought of Vesey pacing up and down the platform of the little station until his train came: imagined him waiting, pale in the intense heat of the afternoon, and at last borne away round the curve of the cutting, into the tunnel, and gone. With her face in her hands, her body hidden in the bracken, she began to weep. She did not so much indulge herself in this great torrent of weeping as become passive while the weight of tears was cleared from her.

A year is too long to wait for someone beloved. In the morning, she would set about living that year, comforting herself across the great waste of days. This afternoon she could not begin. At the end of her weeping, when words began to come again into her head, "It is too long," she cried. She rested her throbbing face in the cool, harsh bracken. She felt that she had cried all the tears of the rest of her life.

In the morning, Caroline, with a kind look and kind untrue phrases, held out her book to her. "Vesey asked me to give you this, and thank you very much. He said I was to be sure not to forget to give it to you."

Harriet took the book and smiled. In the first few pages a blade of grass was stuck to mark a place.

"To-night, will you play hide-and-seek?" Deirdre asked. She took Harriet's hand and spun herself round in a pirouette, absorbed by her twirling skirt, her own fascination.

2

WE cannot always remember our first glimpse of those who later become important to us. Feeling that the happening should have been more significant, we strain back through our memories in vain. But Harriet could always remember that it was through a piece of flawed glass that she first saw Charles Jephcott. In the bus window his figure wavered and thinned, broadened, slanted, so that she had no idea if a fat man or a thin, old or young, would presently enter the bus. Curiosity made her turn her head to see.

To her he seemed so old as to be outside the range of her interest. He sat down in front of her, steadying himself as the bus began to move—an elderly man of about thirty-five. His profile, turned to the passing hedges, was commanding as if it were stamped on a coin, his sandy hair sprang in a straight line from his brow; a heavy signet ring on one hand— a hairy, freckled hand—seemed a further sign of his authority, as was his way of shooting his wrist out of his cuff so that he could see his watch. He sat in the bus with an aloof air as if he were unaccustomed to doing so. A faint smell of spirits came from him. No one in Harriet's world drank anything intoxicating, except at weddings, and she associated that smell with the last bus home and a staggering rowdiness. His manner, though, was so unlike this that she supposed his bout of drunkenness to be over.

The next time that she saw him was in his own home. His mother had come to live at the Old Vicarage where once Dr Garrett Anderson had stayed. Lilian, who had never entered the house before, paused in the hall and looked up at

47

the ceiling, round at the walls, disregarding her hostess for a brief moment, as if there were homage to be paid first.

Julia Jephcott was in her sixties. Mad, raffish, unself-conscious, she had the beautiful and calm air of one who has all her life acknowledged compliments. This air, associated with beauty, lingered after the beauty itself had collapsed and fled. She seemed to be lovely still to herself, as if no amount of looking into mirrors could ruin her illusion. For this reason, perhaps, she wore the clothes of much younger women and a pale, haphazard make-up, which wretchedly emphasised the wrinkled eyelids, the drawn throat. Her white hair was patchily gilded as if it had been brushed over with the yolk of egg. Her charm was unflagging. She had learnt it diligently in Sir Frank Benson's Shakespearean Company. Hours of walking with books on her head had given her a deportment which was now unconscious, and years of being kind to her admirers, of smiling (though one word could not describe the great range of her smiles— tender, gay, brave, mocking, sly, wistful) at nothing, of stressing her words and lowering her voice for scarcely any reason at all, had made it impossible for her now to speak to her gardener or pay a bus-fare without seeking to please and beguile. She was still their servant. She thought nothing of herself.

Even Lilian's standing mute in the hall looking about her did not spoil her welcome. Julia always came out to meet her guests, running down the shallow steps with a suggestion of drapery flowing back from her, her braceleted arms stretched out in greeting, her palms upturned, denoting eagerness and the proffering of love.

While Lilian was making her silent obeisance, Julia came to kiss Harriet, who felt that here at last was somebody to love her, who had singled her out.

Charles did not run to meet people. He stood with one elbow on the chimney-piece in the drawing-room, one hand in his pocket, waiting. From time to time, listening to the

48

voices in the hall, he glanced at his finger-nails, bent them towards him and gave them an aloof dispraisal. He also had a trick, when he was alone or as good as alone, of stretching his closed lips in a tight grimace and rubbing his chin. He did this when his mind was empty, although it gave him a very thoughtful look.

It appeared to Harriet that she was always the one who remembered having seen other people. They never remembered having seen her. She did not like to seem (even to herself) so much more caught up in the importance of others when they cared so little for her. While she was trying to tone down her enthusiasm to something more appropriate, they were attempting to simulate what they did not feel. Sometimes they merely pretended to pretend. Julia could not help but convince.

"Dr Garrett Anderson once came here for a rest," Lilian was explaining.

"Darling, I must confess I never heard of him," said Julia. "My narrow, narrow life and my muddle-headed ways. I am quite a loony about people's names.

"*Elizabeth* Garrett Anderson," said Lilian faintly.

"I would never go to a woman doctor," Julia said. She put her hand up beautifully to her face, the tips of her fingers curved to her cheekbone, her thumb to her chin. "A man is half the battle," she added mysteriously. "Now here is my old stodge. My son Charles. Darling, this is Mrs Claridge and dear Harriet. Say how-do-you-do nicely."

Harriet guessed that only his mother would ever make fun of Charles.

"Are you a suffragette?" Julia asked Lilian.

"No one has any need to be that now, but once I was."

"I have never voted in my life, though I would if I were not so ignorant. You and I must have some talks, and you shall tell me exactly what I have to do. What you once worked so hard for, I must not waste. And I should like to vote before I die." Her eyes misted. She put her hand flat to the

49

base of her throat. There was a moment of nervousness in the room.

Charles had taken Harriet's hand and given it back.

"Tea," said Julia, sitting down on the sofa, "it always seems such an interruption and not very nice, nor worth . . . and one never knows how much, how little, to provide."

She had decided on a great deal, Harriet was glad to see, and every little table was laden with scones and layer cakes and Swiss rolls.

"However," Julia said, shaking back her bracelets, "if we didn't have tea, we could never use the china."

While she was talking, Charles seemed gravely to await her conclusion and, as soon as she ceased, turned to Lilian with some polite and daunting question which, once answered, only could confer silence.

Julia poured tea gracefully, but it all ran over into the saucers.

"My grandmother judged people very much by how they poured tea," Julia rattled on, as she emptied the saucers into the slop-basin. "She applied those arbitrary tests, like throwing witches into water. And being a *lady*" (her voice floated derisively at the word: she handed Lilian her cup) "that hinged on such little things—whether, for instance, one's gloves were buttoned before one opened the front-door. Only the maids buttoned them on the way out. It is still a check, an inhibition, to me. Such trivial things. And what she knew about it all, I cannot say. She was not even what is called one of nature's ladies."

Charles hitched his trousers over his knees, crossed his legs. Harriet, trying not to stare at his mother stared too much at him. As soon as she became conscious of this, she began to look about the room instead, at all the pink and grey cretonne, the cushions embroidered with delphiniums, the firescreen with hollyhocks. In the tarnished brass fender lay all sorts of implements for doing things to fires: long-

50

handled shovels, crooked loose-hinged tongs, pokers, bellows. Not a square foot of wall-paper but was covered with purple water-colours of moorland, or cows wading in ponds, or Persian kittens done in crayon.

When Charles asked her a question, she violently started and he was obliged to repeat it. His mother suddenly lost interest and leant back, fanning herself with a bunch of peacocks'-feathers which she had taken out of a vase. But her smile was at the ready; her look alert. She rarely relaxed more than this, and never unless alone.

After tea, Charles played the piano. The delicate music and his quick hands following one another up the keyboard only underlined his masculinity, as if he played some girls' game with efficiency and despatch. His cigarette trailed smoke from its ash-tray; at the end of the piece of music, he crushed it out, half-turned towards them, paused, and then continued.

Beating at the air with her improvised fan, his mother closed her eyes. Only Lilian and Harriet were left to look about uneasily. Harriet tried to put on a polite and considering look. She loved the music, but could not allow herself to enjoy it among strangers. Sunk too far back in her too large chair she felt helpless, like a beetle turned on its back; and as if she could never rise again, nor find the right phrases of appreciation.

Lilian sat upright with her head slightly inclined as if it were burdened. It was true that music never delighted, only weakened, her.

Imperviously, Charles went from Ballade to Waltz, from Waltz to Prelude. He played without music; mostly, his glance was sidelong down at the keyboard; but sometimes his jaw seemed to stiffen; he would glance out into the garden in an offhand way. Harriet had not imagined that the playing of Chopin could be turned into such a Cæsarist display.

Julia leaning back with such an exhausted look made

51

Lilian suspect that the music was her ruse to take a short rest, and this suspicion antagonised her all the more. She had not cared for Julia from the first; found her subversive and absurd. To have music wreaked upon her was another irritation. 'Perhaps I should ask Harriet to recite,' she thought scornfully, glancing at her daughter spread out so clumsily in her chair, legs bent awkwardly, an expression of taut discontent (which Harriet herself meant to be serious appraisal) upon her face.

Charles finished as abruptly as he had begun, even closed up the piano as if sealing off that side of his nature, and went to fetch drinks. As the tray came in, Lilian was rising to go. Sherry was poison to her, she explained. Gin was worse. All spirits, in fact, were impossible. Her digestion had never recovered from the times in prison. She mentioned this to support herself, to keep in touch with her own world which had seemed eclipsed.

"You were in prison even!" Julia said. "How wonderfully brave and romantic."

But no, it had not been, Lilian thought. Because, once there, she had lost her defiance. The weight of disapproval in the air, the cold discipline and impersonality, the loneliness, had made her beliefs seem an uncharming aberration, her behaviour outré. She could not answer, but most of Julia's remarks were unanswerable. She checked conversations so often that she was obliged to rattle on herself.

Harriet hated to hear her mother mentioning prison. She could not bear that she should have been so martyred and now should dwell on her martyrdom; sometimes, in fact, rather revel in it, as on every July the fourteenth, when she pinned on that badge made like a prison gate and went proudly to London to the meeting at Mrs Pankhurst's Memorial. As a child, Harriet had always averted her eyes from that brooch. Now she was afraid that these two would think her mother freakish. Her quick, doubtful look at Charles met his enigmatic stare. She sipped her sherry. Her mother watched her indulgently, as if confident that a glass of sherry would not turn *her* girl's head, that temptation on a larger scale even would be sturdily rejected.

"And did you go on hunger-strike?" Julia asked in an encouraging voice.

Lilian whitened; but it was to Charles's credit, Harriet thought, that he suddenly (without seeing Lilian's face) sharply said: "Mother, you are being impertinent!"

'I couldn't bear him to say that to me,' Harriet thought. 'I should die of shame.'

But Julia only smiled. "Silly Charles! Women understand one another." Her smile warmed as it included Lilian, suggested complicity. Lilian's answering smile was the faintest tremor. "What an extraordinary statement!" Charles said. He took Harriet's glass and nodded slightly at her. The nod seemed to be instead of a smile. His smiles were rare. Perhaps there were too many in the house already.

"My head! My head!" Lilian said, as they crossed the road to Forge Cottage. "How near she lives to us! That old enchantress!"

"I rather liked her," Harriet said sulkily. "She was so different."

Walking in this warm air stirred up her melancholy. Quiet broke quiet. The still early evening had autumn in it. Grass was tawny; hedges dusty. Under trees late wasps tunnelled into sleepy pears; windfalls rotted. Golden-rod and michaelmas-daisies had begun to be the only flowers in the garden.

She went straight up to her bedroom and sat on the side of the bed, her hands locked tight between her knees, her teeth clenched, as if only by hardness of bone against bone, nails driven against knuckles, could she resist the excavation of her flesh by her passion, support herself against the daily riddling away of her resistance, the unexpected agitations (such as this) which broke up her now painful and lonely life.

She heard her mother go out from the house into the garden and then an irregular clop-clop of shears began; a smell of cut privet, bitter and dusty, came through the window. Harriet rocked on the bed, her eyes tight shut. She began to dramatise her grief; desiring to be struck down. If it could not be love, it could be sorrow. Sometimes, when she had heard old people talking of their memories, of the landmarks in their lives, she was surprised at their public quality—the funeral of the Old Queen, Mafeking Night, the Armistice, the first motor-car, the last lamp-lighter. She thought they dissembled. It is never like that, surely? she wondered: not, at the end of a long life, to see other people's sadness and triumph as the key moments? Or do Mafeking Night and the rest stand in the place of the secret and personal, in the place of what cannot be told and must perish with us—moments when for no reason that we can understand—a warm evening, the scent of leaves, a cock crowing far away—all the air becomes distended with grief. A moment such as this. She began to pace all about the room, putting out her hand to touch the furniture, to steady and reassure herself.

Between the pages of her diary was a photograph of Vesey which she had taken from Caroline's album. Glancing through the photographs one day with Deirdre, she had found that one beginning to come unstuck. The next day, when she was alone, she had swiftly ripped it out and put it in her pocket. No one ever mentioned it or noticed that it was gone; but the sight of the album still alarmed her. She knew now that wrong-doing was only a question of how far she might be driven; that what she wanted badly, she would take.

Now she opened her diary and sat down with the little creased photograph before her; studied it carefully, as if something new might come to light. But nothing did. Vesey looked back at her, and so did Deirdre and Joseph on either side. His hair hung down in a fringe; his smile was wide and

54

rather meretricious, that exaggerated photograph-smile so often seen (as if only happiness should be recorded). She could imagine how it had faded the moment the camera clicked. His arms were over the shoulders of the children. They sat bunched together on the grass; their feet out of focus, too large, like a row of up-turned boats. This poorish photograph (the house in the background tilted, the lawn slanted, roses were pale blurs) was all that was left of some forgotten afternoon, perhaps a year ago. Vesey's book lay open, its covers arching up in the heat of the sun, Deirdre was making a daisy-chain, Joseph had a bandage over his knee. The shadow of the photographer—Caroline, most likely—stretched long over the grass before them. She—if it was she—had rallied them into smiling; but it was a row of sandals she had photographed.

Nothing new was yielded up. Harriet gazed and gazed; but Vesey only smiled his false smile; his hands hung loosely on the shoulders of the two children; she could not even read the title of his book, and now would never know.

Stiff with her grief which had flowed at last, as grief does, into a great sea of boredom, she yawned, stood up and went to the window. Her mother, still wearing her silk dress, snipped at the privet hedge; and from the yard across the road came a swishing sound. She could see the side of the Old Vicarage, a wall with iron balconies among vine-leaves, an old stable with a gilt weather-vane and turtle-doves which flew in the air together, in following arcs, like birds painted on a plate. On the cobbles, Charles, standing well back, was hosing his car. A cool smell rose. Harriet leant out and watched him. Agony receded into dullness. Far away, like insect-voices, dogs barked, children called. A yellow rose growing on the wall below her loosed all its petals: they fell over the path below. Water came now from under the blue gate, twisted out into the road, bearing dust with it.

When a bell rang inside the house, Charles (she could see him between the leaves) crossed the yard at once and turned off a tap. When he had gone, Harriet turned from the window again, yawning.

3

THE disorder in the room was appalling—but had ceased to
fidget Harriet, who now contributed to it, dropped screwed-
up face-tissues on the floor, left dirty cups in the sink. She
had made several such adjustments in her life, experimenting
with cheap make-up, letting down her hems, acquiring all the
mateyness she could in the form of small confidences, by
helping Miss Lazenby with her hair and adding to the
untidiness of this room. At first, willing though she was, the
transition was not easy. Although she never really met the
glances over tea-cups, she knew that just before she looked,
just before they casually turned aside, they were all trying to
place her: not with any particular unkindness: it was only, as
Miss Brimpton would have said, that they wondered.

"I only wondered," she was now saying. "I said to him I
was only wondering if the juniors couldn't keep to their own
separate tea-money. It's very humiliating, I said, when you
come to the end of the week and there's no tea left they've
been so extravagant. Perhaps you'd ask them, he said.
I'll certainly make enquiries, I said."

They all sat round, breathing into their tea, elbows on the
table, before them a litter of buns in bags, butter in greasy
papers, cigarette-stubs in saucers, Miss Lazenby's setting-
lotion and comb.

Harriet found her position among these 'seniors' strange,
hardly tenable. The two juniors were, it was true, only
fourteen or fifteen, fresh from school, useful only for doing
work. Their wages were purely nominal, the manager said,
because they were learning the business; but if they had not

picked it up within a week at most Miss Brimpton would have found something to say. "I was only just wondering about Miss So-and-So," would be what she would find to say to the manager. "Whether she's not perhaps the wrong girl in the wrong job."

The manager feared Miss Brimpton. She had been in the shop before him. How long before altered according to her mood and to the conversation. She was often cagey about her age, though sometimes alluding to herself in a buoyant unbelieving way as 'fat and forty'. "When you're fat and forty like me," she would say to Harriet, whom she took under her wing. Another phrase was "That would be before your time, dear." At first assessment, her blue eyes, her peachy, hairy face, her spreading figure, suggested warmth and motherliness. But her mouth was tight, her look sometimes too steady. Her accent was rather fancy and she was a snob of the most usual kind. But she was a figure of mystery, in that no one could believe a word she said. The others did wonder about her. They were all the time wondering about one another.

Harriet's initiative in going to work in a shop had surprised everyone, especially herself. She wondered how she had wrenched herself out of that almost automatic going back and forth between Caroline's and her home, the ennui and impatience she suffered with the children, her mind more than half taken up with her own miseries, her waiting for some mention of Vesey and for the letter which never came. He had dropped so completely out of her life. The days shortened, but only technically. The time it took to live them seemed endless. She began to look, secretly, for another job. What she had found was the best she could hope for. Lilian had not demurred. She felt a little tingling of pride that her daughter had done something for herself. The emotions she had once reserved for when Harriet should be called to the bar or returned to Parliament she now felt to a lesser degree when the girl went off to work in a gown shop

58

for thirty shillings a week. She only hoped that the other girls were of a nice type. When she was young, she had refused to be sheltered, but the women in the Militant Suffrage Movement had been of a very nice type, especially those who, like herself, had gone to prison. The more elegant and ladylike they were, indeed, the more ferociously militant they had seemed. Young Mary Blomfield, for instance, who had called out as she was presented at Court: "Your Majesty, please end the shame of women in British Prisons!" The bravery of this, which always made Lilian flush, would have seemed unbecoming to Miss Brimpton, who thought that Royalty should not be troubled or disturbed. She wore pastel shades like Queen Mary and the Duchess of York, and had once peered through the railings of 145 Piccadilly to see the little Princesses in the garden. "They have only to be seen to be loved," she had said. "Little cream coats."

"How are they different from any other bloody kids?" Miss Lazenby inquired. She swore a great deal in an offhand way. She was always plucking her eyebrows when they had these conversations. She did so whenever she could spare a moment, peering into a smeared mirror, her mouth open. She had scarcely any eyebrows left, only an inflamed expanse, but that was fashionable at the time. Miss Lazenby was rather free and easy with men, but the men were not always themselves in that happy position. She pinned them down, swore at them, drank a great deal at their expense and had good fun describing to her friends their dufferish attempts at lovemaking. "Tell us at elevenses," Miss Brimpton would say cosily as they flicked with feather-dusters the display-cards, the corset dummies. They were always flicking when the manager appeared. (The juniors were usually out buying cheese-rolls or matching cottons to cloth.) If his voice held any criticism of their attitude to customers (clients, Miss Brimpton called them), or their handling of goods, they retreated nicely, excluded him from their feminine world,

59

threw tissue-paper over bust-bodices—their eyelids so leaden, their look at one another so sinister—that he went back exasperated to his office, or round to a coffee-shop to talk to other men.

Only Miss Lovelace treated him with pity and consideration, and he feared her most of all. Warm, large-bosomed, full of dovelike murmurings, she bridged, and had bridged, for many married men the gulf between mother and wife; she encouraged them in self-pity and was an exciting mixture of paramour and nursery-governess. There was no sort of woman that she had not been at one time or another to somebody. She was extremely compliant and sympathetic, and, unlike Miss Lazenby, exacted nothing. Her success with married men had perhaps deprived her of what she most wanted—a home and children. The long sequence of yielding, of gathering to her, of, finally, renunciation, was only repetitious. She did renounce a great deal and from the best motives. Then the tea-room was a trough of despair on her account. Over their elevenses they turned and tried the well-worn phrases—"no other way", "painful for all concerned", "the sake of the children".

They felt not only her immediate tragedy; but saw time passing for her. Noble, sad; she was left with only her self-respect, which did not seem to mean as much to her as she had been led to believe. She knitted cobweb shawls for her sister's babies, made the finest layettes—tucked, smocked, gathered; wrapped them in tissue-paper and kept them by her longer than she need. No one could quite see what had gone wrong, unless her warmth were to blame. Her sister had been bleaker, so much more cautious, less generous: was beautifully rewarded for her caution and did not care for her reward.

She and Miss Lazenby gave Harriet a great deal of conflicting advice, but Miss Brimpton's ruled through both. Miss Brimpton bade her turn her back on men; no relationship in which a woman might stand to a man could but debase her: she evoked a procession of downtrodden wives, bullied mothers, cast-off mistresses; the jilted, the enticed, the abandoned; harlots, doormats, birds in gilded cages. Were not men, she asked, all ungenerous or tyrannical or both, peevish, bestial? They were also vain-glorious and ugly. They had, she always ended, hairy legs. There she shuddered. She took up her cup and drank tea slowly, as if rinsing her mouth.

Harriet's virginity they marvelled over a great deal. It seemed a privilege to have it under the same roof. They were always kindly enquiring after it, as if it were a sick relative. It must not be bestowed lightly, they advised. It must not be bestowed at all, Miss Brimpton said. It was a possession, not a state; was positive, not negative.

Harriet listened with fascination. She had never before encountered such cordiality: life had never been so undemanding. Her very mistakes were applauded as disloyalty to the firm. "Serve them bloody right," as Miss Lazenby said.

Their hours were long, so they spared themselves any hard work, filched what time they could; went up to elevenses at ten, were often missing while they cut out from paper-patterns, set their hair, washed stockings, drank tea. Nothing was done in their own time that could be done in the firm's. They were underpaid, so they took what they could; not money in actual coins, but telephone-calls, stamps, boxes of matches, soap. They borrowed clothes from stock; later when these were marked down as soiled, they bought them at the staff-price, a penny in the shilling discount.

Lilian watched her daughter growing day by day more colourful from all the beauty hints Miss Lazenby gave her. Her finger-nails, at first timidly pink, soon grew rosier, her eyelids bluer. Miss Lazenby herself favoured a greenish eye-shadow and a mother-o'-pearl nail-varnish. Her white hands looked like the hands of the dead. The juniors were sent running about all over the town for mascara and eye-lash-

61

curlers, pills for reducing, henna rinses. The seniors rarely shopped themselves. One day they all had ice from the fishmongers tied under their chins; the next day, clay was drying stiffly on their faces. They sat round the table and rolled their eyes at one another, but could not speak or smile. The juniors, going downstairs, laughed behind their hands.

"Did you see where it says about hair on the face?" Miss Brimpton asked them. She was reading Miss Lovelace's *Daily Mirror*. "Waxed away," she read. She put her hand to her fluffy jaw; Miss Lazenby took up her mirror and gave her face an unfriendly look. "Even the slightest down can cause embarrassment."

"I never felt any embarrassment from mine," said Miss Lovelace. They all looked in their mirrors.

"It means other people are embarrassed," Miss Brimpton said. They were uneasily silent.

"Would it hurt?" Miss Lazenby asked. "How much is it?"

"Painlessly, magically," Miss Brimpton read. "Price three-and-six."

"Send one of the kids round for some," Miss Lazenby said. "We'll do it lunchtime to-morrow. Be a bit of fun if nothing else. Comb my hair out for me, Lovelace, there's an angel."

But Miss Lovelace had pushed all the cups and newspapers to one end of the table and spread out a blanket for her ironing. She often did odds and ends of washing at the shop, never wore her underclothes more than one day because of the soap-flakes advertisement she had read concerning personal freshness; also liked what she called 'touches of white' on her dark clothes; so was always rinsing through, damping down, ironing.

"I'll go down and make an appearance," Miss Brimpton said. She brushed crumbs off her bosom and sailed away. In the shop, the manager said: "I thought you were all lost." He glanced at his watch.

62

"Lost?" she said lightly. "Dearie me, no!" She smiled at herself in a mirror, drawing in her chin. "What a thing to think!" She laughed, as if he were a fanciful child.

"Where is Miss Lazenby?"

"Miss Lazenby? Oh, Miss Lazenby's—upstairs." She told the truth in such a way that he blushed. "She'll be here directly," Miss Brimpton soothed him.

"And Miss Lovelace?" he went on doggedly. There was only one W.C. She could not be upstairs at the same time.

"Miss Lovelace is a little bit off-colour to-day," Miss Brimpton said daintily. She took a pencil from the frizz behind her ear and began to mark her stock-book.

The manager walked quickly away. She smiled after him. "Run up and tell Miss Lovelace and the others to come down at once," she said to one of the juniors, who sped away, fists clenched by her ribs, elbows back, as if she were running a race.

Harriet did not offer up Vesey to the others; but she was inclined, from friendliness, to offer up Charles Jephcott. He was a solicitor in Market Swanford and sometimes gave her lifts in his car between there and the village.

He drove his car as he played the piano with extreme mastery and decision. He scarcely spoke to Harriet, so what she offered to the other girls was mainly innuendo. They did not guess that what she would not tell was what she could not.

Her position in the shop was lifted by her relationship with Charles. He was of a professional class, like Miss Lovelace's Mr Williams from the Midland Bank. He had a fast car and a worldly air. They watched him from windows.

"Were you pleased with the gladioli?" Miss Lazenby asked Harriet.

"What gladioli?"

"The ones Charles bought at Hill's yesterday. I supposed they were for you."

"Oh, those!" said Harriet.

63

The flaw in this affair, they thought, was that he was unmarried. They did not for one moment imagine that he would ever marry Harriet, and as there was no really good excuse (wife, children) to guard her pride when he should presently relinquish her, no reason for renunciation as always there was with Miss Lovelace, they felt that far from heading for tragedy, all that could happen to her was that she would be quite cheaply jilted. Their admiration, however, though expected to be temporary, was genuine for the time-being and was deepened by Julia Jephcott's one day appearing in the shop with a cold chicken for their lunch and a bunch of violets for Harriet. She did not stint her charm to shop-girls (her last smile had always been, tear-laden, for the gallery): but became wonderfully familiar; chided, rallied them, teased. One of her best performances she gave and returned home wonderfully restored and limbered up. Harriet had gradually become a favourite: Julia gave her six pairs of discoloured evening gloves and one of Sir Henry Irving's books signed by him. To amuse her, she poked fun at her son behind his back: she confided, romanticised, recreated her past. Her remarks, slanting, glinting, were often outrageously unjust and irresponsible. Some of her opinions lay tainted in remote corners of Harriet's mind all her life.

"Where do you *go?*" Miss Brimpton asked Harriet. "I mean when Charles takes you home."

"Home," said Harriet. Because she knew that they regarded this as a lie, it somehow was one.

"Yes, we know, dear; but beforehand."

"I really do go home." And she laughed with deceiving frankness.

"In the end, no doubt. But if you'd rather not say. I was only wondering. Lazenby, you have to heat that wax, dear, before we spread it on. I hope you're careful, Harriet. With Charles, I mean. He doesn't start any silly nonsense, I hope. I wasn't aware, Lazenby, that I said anything so startling. What you, personally, allow is a very different matter. At your age. All I wondered was his mother seemed the actressy type . . ."

"She *was* an actress once."

"No doubt. But all actresses aren't the actressy type. Look at Sybil Thorndike. Charles, of course, may differ from his mother. Not having had the pleasure of meeting him, I wouldn't be prepared to say."

"I'm glad there's something you aren't prepared to say," Miss Lazenby observed. "Who'd have thought it?"

"Anyone else would be insulted at your remark," Miss Brimpton said.

"Quite."

"Pass the nail-file," Miss Lovelace called. She was doing her nails while she stood over the broth she was making from yesterday's chicken-carcase. A smell of nail-varnish remover mingled with the gluey smell of the soup.

The picture of herself evading Charles's embrace had been insinuated by the others into Harriet's mind so long ago that the journeys that really took place, with Charles looking ahead, driving fast, saying nothing, seemed not true either.

Miss Lovelace removed her chicken-broth from the gas-ring so that Miss Lazenby could heat the little pan of wax. As it melted, it added its smell to the others in the room.

"We spread it on and tear it off," Miss Brimpton directed.

"Then we'll have the chicken-broth." Miss Lovelace put the pan back on the gas-ring.

"On the upper lip first, dear," Miss Brimpton advised Harriet. "Slightly downy, if I might say so."

"Anyone else would be insulted," Miss Lazenby said dreamily. "I call mine a bloody moustache."

"Well, that's up to you, dear, what you call it. No one else implied anything. It really does smart at first, doesn't it. I hope the juniors don't come up."

Harriet obediently spread the melting wax round her mouth.

"I'm doing my beard as well," Miss Lazenby said reck-

65

lessly. "Has that soup caught, Lovelace? Something smells funny."

"Now rip it off," Miss Brimpton commanded.

"You do it first, Harriet."

"I can't. I'm afraid."

"The soup *has* caught, Lovelace."

"Miss Claridge wanted on the phone," one of the juniors said breathlessly, putting her head round the door; withdrawing quickly, with a changed expression.

Harriet clapped her hand over her mouth; tears in her eyes. "I can't. I can't ever take this off." She stared in the mirror at her wax-encrusted face.

"Look, like this, oh, Christ!" Miss Lazenby urged her.

"But, dear, the phone!"

No one had ever telephoned her at the shop before. A wild thought of Vesey sprang into her mind and she began to panic. She took an edge of the wax, and giving herself a mad courage with Vesey's name, shutting her eyes, she tore it from her face. She was afraid to look into the mirror or to put her hand to her mouth.

"Dear, you must hurry." Miss Brimpton felt that she could not bear it herself, if whoever it was rang off.

"Vesey! Vesey!" thought Harriet as she ran downstairs, her skirt floating out at each turn of the staircase, her hair flying back from her shoulders. "But it could not be," she told herself, trying to arm herself against disappointment. Yet who else? "And if people ever do break through into one another's loneliness, is it not always done as a miracle; so may not that miracle happen to me? But it will not happen to me," she thought, her foot on the last stair.

She shut herself into the dark cupboard where the telephone was, picked up the receiver and said "hallo" in a voice which did not sound to her like her own.

"Oh, Harriet! This is Charles."

Her affability was too stressed, she knew. "And I expected nothing," she assured herself. "It could not have been Vesey. How could I have thought it was?"

She held the receiver clumsily as if it were very heavy: she smiled in the darkness and her voice was bright and welcoming.

She went back up the stairs very slowly, dragging herself up, her hand on the banister.

The others were already drinking their chicken-broth. Their glance scarcely shifted from their spoons, and their casual manner was a symptom of the restraint which telephones, letters, 'other people's affairs', set up in them. But they would not begin any conversation which might cover her awkwardness or enable her to frustrate their curiosity. If she meant to get herself out of the silence without confiding in them, they would not help her; not being prepared to go beyond minding their own business.

Miss Lovelace scooped up some broth with a broken cup and handed it to her without a word. Harriet began to drink. Miss Brimpton looked steadily in front of her.

"It was Charles," Harriet said, unable to bear any more.

"Really, dear. Salt, Lovelace, if you please."

Miss Lovelace threw across a screw of paper.

"Is he meeting you to-night?" Miss Brimpton asked; now free to go ahead.

"He wanted me to go for a drink . . ."

"Yes, well, dear, you remember what I said . . ."

"And then to go dancing."

"That's much more the idea. Is it the Hunt Ball?"

"I think it is really just a sort of road-house."

"Never mind. It may well be very nice."

"But I have nothing to wear."

"You know you don't have to worry about that."

"And my mouth is hurting dreadfully."

"Mine's giving me hell, too," Miss Lazenby said. "It was one of our lousier ideas, I must say."

"I could certainly never go through it again," Miss Lovelace agreed.

67

'How strange!' thought Harriet. 'He really did ask me to go dancing. I am actually telling them the truth.' Because she had implied it all to them before, they were not as surprised as they might have been. She was even not as surprised herself.

"I should borrow the cornflower-blue crepe from stock," Miss Lazenby was saying.

"Blue is always nice," Miss Brimpton added.

"A new frock?" Charles asked.

"Not terribly."

"You should always wear it."

('No hope of that,' thought Harriet.)

"Blue suits you. Have you got toothache, darling?"

"No, Charles."

Harriet took her hand away from her mouth and smiled stiffly.

"Have another gin, then."

"Yes, please."

Her mother had said: "Where *did* that dress come from?"

"I borrowed it from a girl at work," Harriet had lied.

"How *could* you borrow clothes? Apart from everything else, they are such personal things. They reflect one's personality."

"Then I've got precious little personality," Harriet said tartly.

"It took us years to get rid of those cumbersome skirts and now you all go meekly back in them like a herd of sheep. And all this make-up. You look like a woman of uneasy virtue," Lilian had said with vague distress.

"I always like blue," Charles now said, rather defiantly.

Kitty Vincent, who had tried to try on the blue dress that morning in the shop, said nothing. It was the first of her many kindnesses to Harriet. She sat at the table, her elbows among the glasses, her chin on her hands. Her sleeves fell away from her plumpish arms. She swayed to the music, her

68

eyes half-closed. When her husband spoke to her, she smiled dreamily and went on humming the music and then, suddenly, she opened her eyes. She put her arms up with a lovely gesture—rather like a child asking to be carried—and they moved away across the dance-floor.

"How beautifully she dances," Harriet said.

"Kitty does everything beautifully," Charles said unhelpfully. He kept spinning a half-crown round on the table and slapping it flat. She watched with eyes grown heavy in the smoky air, her hands leaden on the arms of the chair. More half-crowns were added: they lay in a neat row and he played with them absent-mindedly until the waiter brought their drinks. Harriet continued to stare at the ringed and sticky table where the half-crowns had been. She could not move her head, or speak.

Running below the beat and braying of the music was the steady needle-scratch on the gramophone record. Each sound had another underlying sound. She felt that if she could concentrate she would unpeel the outer sounds from the inner one, the one now buried, the last sound before complete silence—the tick of the blood in her wrist, she thought, turning her hand on the chair; the voice of her own mind. There were these layers of sensation. Below the smell of smoke she could also detect the chill smell of the newly-painted walls; rough, scumbled plaster like outer walls; for the room had turned itself inside-out and, in spite of its ceiling, its dance-floor, was pretending to be a courtyard. Linen vines, papier-mâché wistaria hung on a green trellis; lanterns, shutters, garden furniture did not complete any illusion, but added incongruity. Striped sun-blinds canopied the bar, made a bright booth of it, where grenadine and crême-de-menthe flashed like the bottles in a chemist's shop.

Each time Kitty Vincent passed, she lifted her hand a little from her husband's shoulder and smiled.

Her husband, Tiny, was a bustling man, who was Charles's partner. For brains, he substituted bonhomie and he did not

69

let this flag. He always was asked out a great deal because his spirits were dependable. He also remembered things about people, asked after aged mothers, inquired about rheumatism, bad legs, children's tonsils. It was felt—it was a piece of unexpressed etiquette—that one would not give him a pessimistic reply. Children were suddenly seen to be better, mothers on the mend. "Good! Good!" he would say, beaming, rubbing his hands together. Tiny is so kind, people thought. Anyone boorish enough to go on being depressed, threw him out a little. "Oh, bad luck!" he would say, hitting them across the shoulders sympathetically. His flitting eyes would seek the bar.

His relations with Kitty were very rallying, very public. Rarely uneasiness was felt—then only for a moment. Did he not lay an edge of hatred to his teasing: the friendly smack on the bottom, was it not a bit on the vicious side? But then Kitty would smile lazily. They are very understanding with one another, was the general opinion. 'I can take it,' Kitty told herself. Apathy, apathy sank through her. Since her marriage, she had grown fat, because she no longer bestirred herself. "Kitty looks well," Tiny's mother said. Now she had begun to think she was pregnant. The thought of food fascinated her. She read cookery-books, but could not bring herself to eat. She did seem to be ill, retching in the mornings until her wrists were frozen, her legs trembling. "The old girl's hangover," Tiny said. She said nothing about her suspicions for the time-being; for they never discussed anything seriously, except money, and she dreaded all the coy and humorous references. She applied herself gaily to the pub-crawl, the cocktail-party, the Sunday morning session. "I wish Tiny and Kitty would come," anxious young hostesses would think when parties bogged down. And Kitty, needing people so much, did not mind where she found them. She was not discriminating, she had found to her cost.

As she danced with her husband, she glanced at Charles

and Harriet, sitting rather far apart—each, now, with a drink in hand. She thought Harriet looked a little drawn and blurred. She blamed Charles about the gin.

"We should go home," she told Tiny; for her own sake as well as Harriet's.

"As you say, darling. Anything you say. A dead loss of an evening, who can deny it? Charles in one of his moods; little what's-her-name pie-eyed. You half-asleep."

"One more drink!" said Charles when they returned. "And then home."

"I'd like a nice leafy drink," Kitty said. "Mint especially."

When it came, she stood at the table and breathed it. The smell tantalised her. She took a leaf of the mint and pinched it. It was the most exquisite, sensuous pleasure; but teasing. Her senses seemed dreadfully heightened. Even light struck her more forcefully, so that she felt bereft of her outer skin, some poor shelled creature. But she could not drink. As soon as she put her lips to the glass, ice touched her mouth. No, she could not bear it. She put the glass down and turned to Charles. They went to dance. Harriet was left with Tiny, who said: "And how do *you* feel, sweetie?"

"I feel all right."

"Good. Good. Let's dance then, shall we?"

Her eyes had been so much on one level that when she stood up, the room seemed to change.

Tiny was a bouncy dancer. He took a firm grip of her and steered her very masterfully; his thumb in the palm of her hand pressed rather automatically: the other hand fidgeted in the small of her back, even snapped an elastic through her dress. Sometimes, he hummed in her ear, other times gathered her up with a little squeeze.

"Your Harriet looks tired," Kitty told Charles.

"I know."

"What are you aiming at, Charles dear?"

"Girls of that age . . . I seem to have forgotten . . . I seem not to get very far."

71

"And how far do you want to get?"

"Well, how can you know until you have been some of the way at least? Day after day I drive her home. We never do say a word to one another."

"Of course, you are known for your caution, your prudence, dear Charles."

"When you've so wretchedly, so publicly, failed with one woman . . ."

"But that was years ago."

"It made me self-conscious, unwilling to commit myself. I hate to fail. Now I feel stiff and heavy. Can't do all the nonsense like Tiny. I envy him that. You can see how he's making Harriet laugh this minute. I never can make people laugh."

"He doesn't always evoke suitable laughter," Kitty said.

"I envy him," Charles repeated. "I particularly envy him *you*."

She smiled.

"Ah, there you see, it is what I mean. Heavy gallantry. All I am capable of."

"I took it as a lovely compliment."

Harriet was beginning to get the hang of the evening, too late. Tiny helped her. He guided her feet one way, her conversation another—although it was not so much conversation, as, like the dance, a set of steps to be taken. She felt elated with both and when they were to go, was sorry.

Outside, on the main road, cars went by like arrows. It had begun to rain, so that the gravel crunched loosely as they crossed the car-park. When they had said good-bye, Kitty bent and smiled an extra smile at Harriet through the car window, then she drew her collar up round her head and walked away.

Charles drove in his usual silent, steady manner, through a village where the cottages came up flat to meet them in the lamplight, the branches of the trees seemed painted.

Harriet loved this driving at night. This hastening through

72

empty villages and then the deserted streets of the town, was the most undemanding pleasure, like watching a beautiful film without a plot.

Only through the fan-shaped spaces on the wind-screen did the outside scene appear. The rest of the glass was pearly with rain and steamed, so that they seemed cut off from the world in the closest intimacy.

"Are you happy?" Charles asked.

"Yes, I do feel very happy."

Yet when he drove the car under some trees, with the dripping branches all round them and, as he switched off the engines, the sound of the rain on the roof of the car, she felt dismayed and oppressed. This hackneyed situation—according to the girls at the shop—seemed unbelievable in reference to herself.

He turned to face her, an elbow on the back of his seat. Nervily, she awaited the next move, hysterical almost with embarrassment and the sense of their strangeness to one another. Regarding her steadily, his hands breast-high, knuckles interlocked, his thoughts about her seemed explicit upon his face. She watched the tightening of his hands, warily; his signet-ring, his eyes in the ghostly light.

"I wonder," he said, "how you think of me, if you ever do think of me! Is it as hopelessly older than yourself? As beyond all question older?"

"I don't think of your age."

"My mother has told you, I expect . . . it always delighted her to tell the story . . . I was once just going to marry a girl, but a week before the wedding she went off, abroad."

"I am so very sorry," she said.

"Did my mother tell you?" he persisted.

"No."

"Perhaps at last she's squeezed all her pleasure from the incident. She didn't go alone; Mavis, this girl, I mean. The appalling thing was that she went off with a friend of mine.

73

I am so sorry to be telling you all this. I expect it is embarrassing to you . . ."

"No. I only do not know what to say."

"There isn't any more to be said by anybody. Though I wanted to tell you."

He took her hand and held it for a moment against his cheek. "I never did love anybody else," he continued, moving her hand round and kissing it: his eyes shut, his face very stern, she could see in the faint light. "Jealousy is the most absurd pain of all. How one resents it! To be made to suffer it in public—the public indignity, the private pain. The shock of it lays dreadful waste in one's soul; it discolours the whole world, cancels every remembrance of tenderness. One becomes so utterly self-tormenting with doubts and questions . . ."

"Surely it goes in the end?" she asked. "Surely now it is better?"

"Now? Yes, now it is quite over. But for some residue." He raised his eyes and looked at her. "It has its horrible consequences in one's behaviour, one's fears for the future, one's negative caution, one's refusal," he said, and he clasped his fingers very tightly round her wrist as if in an effort to command himself, "one's refusal to commit oneself."

As soon as he began to make love to her, her nervousness left her. What she had dreaded in suspense and embarrassment, she now fastened to. She embraced him with an erratic but extortionate passion. He was profoundly moved, though shocked, by her desperation, and felt pity for her and a sense of responsibility. But to her, life seemed all at once simplified. She was elevated and appeased.

"Harriet! Harriet darling!"

But she would not speak to him or say his name as he so wished her to. She clung to him as if something, somebody, might impinge upon them and disrupt them. Was it not Joseph's voice calling up from that garden, echoing round

74

that empty room? When she realised that it was, she shuddered and slackened in his arms. He construed this wrongly, as he always was to, and could not hope to do otherwise.

She sat now as still as a stone, her face furrowed and perplexed.

"Harriet?"

"I am so cold." She began to chafe her wrists and she laughed and looked up at him, her eyes brimming.

"I will buy you a muff," he said. He stroked her cheekbone with the tip of his finger. "How would that be?"

Charles was much respected in the little town where he worked. Solid, serious, astute, he was a strange son for his mother to have borne, people felt. That she was an embarrassment to him, they could easily understand: that there was war between them few realised—war which stimulated Julia and bore her up; but which had effects of prolonged nervous strain upon her son.

As a young wife, imperious, selfish, dissatisfied, Julia had left her husband and gone back to the stage, taking her baby with her. His early life of dressing-rooms, dozing in hampers, long journeys, being petted by sentimental and uncaring ladies; then, later boarding-school, where Julia never sent a letter to him or a cake on his birthday; holidays with aunts; deprived always of his father: still none of this seemed to leave any visible mark upon him. He worked hard; was the child, one might have thought, of ambitious parents who had his future much under consideration. Other boys liked him, as now other men respected him. He grew to resemble his father in appearance: his reddish hair sprang from his forehead in the same arching line. It was uncanny, Julia thought, that even his mannerisms, his haughty glance at the backs of his hands, his way of stifling yawns, were so exactly reproduced from his father, whom he never saw; who, at

75

last, died. We are complete in the womb itself, she thought in terror. We only unfold. This seemed monstrous to her, repulsive. She liked to think that she had evolved herself, gesture by gesture, thought by thought: tempered, made exquisite by the passing years. But her son had grown out-of-hand. Beyond her influence, undeterred, his father unfolded in him. He put on the signet-ring his father had left to him: he stood on the hearthrug as his father had stood: he followed his father's profession.

Julia tired at last. It had been a strenuous life she had led, with little leisure, too much emotion. She set up house with Charles. If he had known, she did not expect him to tolerate her as he did: he need not have done so. But he had different standards, his father's standards. Not for one moment did he hesitate to do what was so distasteful to him —to live under the same roof as her. Her reasons— economy, loneliness—meant nothing to him. Convention, not convenience, swayed him. It was what his father would have done. If he had been married, the matter would have been arranged differently: then different conventions would have predominated, another allegiance held him. But as he was quite alone, he gave up his lodgings; he found the house in the country near his work. His mother filled it with what he thought rubbishy furniture. His own taste was nowhere reflected—it was richer, more solid, inclined to mahogany and leather and red serge: as in his office, where he loved to be, was happiest.

To draw attention to herself had been Julia's life. Team-work had meant the rest of the cast yielding the centre of the stage to her. As she grew older, her parts limited, she had a wonderful power to disrupt a play, even though she appeared in one act only. The applause, when she walked on, broke all dramatic sequence; her little cameo, as she thought of it, knocked it lop-sided. Her curtain, on her own, was something from another world; for old time's sake, the audience responded: younger actresses were unable to combat the atmosphere of nostalgia. They seemed, beside her, to have only competence.

She could not now reorientate her days without applause. It was as if the sound of clapping were necessary to make her blood flow. Without an audience she was nothing, and she had no audience. Her son was immune to her. She quite failed to captivate the country people, though she had tried at first. She thought that she was ignored. No one asked her to be the president of anything; or to sit on the Bench, which she had intended to do with beautiful mercy, a lovely humanity. She was not even required to open a bazaar, and soon was tired of the Women's Institute which was all she was ever invited to. Listening to other women reading minutes with regrettable diction and phrasing, in sturdy, monotonous voices, or demonstrating how to make deplorable objects such as felt slippers, rabbit's-fur tippets or gollywogs out of old stockings, drove her to an undisguised frenzy. Even at tea-time, all she heard was how pleasant it must be for her to live with her son. Maddened by quite ordinary women, as she thought of them—the lady of the Manor who looked as if she had been bred in her own stables; bossy farmers' wives; Caroline and Lilian, full of earnest talk about child-welfare—she sat with her eyes shut, thinking how hard the chair was. A lot of cottage-women! They made speeches while she remained silent. At tea, no one deferred to her. She was asked to take her turn at washing-up.

"I could never go again," she told Charles in the evening. "That awful village hall and all those dretful women smelling of the lunches they'd just cooked. One's own gardener's wife telling one to pass things along—you know, they hand their repulsive exhibits round, so that one can see how to make them—as if one ever would! Carpet-slippers, I think they called them. Quite unnecessary."

Boredom drove her for a while to illness. She often had her hand pressed to her ribs—a fatiguing but unspecified complaint. The pain began to be there, even when she was alone. "You should see a doctor," Charles said, passing the buck.

"Are there doctors in the country?" she asked scornfully.

"Does Charles take care of you nicely?" she said to Harriet one day.

She was walking about the room, a little cushion in her hand, the fringe she was sewing to it trailing after her on the ground.

"Of course."

"He won't turn you into one of these little suburban gin-drinkers?"

"Why should he turn me into anything?"

"Why indeed? I shouldn't touch that china, dear, if I were you. It *is* rather rivetted."

A whole chariot-race in Meissen china streamed across the chimney-piece. Harriet often rearranged it. Now she stopped, and sat down.

"So you met the divine Kitty?" Julia went on, spite driving her. But spite rarely exhausts itself: it is insatiable.

"Divine?" said Harriet, and now she infuriated Julia by picking up a piece of unfinished embroidery and glancing at it without interest.

"Darling! You are in the most fidgety mood. Do stop touching things. Divine? Why, yes, *divine*. Does she not try to be a goddess all the time—a lovely, blonde, boring Wagnerian goddess?"

"I find her far from boring."

Julia took her cushion over to the window, stood with her back to Harriet, as if she could not see her stitches. Her hands were trembling.

"Then you and Charles have a lovely lot in common," she said. "A lovely, lovely lot to chat about."

She did not want to turn Harriet against her, but the scene was almost beyond her control. Her toe tapped the carpet; long breaths came up from her lungs, as if

78

she would soon let loose upon them a great flight of words.

"How is your mother?" she asked in a haughty voice.

Harriet sucked in her cheeks quickly to hide her smile.

"She is very well," she said meekly.

"Then she is a fortunate woman." Julia turned from the window, the cushion held out with a tragic gesture, one hand to her ribs.

"Are you ill, Julia?"

"Yes, my darling. Madly ill. Ill and bad-tempered—oh, do not," she cried, her arm stretched out forbiddingly, "do *not* say about the *doctor*, as that silly Charles always does. I am beyond all doctors." Now her arm bent with a movement most heavy, most tragic; her knuckles touched her brow. ('You never do see a young actress who can use her *arms*,' she told herself.)

"But, Julia!"

('How these girls throw away a scene, let it drop to the floor and then shuffle about among the pieces,' she thought, cross with Harriet and her 'But Julias'.)

"I am sorry I spoke unkindly of your friends," she said.

"They are Charles's friends, not mine."

"Poor Charles. He does have a disappointing time. He was going to marry a girl—Mavis, or some such name—quite sweet, rather the cocktail type, but what else can they do in these remote places? As long as Charles thought the world of her, as he did indeed seem to, what did it matter? . . . don't interrupt me when I am just going to say something interesting—alas, alas, poor little Charles! Everything ready for the wedding; invitations out; presents in; bridesmaids fitted; banns read; then, oh dear, she wrote a touching little note on pink paper—I am inventing the pink paper. I could not possibly remember—and by that time she was in Paris with the best-man's brother. Such a hue and cry! I was the only one not inconvenienced. I had nothing new . . . some affair I was wearing in *Hay Fever* . . . grey with feathers

. . . a bit grubby round the collar, but quite good enough for a provincial wedding. You can imagine Charles—the set jaw, the stalking about. Oh, God, we all felt fools . . .'"

"Please don't!"

"Please don't *what?*" She was getting into her stride, beginning to cheer up.

"You shouldn't tell me. It *is* Charles's story. No one else's."

"No one else's! It was the whole town's. Nothing but that all round the coffee-shops for weeks. Don't be such a little prig. I hate a woman not to like to gossip."

But soon Harriet made an excuse and went home.

'Charles has been turning her against me,' Julia thought. 'Something has changed.'

She took the little botched-up cushion and held it to her eyes.

A flurried shame had beset Harriet after her evening with Charles. She did not again write in her diary: life became confused yet tasteless; her own part in it dubious. She did not want to meet him again and did not know how to when she must. She never had loved Vesey so deeply as when she had been so demanding of Charles's embrace. Absence had made, she realised, her heart grow fonder and her body weaker. At the most personal moment, she had lost the personality. That this could be so shocked her. Such a revelation, through her own behaviour, of the nature of love was unbearable to her. That Charles took, when they met, no cue from her past actions was a source of gratitude.

He no longer drove her home in silence; for there were people now they had in common, whom they could discuss: Kitty and Tiny especially. On Sunday mornings they met at one of the more falsely rustic pubs near the village; later, the four of them went for long walks across country, coming back in the darkening afternoon with branches of berries. The evening clouding the landscape and engulfing the bare trees smote Harriet painfully. Walking with Kitty, whom she had grown to love, she hoped sometimes that she might find words to express her longing: her loneliness: to share, to confide. But she never could find the strength to indulge in the weakness.

She returned home at tea-time, to the bright cottage room, with the firelight pink in the copper plates on the dresser, Lilian sitting on the rug making toast, one hand to her rosy cheek.

"You should bring Charles to tea," she said, turning the toast on the fork.

"He feels he should go back to his mother."

"I hope *you* don't feel the same."

"Of course not," Harriet lied.

Soon church bells would beg to ring—a steady clangour in the sharp air. The feeling of Sunday evening began to pin her down: thoughts of mortality, of the churchyard with its bleached crosses; her mother; guilt; pity; the burden of owing too much. Only when she was a mother herself would she know that those feelings were unnecessary; that she owed her mother nothing; that the pity was mutual and that, far from fearing middle-age, one took refuge in it and felt no tragedy in the mere fact of years having gone by; that at forty she would not envy the girl she was at twenty. She mourned her mother's lost youth more than her mother did, and looking at old photographs, felt sickened by pity for the wise innocence of her mother's face when she was a young woman; how, for instance, maternity was awkward in her: she held her baby, who was Harriet herself, as if she were a little girl with her best doll.

"Oh, I am getting old!" Lilian said, for her bones cracked as she stood up from the hearthrug. She did not know how her words pained her daughter.

"Charles always says how young you look," Harriet improvised.

"It is kind of Charles," Lilian said, irritated by the girl's

81

lie. She knew that she looked much older than her years.

Later, they took their sewing and sat down on either side of the fireplace. The long evening began. Lilian bent over her embroidery-frame. The pale wreath of flowers in petit-point encircled Harriet's initials. Sometimes the strands of silk caught against her roughened hands.

Harriet's own work needed little attention. As she cobbled up her stockings, her thoughts ticked over and over in her mind and she glanced across at her mother often when she was not looking.

"Grey velvet," Harriet said.

"But that's absurd," said Lilian. "When you're my age, yes. Then you'll regret all the white frocks you can't wear any longer. A nice simple white frock is always suitable for a young girl."

A beautiful, not a suitable frock, had been what Harriet had wanted. She could imagine how mottled, how red-elbowed she would look in white tulle.

"You could have had that black velvet," Miss Lazenby said, when the subject was opened at the shop. "Only some old cat bought it Friday."

"Black velvet's always flattering," said Miss Lovelace.

"You don't need to be flattered when you're nineteen," Miss Brimpton said. "It's when you're fat and forty like me. . . ."

"Oh, go on!" Miss Lovelace said, dutifully, mechanically.

Evening frocks had suddenly changed. From being short, spangled, fringed, waistless, they now swept the ground. Instead of ostrich-feather fans, there were Spanish shawls to manage. Caroline and Lilian disapproved: long skirts, they feared, would threaten the status of women.

"Oh God!" said Kitty Vincent, when Harriet described the conversations to her. "I like to *wear* clothes, not talk about them. The same with sex," she added vaguely. "Talk, talk, talk." She was trimming a hat, for doing which she had a

82

flair. "They must drive you well-nigh crazy at that shop. Don't listen to them. What you wear's your own private thing. Whom you love, too. . . ." Her glance was carefully for the hat she was trimming in her hand; sidelong and appraising.

'What has sex, love, to do with this?' Harriet wondered.

"They say ospreys are pulled out of living birds," Kitty said. "Do you think that is true? One hears such frightful things. It's the middle-man who corrupts us all the time. After all, who would snatch feathers out of a poor bird just to decorate herself? When it is so remote, though, another country, other people . . . furs, too, of course! The other afternoon, at the committee-meeting for the dance, I began to count all the little moles that had gone to make up Mrs Crockett's coat . . . it came to a hundred and something! and I couldn't even *see* the back. What a horrid massacre; what bitches we are! I thought."

She put on the hat and stared at herself in the mirror with great dissatisfaction.

"At nineteen," she asked, "does one look forward to dances? I forget."

"I look forward," said Harriet doubtfully, "yet half *dread* . . ."

"Dread what?"

"Why, seeming dull, I suppose."

Kitty laughed. "I dread the others seeming dull," she said. She took off the hat, as if she were cross with it. Her laughter had soon faded. She sat looking into the mirror in an absent-minded way. Presently she sighed, stood up, her hands on the dressing-table. It suddenly occurred to Harriet that she was pregnant.

All the happiness she had felt a moment before at being in Kitty's bedroom listening to her, watching her, dissolved. The intimacy had not, after all, been intimacy. That Kitty should have chattered about feathers and furs and hats and kept secret a matter of such importance made Harriet feel

83

roughly excluded and disregarded. Ten years was still apparently to be a barrier, as it had been in the nursery, at school. Mingled, too, with her feelings of hurt and disappointment, was envy; emotionally, physically, she was envious of Kitty and would not speak, was sullenly antagonistic.

"There," said Kitty, tidying her dressing-table. She took up a silver button-hook and swung it from her finger. "And as I expect you must notice . . . I can't think why everyone doesn't notice . . . I am quite obviously in the family way. Do not wince, dear Harriet, at the homely expression. I've tried the others over to myself and they're all prim or solemnly poetical or medical. . . . I find vocabulary a great drawback . . . one is forced to make jokes . . . though heaven knows it isn't funny. If I could find the right phrase, I could tell even Tiny. . . ."

"I am so pleased," Harriet said. She sat on the edge of the bed, swinging her feet backwards and forwards. She looked up and smiled, feeling suffused with happiness.

"It's like 'womb'," Kitty meandered on indignantly. "What a word to be stuck with—so sinister, so Biblical!"

Nothing was heard of Vesey. Harriet gave up going so often to Caroline's in the evenings. No crumb of news ever came her way to reward her for the dullness of sitting with Hugo and Caroline after supper in the peace and bliss of their domestic life—Caroline mending, her horn-rimmed glasses slipping down so that she peered over them when she looked at Harriet; Hugo reading a boring book about some war or other, reaching forward from time to time to throw a log on the fire. He sawed these logs himself on Sundays and watched them wistfully as they burned, dusting his fingers on his trousers, watching sap dribbling out and, at last, the great antlers of flame branching up and over.

Lulled by the ticking clock, the sizzling and explosive fire, Harriet would sit fondling the dogs' ears, trying to draw the conversation towards Vesey, without being suspected of doing so: but Vesey had been blown away like a leaf in the wind: he left no mark, it seemed: no remembrances. She was not old enough to know that if she had asked outright, they would have suspected her less, though could have told her no more.

Now that she went there seldom, it was strange to her to cross the lawns again and push open the front door, which once she had entered every day.

It was almost Christmas-time, and the countryside drew apart from the town, uncompromising in its darkness at night, with its dripping trees, the solitary figures of its landscape—the child going with a milk-can in its frozen hands towards the farm at dusk; the women snatching in her washing hastily as if night were a thief; and now Harriet on her bicycle with its wobbling light cast down upon the rutted lane.

Caroline's windows were yellow; the fir-trees raised great tasselled arms about the house; the garden creaked and dripped. When she pushed open the hall-door, dogs padded towards her; there was a smell of vegetarian food, a far-away sound of washing-up. No voice answered her call. When she opened the sitting-room door only Vesey was there.

"I . . . I wanted Caroline's fan," Harriet stammered foolishly, shocked.

Vesey put out a hand and turned off the radio, but did not rise.

"Is that all you have to say to me? That you wanted Caroline's fan? How disappointing of you, Harriet!"

"I didn't know you would be here."

"You could still have welcomed me."

"I do," she said faintly, and sat down on the edge of a chair. She stared with great absorption at the fire. "How are you?" she went on, mustering an arch sociability. "How is Oxford?"

"Full of bicycles and tea-shops, you know," he said vaguely. "It smells of umbrellas. Umbrellas and toasted tea-cakes, worm-eaten wood, damp clothes."

"Don't you like it?" she asked eagerly.

"Even in bookshops the rain runs off umbrellas into little puddles on the floor."

"But it can't rain so very much more than in other places, surely?"

"Probably not," he said carelessly. "It would not be so noticed, elsewhere."

Oxford, it seemed, had not come up to expectations. Harriet tried to be sorry; but was only cheered.

"Why, Harriet!" said Caroline. "I didn't know you were here."

"It is surprises all round," said Vesey.

"I came to ask if I could borrow your fan for the dance; the grey feather one. I would take great care of it."

"Of course, if Deirdre hasn't broken it. Vesey is here, you see."

"Yes."

"What dance is this, Harriet?" Vesey asked. "I had not visualised your life so gay."

"It is just a dance at The Bull," she said.

He felt a sense of change, of loss. He longed to say to someone—and who could it be but Harriet?—"I can only fail. Never expect anything. Because of some flaw in me, some wrongness, I can neither succeed nor admit defeat and between the two wait cynically for nothing whatsoever. When I am touched, I give a false note, like a cracked glass's. A note of cruelty, or scorn."

"You should come too," Harriet was saying.

Caroline had gone off to fetch the fan, and Harriet went over to him and stood near-by. 'Prove to me,' she willed him, 'that love is not what other people describe, not what has happened to Kitty, not what the girls at the shop discuss —a trap, an antagonism; or, as it is under this roof, a dull

86

habit.' She stood very still, her head raised a little as if she were straining to hear something. 'If I could find out,' she thought, 'if it meant the same to him—being in that empty house that evening, or if he has forgotten already—for people forget such important things: or they pretend that they forget.'

"Would you like me to come?" he asked.

"Yes."

"Who is taking you?"

"Charles. Charles Jephcott. But it would be all right."

If it wasn't, she didn't care.

"What are you going to wear?" he asked her.

Then a surprising, a beautiful thing happened. He leant forward in his chair and took her hand, sat studying it carefully, parting her fingers one from the other.

'And this evening, when I set out,' she thought, 'I had no idea . . . I expected nothing miraculous.'

"Your frock," he insisted gently, pressing her hand.

"It is grey velvet." Now the frock seemed wrong. She wished that she had not won that battle with her mother.

"Speak up now! You have nothing to fear," he said. "A pink rose you *must* have, tucked in the waist."

There were no waists that year, but somehow she would have one.

"Or bosom," he added.

She blushed. There were no bosoms either. Her own was flattened under a pink elastic bust-bodice.

He folded her fingers into the palm of her hand, enclosed them tenderly in his own. "Your poor little bones," he said, crushing them together.

Then, hearing someone on the stairs, relinquished her. He turned aside and switched on the wireless. It was his favourite toy. The ranging from station to station matched his own restlessness.

"Here we are!" said Caroline. She flicked open the fan and belaboured the air with it.

87

"You do know how to brandish a fan," Vesey said with steady admiration.

Terrible shrieks were coming out of the loud-speaker horn. Caroline put her hands to her ears. Harriet's eyes were stars.

"The rose looks dreadfully theatrical," Lilian said.

"You must allow me to dress myself, mother."

Harriet broke off the red thorns and tucked the rose into her bosom where it scratched uncomfortably.

"If you pinned it to your shoulder, perhaps," Lilian went on.

But Vesey had said 'tucked' not 'pinned', had said 'bosom' not 'shoulder'.

"There is Charles," Lilian said. She hurried downstairs to open the door.

Charles came into the hall bringing a smell of frosty air with him.

"These are for Harriet," he said, holding out a spray of pink carnations and maiden-hair fern, "and the chrysanthemums are for you." He kissed her cheek and put the flowers into her arm. "You look unwell, Lilian."

"You shouldn't kiss me," she said. "I think I have a cold, a chill. As soon as you're gone, I'll get to bed; but don't say anything to Harriet. How kind of you, Charles! What a lovely bouquet!" She gave him a glass of sherry she bought at the village shop and took the flowers out of the room.

Charles poured the sherry back into the decanter and sauntered about. He loved the photograph of Harriet as a little girl. Anxiously, her eyes looked up at him; a Persian kitten struggled in her embrace. The camera had barely clicked in time, he felt.

The fire was very low. He stooped to put a log on, then remembered that Lilian was going to bed.

"Oh, God!" Harriet groaned, staring at the carnations. "I can't wear *those*."

88

"What *do* you mean?" Lilian said. "Of course you *can* wear them, and *must* wear them."

"But they're not right."

"They're perfectly right, much more suitable than that rose, which will fade at once, and even if they were completely wrong, it doesn't matter in the least."

"It matters to me," Harriet said tragically. She took the rose from her breast and flung it on one side.

"But, Harriet, only *people* matter, and not hurting them."

"*You* say that to *me!*"

Trembling with vexation, she pinned the carnations to her shoulder.

Lilian sighed. Try as she might, she could not remember ever having made such a fuss over a triviality when she was young. 'I must have forgotten,' she thought sadly, going round the room gathering up Harriet's clothes.

"How lovely you look!" said Kitty, stooping to kiss her. She always seemed so Edwardian when she kissed other women: it was the merest inclination, the softest touch, cheekbone to cheekbone. While she was being kissed, Harriet glanced over Kitty's shoulder at the room. She did not want to be seen looking for Vesey. She wanted him to find her.

Kitty, Charles, the Elliots, even Tiny, were like home to her, safety; but her adventure was elsewhere. One dance with Vesey would be enough; the thought that she might be under the same roof and meet his glance across the room filled her with the happiest anticipation. She was glad of the others, who gave her confidence—dear Rose Elliot, whose shiny satin exposed her sad shape so cruelly—highlights drew attention to her little rounded stomach, her spreading hips. 'If I were like that!' Harriet thought, 'for Vesey to see.' She felt gay at the absurdity of the idea.

Kitty's face seemed altered. Such a radiance, a transfiguration that Harriet could only think of flowers—that

Kitty would make them bloom by just lifting her hands. She had all magic in her. That no one else saw this, could only amaze: that Tiny should say: "The old girl's getting fat," and only Harriet know that bliss was in the air, that Kitty was a tree in blossom!

"Come, Harriet!" said Charles.

She stood up and put her hand on his arm. While they were dancing, she was glancing over his shoulder at the door.

"I can't be bothered to change," Vesey said to Caroline. "I'll go for a walk instead."

"Is something wrong?" Caroline asked, embarrassed and distressed. "Nothing at home? Of course, we love to have you here," she added. "It was a lovely surprise. You know that."

"Oh, yes, yes," Vesey said, hoping to avoid thoughts of home.

He had come down from Oxford in the afternoon. Letting himself into his parents' flat, he felt its emptiness. There was no one at home and letters lying on the mat: the usual little sounds of an empty house—clocks rustling, curtains moving, the water in the pipes. Then he heard a door gently open and shut. A young man came out of his mother's room, hesitating in the dark passage. "Are you Vesey?" he asked.

He was very pale.

"Yes."

"Ba . . . your mother . . . would like to see you. We were lunching together and she was taken ill. She suddenly felt ill."

Vesey waited.

"She's lying down now."

"Oh, is she?"

"Yes. I'm glad you're here. I didn't like to go . . ."

"Of course not."

"We were having lunch together . . . 'I don't feel

at all well,' she said. 'I won't stop for coffee'."

Vesey watched him warming to his story.

"But now I expect you'd . . . I'm late already . . . I'll telephone, tell her . . ." He put out his hand and Vesey sullenly took it.

The young man said some of the things over again and at last he was gone.

'There's one thing I can't do,' Vesey thought. 'I can't go in and see her.'

He went into the kitchen and wandered about. Then he had to go to her. He opened the door and she was lying on the bed, the curtains drawn. She looked drowned in the greenish light, a middle-aged Ophelia.

"Is there anything you want?"

She turned her head wearily on her pillow.

"Nothing, darling."

It was true, then: she was ill.

"Sure?"

"Only not to worry your father with this. I'll get up in a little while."

So it was not true, then? When had she ever tried to spare his father any worry?

He went out and shut the door. The next day he rang up Caroline and came down to stay.

'I shall never be sure,' he thought now, walking along the dark lane, his fists tight in his pocket. 'And I must never think of it again.'

At some point of the evening, Harriet abandoned hope. There had been the dismaying moment when doubt began, and then, much later, the moment when she could no longer even doubt, when she stopped looking at the door and into her mirror: she felt enervated, her vitality run down. 'He will do this to me always,' she thought. 'He only thinks of me when I am with him. What I wanted answered last night is answered now.'

The lights dipped down over the room and then, with great daring, flashed crimson, so that all the glasses seemed to hold red wine and all the white flowers became rosy.

Harriet danced with Henry Elliot. His grave, quiet manner soothed her. He said: "Kitty enjoys herself," watching her dancing with Tiny. Then he said: "She works among us like yeast," and he smiled at Harriet.

Tiny was not satisfied to be dancing merely with his wife. He wanted to dance with the whole room. He tapped other shoulders in passing; gave a phrase here, a wink there; squeezed elbows; slackened their pace past the tables of his friends; tried to rally them on to the floor; chid them for drinking. Kitty smiled with lovely patience; her eyes scarcely lifted; in a dream of her own. "The old girl's shot away," Tiny explained. "Poor itty bitty Kitty. Me wife's drunk."

'God grant me patience!' Kitty thought.

The dance had been like all the others. To-morrow in this room business men would eat their lunch: the gilt baskets of chrysanthemums would be gone. Already, wives were slipping out to fetch their furs from the camphor-scented cloakroom. When the band began to play God Save The King, Harriet and Henry stood side by side, the backs of their hands touching. Kitty half-turned her head and smiled. And Harriet smiled back. She was exhausted with disappointment.

Going home in the car, Kitty was sorry the evening was over. When Henry asked them in for a drink, she would have said yes; but Tiny had begun to think of the morning. His party mood dropped off him. But Kitty felt elated still; not ready for bed. She tried to lull herself, and, going through the dark streets, thought about her baby, imagined its strange progress towards life; a stranger journey, she thought, than any it will take after it's born; a more complicated evolution. May it make me patient and contented!

Tiny had slackened; all his good spirits gone. He drove in silence, as if he were alone. When she spoke to him, he started, seemed guilty at his own thoughts, leant forward and wiped the steamy windscreen with his glove, peered at the road ahead as if he were trying to find composure.

"Tiny, I find I'm pregnant."

She pressed her fist secretly to her knee.

"You're what?"

But she would not say it again.

"You're pulling my leg," he said uncertainly.

"It's true."

He was ruffled, put out. She need not look at his face in the fleeting lamplight—indeed, could not, since he, each time they passed a lamp, looked hard at her.

"You can't be serious."

"Is that all you have to say?" she asked wearily. (And it has only just begun, she thought.)

"Well, hell, what am I supposed to say?"

"Nothing, nothing."

She had stopped trembling. She felt very still and quiet in her mind, at peace in her hatred, as once she had been at peace in her love.

Charles took the photograph of Harriet as a child and staring at the anxious little face and brushed-back hair, said to the real Harriet: "Would it seem too absurd to you if I asked you to marry me?"

She was unpinning the carnations from her dress.

"Of course not *absurd*, Charles."

"But out of the question?"

He put the photograph back on the chimneypiece. She twirled the carnations round and round between her hands and could not answer.

"I am much too old for you."

She shook her head.

"Well, of course I am. But I had wondered if we might

not be happy all the same. Looking round at other people's marriages, I had come to the conclusion that the things which seem important may really not matter in the least. . . . Why cry, Harriet? Why cry?"

"I didn't think anyone would ever ask me to marry them."

"And now it's the wrong one. And why should no one ask you to marry him? You must have more confidence in yourself. Remember that you are gentle and lovely and honest . . ."

"Hard working and sober," she added, trying to smile. "But Charles, I truly could not."

"Heavens, how cold your arms are!" He looked wretchedly at the ashes in the grate. "I would always love you and cherish you . . . try to make you happy."

The word 'cherish' moved her deeply. She put her cold arms inside his coat and leant her head against his breast.

"Is there some other sort of person you love?" he asked. He did not think there could be an actual person, but felt knowing about young girls and their romantic fancies.

"No one else. No one else," she said quickly.

"It shan't be like Kitty and Tiny," he promised her. "I would consider you and love you all the time; with other people, and when we were alone."

"I know," she said.

He remembered the evening in the car, and her vehement embrace which had disturbed him then and often since.

"Whom do you love?" he asked, feeling her now taut against him.

"No one. No one," she cried.

"Hush, we shall wake your mother." If only there were a fire, he thought, and we could sit beside it and talk. "You're tired, my darling. It's that damned shop and all those long hours you work there. I wish you needn't. I'm sorry I worried you." He put his hands under her hair at the back of her head and tilted her

94

face up and kissed her. "Go to bed. Forget it all."

"Yes."

He chafed her arms gently and led her to the bottom of the stairs.

"Good-night, sweet Harriet."

"Good-night, Charles."

Halfway-up the stairs, she turned, remembering, like a child, and said: "Oh, thank you for taking me."

"Shush!"

He watched her go on up to the landing, then he turned off the hall light and let himself out of the front door.

As soon as the door shut, Harriet was aware of a soft moaning in her mother's room, as of someone very ill, turning and turning to evade pain. Very fearfully she opened the door upon darkness. Lilian lay on the bed in her day clothes, her body stiff, her face yellow. She turned only her eyes towards Harriet.

"Mother, what is it?"

She dropped down on her knees beside the bed. Lilian's hands were like ice to her touch, though she was cold herself.

"Don't come near. I think I have 'flu."

"How *could* you let me go out?"

"I didn't know. It became worse afterwards. Don't come near me, Harriet."

"You're so cold."

"But my head is hot. If I could just have more hot-water bottles."

"Of course."

Lilian had never before been so ill that she could not manage for herself. Harriet had no idea what to do. She darted off to fill kettles and then came back to undress her mother, whose stockings were stuck to her legs, cold with sweat.

"I am sure I should call the doctor."

"In the morning, perhaps."

"I mean now."

95

"One doesn't bring doctors out in the middle of the night for 'flu."

"It may not be that."

Lilian, trying to raise herself, was sick, her body concaved with pain.

Harriet banked her with hot-water bottles and knelt down by the bed, holding her hand. She could hear cocks crowing, but it seemed still in the middle of the night. Soon the violence of the pain alarmed her. She was afraid to leave Lilian, but there was no telephone in the cottage. She slipped out of the house and across the road. A steeliness in the sky was the beginning of the day. The ground was like iron, branches encrusted with rime. At the Old Vicarage windows glinted darkly. She tugged at the bell, then stood back on the path looking up at the house, striking her hands together in impatience.

Charles, seeing her still in her velvet dress, felt suddenly that he himself had driven her to some act of desperation or recklessness. She could not at first make him understand, her teeth so chattered with the cold.

Julia came out of her room and leaned over the banisters, superbly furious at being disturbed; her hair on her shoulders her wrap trailing. It was as much as she could do not to call down, "How now!"

While Charles was telephoning and trying to send his mother to bed, Harriet went back to Lilian. She began to light a fire, attempted other little jobs, abandoned them all and returned to her mother.

"Darling, I was so hateful to you before I went out. I can't forget it."

"Caroline! Caroline, where are you?" Lilian cried, piteously. Tears ran unchecked out of her eyes and over her face. Last words have no more meaning, perhaps, than any others; but those were her last words to Harriet.

When she was taken to hospital, she was unconscious. For two more days Caroline and Harriet sat on either side of her bed, but although she opened her great sunken eyes and moved her mouth, she did not speak again and was not anyone they knew or recognised.

"If only she would speak!" Harriet whispered. She stroked her rough hands. "Can she hear?"

"No, I think she can't."

It began to snow. The flakes turned slowly over the hospital gardens, and against the leaden sky, drifting hopelessly across the dusk. Harriet went to the window and watched them. She was only waiting for death, she knew. She prayed that she would behave well. Then, "I wasn't good to her," she suddenly said.

"You were always good."

"No. We quarrelled."

"It can't be helped. One takes it out of one's nearest and dearest. It doesn't matter. It's the other side of love, part of the same thing."

"The doctor blamed me."

"No. You did all you could."

"If I had been quicker . . . I should have been quicker. She must often have been in pain and said nothing."

Caroline had tears as hard as bullets beneath her lids. She could not comfort Lilian any more: could only try to console her daughter. A long intimacy was over. It had been compounded of trust and suffering and love. It had no flaw in it, as Harriet's relationship with her mother had flaws. At the moment, with middle-age upon them, which they had awaited together, she felt she could dispense with this friendship less than anything else in her life. Now she would have no one to run to with her few jokes, her many enthusiasms, her allusions, her memories. 'We went to prison together,' she thought. 'I held her bouquet at her wedding. I comforted her when she was a widow. She took new-born Deirdre in her arms to Hugo; but more than that we had our day-to-day life; the subtle and allusive letters women write to one another; the informality; the insinuations; the ease.' She put her hand to her aching throat and watched Harriet at the window playing with the blind-cord.

From time to time a nurse came in and took Lilian's wrist between her fingers, then laid her arm back on the quilt, as if there were no more to be done.

Harriet watched the cabbages down below in the garden filling with snow. In the roads it scarcely lay, but the gravel paths showed footprints already and the cabbages were soon white like peonies.

The Matron came in as if she had some instinct of approaching death which had summoned her from another part of the building. Harriet put her hands over her ears, her brow against the window pane. Her eyes were hot with tears.

"She's gone," the Matron said, and she drew Harriet's head down against her shoulder, briskly kind. A nurse went hurrying along the corridor.

Harriet went over to the bed and looked at her mother's hands. She could not yet look at her face. All the Sunday evenings of her life seemed to oppress her with piteous strangeness. There was a small scar on a knuckle, which would not heal now, she thought. She could only be distracted by such little things: could not take in the enormity of loss.

Then, with great resolution, she looked at her mother's face. Calm, austerity, a remote nobility were the same barrier as the wildness of pain had been. Her mother was never any of those things. She had been reserved, but timid: full of wavering courage and unwavering integrity: nervous, ill-at-ease, uncompromising, loyal.

She put her hand for a moment on her soft hair. As a child, she had often stood on a stool behind her mother's chair and brushed her hair and combed it while Lilian sewed, or read.

"Come, Harriet, we want you with us now," Caroline

98

said. She bent and kissed Lilian's forehead, then put her arm along Harriet's shoulders. Harriet looked desperately round the room. Then she followed Caroline. They walked down a long corridor, past half-open doors. Outside, it was dark. Charles was pacing up and down on the snowy gravel beside his car.

"It's the way people treat you," Miss Brimpton said. "As if you can't be a lady just because you work behind a counter."

"Well, of course you *can*," said Miss Lazenby. "If you want."

"Sometimes circumstances force you to do things one wouldn't have thought possible. It isn't very pleasant when they're the very people you've been brought up to treat as one's equals." She smoothed her dress with her plump hands, brushing biscuit crumbs on to the floor. "Starvation itself," she added, "wouldn't keep me in a post where I was not respected."

"Oh God!" said Miss Lovelace, looking out of the window at the street below. "If only I could be one of those women down there shopping. Even a poor one with a great fish-basket and someone's supper to buy cheap. Someone to haggle for."

She dropped her cigarette-end on to a passing bus and shut down the window.

"That's better, dear," said Miss Brimpton, shivering.

"*Need* you fry meat in here, Lazenby?" Miss Lovelace said. "The smell gets into my clothes and I'm going out to-night."

"I'm not frying: I'm grilling."

"One of the juniors is going to Lyons for me. I thought I'd have a nice individual fruit-pie," said Miss Brimpton. "Being pay-day. Harriet, dear, won't you join me?"

She offered the individual fruit-pies instead of words of consolation, which they had between them decided to eschew.

99

"A nice black-currant one, say? There, you will? That's a good girl. I'll tell her to bring two. Your chop has caught, I think, Lazenby."

They were dubious and a little jealous that Miss Lazenby should do herself so well. Miss Brimpton with her cheese-rolls and tarts and sugared buns was in a state of perpetual fulness and yet perpetual hunger; and catarrhal, too: but buying meat for oneself seemed a peculiar extravagance.

Miss Lovelace ate nothing. She had bought some satin instead. She pushed the cups and newspapers to one end of the table and wiped it down with Miss Lazenby's face-flannel, which she hung back on the dresser. Then skilfully and beautifully, she began to shear away at the peach-coloured satin. They watched it lying in a voluptuous, lustrous pool on the table—Miss Brimpton doubtfully, Miss Lazenby enviously, and Harriet without seeing it at all.

The strange viability of the body—she had seen it in her mother—she now seemed to experience herself. Divorced from, divested of personality, she was yet alive; as she supposed her mother must be said to have been alive in the last days before her death. But it was no existence to which she had previously a clue, and only mechanically did she rise in the morning and go to work, and perform the leaden, tiring movements of her daily life. She could sit still for a long time without moving her eyes even, but she did not feel that she suffered or felt any emotion. She was thought—by Caroline and Hugo, by Charles—to be behaving too well; but it was more true that she was not behaving at all. They had hoped that with the ordeal of the funeral over, she would allow herself some expression of grief. When Charles gave her a large brandy, she drank it calmly as if it were a glass of milk. It was her stomach which refused it; as if it was, all along her body which pulsed, breathed, dictated, forbade, demanded. As much as she wished anything, she wished to be at work, to have her daily life in the shop with the other girls—to feel time passing over her, as if it did so above a crust of ice. And Miss Brimpton, with her fruit-pies, did as well as anyone else with her: and better than many—better than Julia, with all her enfolding drapery: better than Caroline with her careful carelessness. Tiny avoided her. He jibbed at all grief which could not be brushed aside.

"You will get over it, Harriet, I promise you," Charles had tried to assure her. It had been the moment when she most nearly faltered, picking up the book her mother had been reading, the place marked by a letter. She took the letter out and put the book back on the shelf, afflicted by her utter non-comprehension of the mystery of death. Her arm dropped against her side. He was pained to see the heaviness of her movements and tried to prevent her faltering again; tucked away from sight all the reminders of how recently her mother had been about the house. When, later, she found Lilian's petit-point, the half-finished garland of flowers, thrust into a cupboard, she knew that Charles must have done this and was touched by his concern for her. With something perhaps more painstaking than imagination he tried to circumvent her distress, to help her through days which could only pass, hoping that she would use him as she must, to lift herself out of darkness as soon as the will to do so came back to her.

She was with him a great deal; polite, silent, smiling. At night, he took her to Caroline's. Harriet acknowledged their kindness, their goodness to her; but the only time when reality touched her was when, on the day after her mother's death, when Vesey had gone back to London, saying nothing, she found a little piece of folded paper in her jacket pocket. She carried it with her to work. It was never away from her, and in moments of stress her fingers felt for it and held it, the only writing of his she had ever had—"Dear Harriet, I am sorry. Love, Vesey." It had seemed—and still did seem—a message from some outside and more natural world: brusque, simple, it comforted her. She carried the paper

101

secretly with her and its words always in her heart.

Once, when she thought she was alone, Charles saw her go over to the window and take the note from her pocket. Rapt, reflective, she looked out at the wintry garden. When she turned round, he had his back to her. He stood at the chimneypiece and—his old trick—was examining his finger-nails.

"What is it, Charles? I didn't know you were here."

Her voice had its first lift in it, its first unestimated calm.

"You are so precious to me," he said in his off-hand way, "and I such a bore to you."

'The old-fashioned ways were easier,' she thought. 'When one had refused a proposal, one kept away. Not this drifting on, always together. Yet what should I do without him?' she wondered in a sudden flash of honesty. It was difficult to imagine.

Later, seeing her discarded jacket on a chair when he was alone in the room, temptations from what seemed terribly long ago beset him; pains he had forgotten. It was as if an unkind hand raked up dead leaves in his heart. He took the paper from her pocket and read it. His face was scornful because of his contempt for himself; contempt at having so weakly fallen into the old ways, of pain and secrecy and suspicion.

He went over to the window where she had stood and looked out at the darkening garden. His mother came up the path with a red and silvery cabbage in one hand, a knife in the other. She held the cabbage away from her, as if it were some loathed thing. It might have been John the Baptist's head, so dramatically did she carry it.

'Vesey', he thought. He barely knew him: and that but as a young boy. Feckless, penniless, indolent. But young. He remembered—walking up and down the room, and some-times stopping short when intolerable ideas presented themselves—firstly, Harriet's embrace in the car; secondly, her comforted face as she had read that note. What hopes

102

did she have from one so debilitated? · (Yet so young!) And if hopes; then built on what?

In the kitchen, Harriet helped Julia; chopping, shredding, rubbing pans with garlic, larding with anchovies. Julia was in one of her cooking phases. A cabbage was a great labour to prepare; into it went onion and apple, vinegar and sugar, cloves, butter.

"I have Russian blood in my veins," she said, and held out her wrist to Harriet as if something special might be visible there. "On my mother's side."

'She will soon tire of this,' Harriet thought. 'Then someone else will have to clear it up.'

"At Christmas," said Julia, "we'll have the most wonderful tree. I have some little trumpets made of silver glass and some spun-glass birds. What poetry there is in ordinary domestic life, the rhythm of a house . . . what are you sniffing at, darling?"

"This," said Harriet, dubious over a basin. "What is it?"

"Sour cream for the bortsch. Don't tell me you are like Charles and loathe it?"

'Who is she cooking *for?*' Harriet wondered. Aloud, she said: "How dark it gets!" Her low moods were physical like a nearness to fainting: without warning they gathered her up and enveloped her, especially now in this time—the late afternoon—which was like a gulf between living and dying, full of terror and poetry and panic: isolating, it drew a moat around her. To be moving was a little comfort to her—it proved that she could—or to speak. She crossed the kitchen quickly and snapped on the light. It rained down harshly on the litter of bright food, the tableful of crockery.

"Darling, what a sudden glare," said Julia.

Later, on her way to the drawing-room, she met Charles in the passage. It seemed strange that though they hesitated, neither could discover any words trivial enough for the occasion. Surely, both felt, they could find some phrase to say to the other: but no words came, and they went on

103

without speaking; he sinking back against the wall to let her pass. It seemed to Harriet that they were like total strangers glimpsing one another as they sped by on opposite escalators, borne apart, incurious.

But now that the evening had come she was more confident. She could even believe that for everybody there is perhaps another person who will not fade on approach; with whom it might be not entirely like those fishes in tanks, crossing and recrossing, weaving their way through the water, fearing only, it seems, to touch one another; gliding upwards and away instinctively when their paths threatened to meet.

She tidied Julia's drawing-room which was a great litter of Sunday papers. An out-of-date magazine with Julia's photograph had its yellowed page exposed as though by accident. 'The sadness one sees looking about among one's friends,' she thought, and she drew the curtains smartly across the windows as if she were insulting the dark evening outside, 'is chiefly the sadness of them being themselves. What that seems to do to other people.'

·She did not contemplate ever looking back to say her life had been the same. Because she was sure that it would not be, she began to hum as she tidied the room for the evening. A few miracles had happened, others, given time, would no doubt follow. Any morning a letter might arrive, or she would come home from work to Caroline's and find Vesey sitting there.

"It is lovely to hear you singing," Charles said when he came in.

"Was I?"

"Don't stop."

"How could I go on?" She laughed.

"Oh, darlings, darlings!" Julia cried. "Something's curdled. It is so vexing, after all my pains, so devastating!"

She sank down in the middle of the sofa and rolled her hands up in her apron.

"When I put in the lemon-juice it all went funny . . . speckly, flaky, you know; *curdled*—that's the word."

"Have a drink, mother."

"A drink? You can't console me with your drinks. Your answer to everything. Do you realise that, Charles? Pain, loss, disappointment. A drink. So easy to offer, so useless to receive."

"A glass of sherry?"

"Your taste in sherry is hardly mine. Dry, light, sharp, thin. I always loved a full sherry, rich, with some *body*." She curved a hand in the air. "What I find I can now say for your father is that he liked a good sherry."

"There is a brown sherry you would like . . ."

"Then bring it, bring it. Don't stand there like a shop-assistant. I beg your pardon, Harriet. Try not to argue so, Charles, as if you were hoping to sell me something. It's hardly gracious to make such a song and dance beforehand."

She took her drink and sipped it, sitting there in her apron. "There won't be any soup now. I feel so weary. I'm not a young woman any more." Harriet tried to dispute this, but was interrupted. "Oh, how did that old magazine get here?" Julia asked. "Where can it have come from?"

"You must have left it there yourself," Charles said seriously. "I wouldn't have done."

"I love a nice talk," Kitty was saying. She might instead have been pouring out the coffee, Charles thought. He sat watching the empty cups as she chattered, and presently leant forward and managed for her. "But how miserly we are!" she continued. "Our boring, miserly conversations." She looked round the little café with contempt. "One person brings out a pocketful of coppers, sorts them out, hands over a penny; then the other one fumbles and presently gives a halfpenny change. I should like to find someone who suddenly handed out a five-pound note, wrapped it round a sovereign and threw it into one's lap.

105

E

One gets so lowered by nice recipes for rice-puddings, and what girlie said to Daddy. Oh, what girlie said to Daddy bores me most of all. Funny little remarks the kiddies made! Dear Rose is greatly at fault over that."

"Kitty!" said Charles. He leant over the table and gently shook her wrist to stop her talking.

"It was sweet of you to bring me to coffee," she said. "I had forgotten Tiny was going off to defend the murderer."

"Oh, hush, darling. You will do us all irreparable harm. The man's not a murderer until he is convicted."

"If he did it, he is," she said calmly, licking doughnut sugar off her fingers. "That's where I so disagree with you. Even if Tiny gets him off, he's still one if he did it. Those things seem simple to women."

"Tiny has no right to discuss it with you . . ."

"He didn't discuss; he mentioned. And not even you can stop me from reading newspapers and coming to my own conclusions. This is the first time you've ever brought me out in the middle of the morning . . . I wish we could do it often and get gossiped about. Those women over there already have their eyes on us . . ."

"I brought you . . . I asked you to come, I mean . . . for a special purpose; to ask you something—though it's difficult to get a word in edgewise."

She waited, he thought, apprehensively, her eyes anxious above her cup as she began to drink her coffee.

"What is it?"

She knew by his slight hesitation that he would say something unpleasant.

"You are a dreadful chatter-box, Kitty, but I always did respect your judgment."

Yet when he considered her marriage he began to wonder why he had said this.

"How boring of you," she said, setting her cup down, glancing out of the window. "Oh, Charles, *look* at Rose over at the greengrocer's. Can she know her petticoat is hanging down such yards? Should we lean out of the window and shout to her?"

"Let me say what I am going to say."

"Well, then?" She resigned herself, gave a last look at Rose and said: "It will be bound to be unpleasant or you would have babbled it out without all these preliminaries. I hate preliminaries."

"It is only, I think, unpleasant—no, not that; vaguely disquieting at most—for *me*. Something about Tiny's attitude to me. It is constantly borne upon me that something is wrong. His avoidance of me becomes something *I* can't avoid. Please don't say 'nonsense' or anything like that. One has to face such things."

"Oh, no," she said quickly.

"If he knows I am going to a place, he won't go there himself."

"It's perhaps Harriet. He feels uncomfortable with the bereaved. They are greatly unpopular with him."

"I am not all the time with Harriet. She is not in my office with me."

"I wish after all I had not come for this coffee. Even saving sixpence and being gossiped about doesn't make it worth while."

"Your hedging convinces me that I am right."

"Why not ask Tiny himself?"

"Yes," he said uncertainly.

"You are different from one another. You are so serious . . . perhaps you seem—oh, to *him*, I mean: not at all to me . . . She laughed and laid her hand over his ". . . a bit too solemn; an old stick-in-the-mud." He felt the pressure of her hand. "Unlike his friends. His other friends."

"Unlike Reggie Beckett?" Charles said lightly.

"Oh, awfully unlike Reggie Beckett."

"You don't like him?"

"Well, you see, I don't like any of them. They bore me so madly with their racing-talk—all that about ponies and

107

monkeys. I just call them the b'hoys. They never have come even to adolescence. Have they?" she asked, with her wavering, anxious smile. How can we forgive, she wondered, the one who cries Woe! Woe!, who initiates disaster, who reveals the first cat's-paw across our calm? "I mean, they must be panicky inside unless they just are as innocent as children."

"You sit there feeling superior?" he asked, suddenly smiling.

"No, I sit there feeling evil, malevolent, guilty."

"You have nothing to feel guilty about."

"I have my thoughts," she said proudly. "The same as other people."

"Silly Kitty. I adore you."

"Speak up, for pity's sake."

But when he opened his mouth as if he would obey her, she laughed and blushed and put out her hand protestingly.

"So Vesey is leaving Oxford?" Caroline said. She folded the letter Hugo had given her and put it back in its envelope. "*Now* what will he do?" she wondered aloud.

"He scarcely gives anything a chance," Hugo said.

"His mother spoils him."

"He should have been made to stick it out. A mercy for all of us that the war was over in our generation. What all these problem-children would have made of it can be imagined." 'Problem-child' was a new term, which attracted him.

"Vesey is a bad boy," Joseph said with certainty; then: "Why is Vesey a bad boy?"

"Mind your own business, Joseph," Deirdre said, her eyes on her mother's face.

One of Harriet's hands clasped her knee tightly, under cover of the table.

"I foresee a sad future for him unless he pulls himself together," Hugo said, and glanced at his own son.

"Yes, I think he is a bad boy," Joseph said. "A very bad boy. He did eat some meat," he added. "I saw him once."

"Don't tell tales," Deirdre said loudly, now looking at Hugo for approval.

But Hugo didn't care either way. Other people's failures, with their children move one so little: even one's own brother's. The concern so soon turns towards comparison with one's own affairs. 'Not done too badly,' he thought, meaning Deirdre and Joseph. 'Sometimes lost patience, been unjust. But on the whole hasn't worked out so badly so far.'

So Vesey's falling-off only spread complacency in Hugo's heart, and "We've done all we could," he said, "though it's worrying for his parents, I've no doubt."

"There are the books to sort out for the Jumble Sale," Caroline said. "Yes, I agree. Very worrying for poor Barbara, I expect."

She was not, when she stood up with the tips of her fingers resting on the table, saying Grace; but collecting her thoughts. As she grew older, this became more difficult. Many affairs were on her mind: many people. Sometimes she failed to recognise acquaintances, but they had grown so thick and fast upon her as her busy life went on that her mind and memory could contain no more: for there was a limit (she excused herself in her own heart as she could not to the offended) to what one can retain. When new people come in, after a certain point others must drop out. So many faces, in the village, the town, on committees, at meetings, that she could not tidy them in her mind. She had not weeded them out, as she was now, moving away from the table, about to weed out her books.

It was assumed that Harriet would clear the table. As she went in and out of the room, she could hear how they progressed with this weeding-out. It was much more, she thought scornfully, the opportunity of ridding themselves of rubbish than beneficence which made them so zealous.

That clearing the house might have the by-product of bolstering-up the Liberal Party gave great satisfaction.

The dining-room books were only an overflow, so that any reason for wanting to keep them was likely to be sentimental, any reason for wanting to buy them second-hand utter lunacy. Who would be inclined to read them? Mottled, clenched together, they had the unpleasant smell of books which have been behind glass. Caroline, sneezing, took them out in armfuls, kneeling on the carpet.

"We should be quite ruthless, Hugo," she said, pushing her spectacles up her nose, peering at a row of titles. "They are only decaying here and it would be a wonder if we ever took any of them out to read. What an enormous spider! It amazes me that they can go on living shut up in a cupboard year after year: years it must be since I opened this door. Oh, it is dead, anyway. Well, there's one we don't want, to begin with. *The Roadmender*. Falling to pieces. Smelling bad."

"That was Vesey. He left it out in the rain and ruined it. Scarcely apologised afterwards. I was very annoyed at the time. My brother gave it to me." Hugo turned the book sadly in his hand.

"In that case . . ." Caroline said.

"No. After all, we said we'd be ruthless and we must be. It's useless to harbour it."

At the Liberal Party Jumble-Sale he felt a good home would be found for it, as if it were a shabby kitten. He threw it into the arm-chair with the other rejects.

"*Mothercraft Manual*," Caroline said sadly. "No more call for that."

"We hope," Hugo said, as husbands feel they should.

Caroline remembered how she had turned those pages in anxiety and despair. Few of the horrors had happened to her—neither of the children had had convulsions or pushed beads up its nose. She threw a pile of Jules Verne into the arm-chair.

110

"Steady!" said Hugo. "Joseph may like those later on."

"Oh, I doubt it. Boys don't like the same books nowadays." She tossed some more of Hugo's youth away—Captain Marryat, Ballantyne.

"But, Caroline, this was a *prize*," he protested.

"Oh, was it, dear. Sorry. Keep it then."

"I intend to. All right for this *Little Women* to go, I suppose? There's another one in the sitting-room."

"I think I'll keep that for Deirdre. It's rather a nice copy. My Aunt Hester gave it to me."

"Well, then, the one in the sitting-room can go. Harriet, I wonder if you'd mind fetching it?"

"My mother gave me that one," Caroline said in a shocked voice. "She used to read it to me after tea. We both cried dreadfully."

"All right, dear, all right."

He carelessly tossed aside another book, then some memory checked him. He retrieved it and cautiously glanced at the fly-leaf.

"Well, here's one we *won't* send. Here's one there's no argument about. Harriet, look! There's a book I'd never surrender. Never. The first book—I think I am right in saying—that Caroline ever gave me. You'll see, she's written in it. *The Story of an African Farm*. 'Allons, the road is before us,' she's written. 'Hugo from Caroline'. We were just engaged. I've always treasured that and always shall. The Liberal Party can go bankrupt before I'd be induced to give them that."

He replaced the book with dreadful vehemence on the top of the bookshelf.

'They're all right,' Harriet thought. 'Always have been. Smug, satisfied. Allons, the road is before us, indeed! To be so sure, to be so exclusive!' She could not imagine ever putting such an inscription in a book for Vesey. No road was before her. Only a thicket of briers, she thought, carrying out the last trayful of crockery.

111

"Do you remember this?" Caroline asked Hugo. "*The Golden Bough.* You read it to me when I was sewing for Deirdre before she was born. It does conjure up Viyella and feather-stitching. And discomfort. I used to twitch so and get a sort of toothache in the ribs."

"The headmaster of my prep. school gave me this when I left. *Stanley in Africa.*" He wavered between the two heaps, then blew dust from the pages and put it on top of *The Story of an African Farm.* It had meant something at the time. He thought it always should.

"I didn't say anything when Harriet was here about Vesey wanting to go on the stage," Caroline said in a low voice, an open book held up as a sort of disguise in front of her. "You know what some girls are like about the theatre. It fascinates them."

"If it wasn't one thing, it would be another," Hugo said vaguely.

"But Barbara said he has always felt bound to do this. Perhaps it has been the trouble."

"Once it was to be an author," Hugo said scornfully, as if the boy swung from one dubious ambition to another. "Well, let him try. Let him be an actor, I say. Let him starve in this repertory theatre. He'll find there's no sort of usefulness in the life unless one goes fairly quickly to the top. Let us see if he will do that," he concluded, comfortable in the certainty that Vesey never would.

"I thought say nothing to Harriet for the time-being. Nothing to unsteady her. It may all blow over. What is that you have, Hugo?"

He handed her some pressed flowers—once white violets, now yellow, and tissue-thin.

"We picked them that afternoon we walked to Stoner Hill."

"Yes, of course."

"They were in this book."

She sat looking at the dead flowers. "I wish," she said,

112

after a while, "I wish that Harriet would marry Charles: that she could *settle*." (Her voice matched the word: it seemed to come to rest: she smiled). "As we have done," she said.

"Harriet, dear, you do watch me so. It makes me feel uneasy. I know I am not looking my best."

Harriet blushed. "I think you look so beautiful," she stammered. "I'm sorry."

Maternity-dresses in those days seemed always to be navy-blue with touches of white. Kitty's crossed over discreetly in the front, then tried to avert attention either to her elbows, with a fall of accordion-pleating, or to the frilled jabot at her throat. She now had a much more capable look; planted her feet down more firmly when she walked.

"I envy you so," Harriet said simply.

"It is when one does—at your age, thank goodness, when it is ahead probably, not past. Lucky it's that way round."

"When you tuck that cushion in the small of your back and hold your sewing up high over your stomach, I think 'one day I hope I'll do that'. It looks so nice."

"It isn't playing with dolls. When it comes you'll only feel cumbersome."

"I won't mind."

"You'll spend your days thinking of the flowered voile you'll have in the summer when it's over."

"Is nothing ever right at the time, then?" Harriet asked in bewilderment.

"I'm teasing. Because you made me feel self-conscious. Once, when I was younger, a man told me I had a lovely profile. Then I had to be so careful not to keep turning it towards him, as if I were asking him to notice or remark on it again. I became very fidgety, shifty. I got into difficulties in cinemas. Began to look at everything lop-sidedly, squinting, *louche*. People who are often complimented are not so thrown out."

"Someone is coming up the drive with Tiny."

113

"Man or woman?" Kitty asked. With her weight on her wrists, she struggled up from the sofa, brushing bits of cotton from her creased frock on to the floor. She felt her child heave over, like a disgruntled sleeper, disturbed.

"A man," said Harriet.

"Reggie Beckett," Kitty said, standing by her at the window. She half-raised her hand, but they did not see her. They came slowly up the gravelled drive, between the ragged shrubs, heads bent as if they discussed some grave matter.

"Heaven knows," said Kitty, "how anyone so babyish, so fat, cherubic, could seem to be so closely connected with doom. It is strange how some people *threaten*, by just being their cheery, silly selves."

"I can't imagine how *he* does," Harriet said. Her laugh smeared the window-pane and she wiped away the mark with her cuff. "He looks like those angels in the corners of maps, blowing wind out of their fat cheeks."

"He'll coarsen," Kitty said. She turned away from the window. "And he does threaten."

"I'll let them in," Harriet said. Kitty sat down again and took up her sewing, waiting to hear their loud and echoing greeting break loose in the hall.

PART TWO

I

"So this is your province," Vesey said as they danced. "You know everybody here but me. I know nobody but you. Why did you say that you couldn't tango?"

"I didn't know that I could. I usually sit down when one begins."

Most other people were doing that. Almost alone on the floor, she felt watched, especially by her husband who usually went to the bar when the band played anything of this nature, but now sat at their table fanning himself with Kitty's black lace fan.

"I can't!" Harriet had pleaded, as self-conscious as a young girl. "I can't tango."

"You can with me," he said smoothly.

"But not quite yet!" she whispered, looking at the empty floor.

"Now."

He was so sure, that he could risk her humiliation, could take her out to dance alone while her friends turned their chairs a little from the tables to watch. He simply did not allow her to falter and her nervousness began to change to elation. She wished that they might never stop; believed that they might not; for time, with its dwindling, filching ways seemed triumphed-over. They were suspended in some magic which caught up also, meaninglessly, gilt baskets of azaleas, some paper streamers and a great chandelier like a shower of grubby acid-drops. Remotely, the figures of other people drifted at the perimeter of their enchanted space of floor. They dictated their own music.

115

'After nearly twenty years, I have had my dance with Vesey,' she thought. "There was the other dance," she said, "in this very room. You said you would come, but you didn't: I watched the door for hours over Charles's shoulder, until I could not any more." For the first time she almost lost the pattern of the dance. His *extra* grip steadied her.

"We must go on with this," he said. "The alternative would be to go back to that table where they're all sitting and waiting. Charles would stand up and bend over you solicitously as if I had been doing you some harm."

"Why *didn't* you come that time?"

"I can't remember."

"When one is middle-aged, one can suddenly ask lots of questions."

"Do the answers still matter?"

"It was nice just dancing," she explained. "Let us not talk again."

It bore no relation to any other dancing she had done. She had been shuffled, bounced, jostled round the floor, trying to keep up, trying to think of something to say or to guess what had been said, grasped either too tightly or too slackly, smiling, hoping to look starry-eyed with enchantment. Now they danced with perfect, grave precision and in silence. They made some ritual of the dance, some pact, as if they were alone; ecstatic, in its true sense. They made an exhibition of themselves, Charles thought.

He would not in his turn ask Vesey's partner to dance with him. For one thing, he could not tango: for another, he thought that she was drunk. She had left the bar only once or twice when Vesey had led her away on to the floor. Then she had drooped against him: they had scarcely progressed, locked together indifferently, rather as if they were strap-hanging in the tube at rush-hour. Back at the bar, she became, glass in hand, reanimated, the centre of a knot of men, whose laughter at her *double-entendre* seemed to amaze her. Surprised, her eyes unflinching, her glass held in both

116

hands against her breast; at last, the meaning they had got from her meaning permeating her innocence, she flushed, drew in her cheeks, sipped her drink as if it were her bedtime glass of milk. They were bad men, she told them. They thought her an absolute scream. If, they said, she could put up such a good show on the stage they would almost face *Hamlet* and the hard seats at the Town Hall to see her again.

"I am better when I have a hangover," she promised them. "I am more distracted. I give out flowers in all directions. Sometimes," she tempted, "put in the rude bits that I am supposed to leave out."

Vesey had to speak, for he felt the music to be unwinding to its conclusion. He knew himself to be at the stage which initiates falling in love, that he was committed to it and would feel pain if he turned away, did not give in to the desire to unpack his life in her presence, to lay before her treasure after treasure (or, rather, loss, laughter, disappointment). As, when a child, his mother had returned from abroad—the cases lay opened round the room: carrying frocks over her arm, casting crumpled underclothes into a basket, "That is for you," she would sometimes say, tossing a little package to where he sat on the bed (a musical-box from Switzerland, a tie with a design of postage-stamps from Charvet, a bunch of sugared almonds arranged like flowers): out of the boxes she would shake her more recent life. He would finger the bottles and jars, sometimes explore, impertinently she apparently felt, for she would snap things away in drawers, saying repressively, meaninglessly: "That is *mine*," meaninglessly, because he had not supposed that it was not. To share the unpacking, delving, with Harriet would delight him: to do so in no sort of order, to be arbitrary, indiscreet, and she the same.

"Next week I go on to Guildford," he told her. "Though that's not important. It doesn't matter where I go. I want us to talk to one another."

"You must dine with us," she said allayingly.

117

"Don't be absurd. Dine! I haven't dined anywhere for years. I have to be at the theatre. I never go anywhere except late at night like this."

The music had stopped. He stood clapping vaguely, looking at her. "When?" he said.

"Vesey, it's no good. I am afraid it might make Charles unhappy."

"Can you not have your own friends?"

"Yes. Don't play with words."

"You played with words, asking me to dinner."

Everything she had once wept for, now, offered, confused her. They were walking slowly back to the table.

"I have a daughter of fifteen," she said.

"It is hard to believe," he said with weary sarcasm. He swept her daughter on one side with the sort of answer he despised. He ignored her implication. They had wasted time out there, just dancing. "To-morrow afternoon, meet me somewhere, anywhere."

"You could come to the house then," she said primly.

"I don't want to. If it's a thing that will make some difference to you, I will, though. Do you ever see anything of Joseph or Deirdre?" he asked in a more social voice.

"I see them themselves," she replied.

Charles stood up, his hand on the back of a chair, rather posed-looking, as if he were having his portrait painted. Vesey stood beside him. They seemed to be encouraging dignity in one another. A slight awkwardness had fallen over them all, though Rose Elliot tried to overcome it with compliments on their dancing. "Quite Spanish," she insisted. The awkwardness only grew. Harriet felt exposed, but by her own hand. They deprecated what they congratulated, she knew. When Vesey went away they relaxed a little. "Dark horse, Harriet," Tiny said.

At the bar, Ophelia waited with mad impatience for Vesey to return. When he did so, she pretended that it was she who had erred, who had abandoned him. She drooped with penitence. She made a shelter for her eyes with her hand, caught-in her lower lip, seemed to await a reprimand.

"I'm going home," Vesey said. "I'll get a taxi."

"I'm not ready," she said steadily, not any more a drooping little girl.

"That's up to you."

"You bad-tempered little so-and-so," she said swiftly.

Tiny had come up to the bar and she leant her shoulder against him.

"I have to go home," she said pathetically.

"Nonsense. Only just beginning. The first five hours are always the worst."

Vesey thought: 'If she doesn't come I'll save the taxi-fare.' He would walk all the way back to the boarding-house. But she went, lingeringly, protestingly, to fetch her tweed coat from the cloakroom. She hung it over her shoulders then put her arm through Vesey's. He did not look back towards Harriet. She saw them go, in a swift glance, as she leaned forward to unstrap and strap her shoe-buckle, not wanting Charles to notice her look.

'The air is lighter,' Charles was thinking, 'sweeter. May we never be so menaced again!'

The band played so much nonsense nowadays that it was some time before there was a proper fox-trot and he could ask his wife to dance.

One by one, the other cars slipped off into the darkness; but here they still shuddered, pulsated, at the kerbside. Rose Elliot had gone back for her gloves. Charles tapped his shoe to some imagined music—a martial tune, Harriet was sure, looking at him.

"Kitty's getting fat," Henry Elliot said, watching her getting into their car, which went down on one side as she put her weight on the running-board.

But there was Rose at last, hurrying down the drugget to the glass doors. Her husband yelped ungallantly with pain

119

as she trod on him getting into the car. She took off her shoes and put her feet in her muff. Her thighs ached; her toes felt broken.

"Surely it is time we gave up all this dancing?" she said, settling down. "And yet there is Harriet, as fresh as paint."

"No, I'm tired, too," Harriet said quickly.

"All this dancing!" Charles repeated. "Three or four times a year at most."

"I can't any longer do the things they have, can you, Charles? Rumbas and so on."

"Englishwomen should never rumba," he told her.

"But you could not dance with one another. . . ."

"Harriet's tango was something we shall all remember," Henry said. He sat neatly on the little tip-up seat of the taxi, his eyes shut, his arms folded tidily across his chest. He looked like a collapsible model of a man, especially designed for carrying in taxis.

"Yes, Harriet's tango! Goodness, *he* didn't look English," Rose said.

"There you are!" Charles nodded at Harriet.

"What do you mean, 'there you are'?"

"I always said he looked a dago."

"Holding your hand behind your back in that funny way," Rose said, yawning and yawning against her fist. "I should think you were embarrassed."

But dancing like that is impersonal, Harriet thought: so formal that it transcends the closest embrace. Though she would not have explained this, even if she had been able.

Rose said: "She danced well, though."

"And getting up," Charles complained, "the moment the music began. No one else on the floor. No one ever gets up for a tango until it is nearly over. If then."

"He's half Irish," Harriet suddenly said. She could not imagine why she wanted them to know that.

In the cloakroom, leaning to the mirrors, side by side, Kitty had asked her: "Who was it?"

120

Her powder-puff pressed for a moment to her chin, Harriet had said: "He is Vesey. Years ago I knew him."

"Before you knew Charles?"

"When I was a child."

The powder-puff began to rotate again about her blank and puzzled face.

"I have never heard you mention him. Did you never see him again?"

"I saw him once," Harriet said. "A few years ago. At a memorial-service to his aunt."

Kitty dragged her shoulder-straps up, for they cut in to her plumpness. Without taking her eyes off herself in the mirror, she said: "You gave no such impression. I felt something rehearsed yet fatal about you, a part of a ballet, perhaps—yes, that—his just coming out of the crowd and claiming you, then disappearing . . . the clock might almost have struck twelve." She tucked her hair into her fur collar, dropped sixpence into the saucer.

"Follow me!" she had said, and she put out her hand and took Harriet's as if she were blind and must be guided from the room. Harriet laughed; she felt the warm kid stretched tight across the hollow palm; for nothing Kitty had ever fitted now. Her flesh was always ahead of dressmakers. Rosy, pearly, she was like a great, idle and voluptuous goddess painted on a ceiling. Clouds should have banked about her; cherubs caught at her fluttering ribbons.

Now, in the taxi, Rose was asking: "Where did he come from?"

"The past. From the past," Charles said, his voice dressing the words up in absurdity. He really was behaving badly.

"How romantic!" Rose murmured, cramming her feet back into her shoes, for the taxi was running down between laurels to the boys' school where Henry was headmaster.

"Light on in the small dormitory," he said, peering up at the front of the house.

"That will be little Stuart's ear-ache," Rose said. "Matron

121

will be terse with us, and us breathing whisky all over her. Good-night, my dears."

"You danced beautifully," Henry comforted Harriet, taking her hand. "You surprised us all."

"I think she did that," Charles agreed.

As the car turned, crunching deep into the wet gravel, they saw Rose hobbling into the porch; Matron still, at this hour, starched and white, opening the door to her, and Henry standing in the rain against the black wet laurels. He raised his hand as they drove away.

"Dear Henry!" Harriet said. 'Dear irritable Henry,' she thought to herself—for his very faults seemed a refuge to her at this moment, part of the fabric of her daily life with which she had for long camouflaged her desires. 'My world and my province!' she thought, and she turned her head sharply as if to avoid that word of Vesey's, which he had used earlier in the evening. She tried to look out of the window, but beyond the silver drops on the glass, which turned gold when they passed a lamp, she could see very little. A string of blurred lights went up and over the hill. The quiet avenues and crescents were darkened and rain-swept.

Charles, who had had so much to say in the others' presence, now had nothing to say. His coat collar was up to his ears, his hands were deep in his pockets, he sat hunched up in the far corner, away from Harriet. 'Marriage does not solve mysteries,' she thought. 'It creates and deepens them.' The two of them being shut up physically in this dark space, yet locked away for ever from one another, was oppressive. Both were edgy.

"Coming on faster now," said the driver, over his shoulder.

"Yes," they both tiredly agreed.

"Shouldn't wonder if it went on all night. . . ."

Charles stifled yawns against his gloved hand. Harriet began, too; for it was infectious, she found.

"Once it's begun," the driver added.

"Here we are," Charles said sharply.

Jessica Terrace looked like a row of paper houses. No lights shone from any of the windows or the fan-shaped glass above the doors. The evergreens were glossy in the rain, unseparated from the pavement, for the iron-railings had been taken in the war. The façade seemed to have so little depth that even Harriet, who had lived here for sixteen years, could scarcely believe that, behind it, passages ran away towards kitchens; that in remote parts the front-door bell could not be heard, and that, in back rooms overlooking the narrow gardens and level with the top branches of a mulberry-tree, her daughter and the young maid were asleep.

She loved the lulled sensation of being driven at night and was reluctant to leave even this musty car. "Wake up!" Charles said crossly. They had stopped by the familiar street-lamp. She said good-night to the driver and hurried towards the steps, her head bowed in the rain.

The lamp shed light down through ivy-leaves upon the white door. Waiting, shivering, for Charles to sort out his keys, she stared before her at the iron knocker—a hand grasping a wreath of roses. To-morrow—in a few hours really—Vesey would stand here. Inside the house, she would have been awaiting him, tense in the middle of the room, away from the windows, listening for the sound of his banging with that iron ring upon the door. 'If he did not come!' she thought. 'If something happened, so that I never saw him again!'

"I am being as quick as I can," Charles said; for her shivering he took as a reproach. Perhaps as a result of years with his mother, he was very prone to take things as a reproach.

Inside the narrow hall, the little white cat, Blanchie, made her uncertain, sideways approach, wove her way between their legs, purring. On a chair, Betsy's satchel was packed ready for the morning beside a bunch of flowers for Miss Bell.

"I wonder if Elke did the hot-water-bottles," Harriet said,

123

beginning to go upstairs. As she went, she looked over the banisters at Charles. He had pulled off his white scarf and stood there swinging its fringe at the cat, looking thoughtful and absorbed. She could not guess what his thoughts were. Against him, against his calm and decision, she felt confused and incoherent; and, looking back on her married life, it seemed a frayed, tangled thing made by two strangers.

Betsy awoke at the sound of a car door slamming. She had fallen asleep in bed over her homework with the light on. The corner of the book on which her forehead had rested had engraved a ridge into her flesh; one hand, bent up awkwardly under her ribs, had pins-and-needles. She could not bear the high-strung, tingling sensation as she tried to uncurl her fingers; but now she heard her mother's muted, late-at-night voice in the hall below. She put out her numbed and wobbly hand and switched off the light, then hid her book secretly against her breast, her poor hand drawn down under the bed-clothes, diffusing its prickling up the inside of her arm, so that it was difficult to lie still and feign sleep, even with her mother's step on the landing. She felt dreadfully the need to turn her head and stifle giggles into her pillows. When her mother came into the room, her eyelids wavered uncertainly. She felt that if her life depended on it, on pretending death, as she had read of people doing in books, the rising hysteria could not have been controlled; she was certain that she would cry out to break the strain, that she would begin to laugh helplessly.

Her mother straightened the slithering eiderdown, even lightly touched her hair. Betsy lay rigid, feeling Harriet's presence heavy above her, smelling what she politely thought of as her mother's party-smell. When Harriet had tiptoed from the room, the need to laugh went with her. Relaxed and deflated, Betsy found a less theatrical attitude, knees drawn up, ankles crossed, her hands bent towards her chest like paws. Compact, folded, she might have been lying in the

124

womb, as she composedly awaited sleep. She was glad that her head ached. She hoped to look tired to-morrow for her lesson with Miss Bell. She hoped to work with a pale intensity, a brittle fervour; to keep going by her nerves only; to be driven by her will. It would be wonderful if Miss Bell should think this, or comment on her fatigue—if only she could avoid her mother (who was more likely to do so) remarking on the same at breakfast.

Life was quite beautiful, she thought. It unfolded wonderfully from one Greek lesson to another; and every day was happy with the proximity of her loved one.

The bedroom was untidy, for they had gone off in a hurry. Harriet unpinned the carnations from her frock and put them in water. She had promised Betsy that she could have them for Miss Bell (for whom all flowers had been designed), though it did seem impolite. In the end, even knowing things to be wrong, she usually gave in.

When she had done that, she began to undress quickly, as if it desperately mattered to her that she should be in bed before Charles came up. Beyond their familiarity and nakedness, they could now sense their true isolation and were more perfectly strange to one another than people passing in a street.

She was only washing when he came in.

"That kitten!" he began at once as he closed the door. "Now it has wetted the hearthrug. It will have to go."

His eyes rested with indifference upon her as she dried her arms.

"Yes, she will have to go," she agreed.

"The place smells like the cat-house at the Zoo."

"I know."

She began to brush her hair.

"Tired?"

He looked carefully at his face in the mirror, as if to discover if he were tired himself.

125

"A little," she said cautiously.

Getting into bed, her feet recoiled. Elke had, of course, forgotten the hot-water-bottles.

"I'll fill one for you," Charles said.

"Oh, of course *no*."

"You won't sleep. You'll lie and talk." To save himself from this, he went off.

She sat up in bed, patting skin-food round her eyes. Down in the kitchen, Charles pottered about: the kettle began to hum. The house was full of noises—sometimes Betsy turned, with a murmur, in her sleep; Elke, the Dutch girl, snored relentlessly; ivy hit the pane; water lurched in the pipes.

When Charles came back, she took the hot-water-bottle gratefully, for her teeth were chattering. She went over on her side in a ball, curled round its warmth. When Charles got into bed he tried to unclench her, as if she were a hedgehog rolled up for protection. She went tighter and tighter.

"My darling Harriet," he said, lying on his back, away from her, resigned. "No one there to-night was as beautiful as you. I always know that, wherever I go, no other woman will be as lovely." But he could not uncurl her with flattery either.

He put out his hand for hers. She grasped it hurriedly as if to stave him off. Tears ran silently out of her eyes, slanting across her face into the pillows. He knew by her quietness that she was weeping. "Habit teaches me nothing," he said. "All these years can't prove to me that you are mine. The disbelief dies hard." He ran his arm along under her shoulder and kissed her, careful to avoid her tears.

By morning, the rain had dwindled into a fine mist. Betsy's red woollen gloves were furred over with moisture, her blonde hair hung lank on the shoulders of her reefer-coat. The clothes she wore now and those Harriet had worn

126

as a schoolgirl were almost the same—the felt hat with its band and cockade, the blouse and tunic and tie. Less than anything in England, Harriet would think, has the English schoolgirl altered. Checking the clothes at the beginning of the term, she felt, as regards herself, a mixture of nostalgia and relief.

Betsy, even at this early hour, on a morning which people called 'raw', felt quite gay with anticipation as grown-up women are inclined to feel after tea. She went along at an uneven pace which varied as her thoughts varied. When Father Keogh, startled by her steady look, said 'good-morning', she almost shied back against the railings, and certainly dropped her Xenophon in the thin mud on the pavement. 'He is trying to convert me,' she thought, feeling herself menaced from all directions—Rome, for instance; and then there was the White Slave Traffic, of which she had heard. Desired, endangered, she went on precariously to school, her Xenophon held awkwardly in her gloved hand.

Always she seemed to herself to be doomed; could not imagine how she had reached the age of fifteen without disaster, nor why no one had kidnapped her as an infant. At times, she was so certain that she would be arrested for some crime she had not committed that she assumed a special nonchalant way of walking down a street so as to avoid suspicion; sauntered, looked in shop-windows; then, suddenly wondering if she might not perhaps be taken for a prostitute—of whom she had read a great deal—would step out more briskly, her eyes on the pavement.

There had lately been a murder in the town. Every day she felt compelled to go home by the streets which would take in the place of the crime. The little tobacconist's-shop fascinated her. As if she really were the murderer, she was fatally drawn back to the scene. She did not encounter the police, but imagined them watching from upper windows. For this crime, luckily, she had a dramatic alibi. At the very time that the poor tobacconist was being battered with a

127

meat-cleaver, she was being confirmed by the Bishop in St Giles's Church.

Going along to school this morning, she imagined, as she often had, being questioned in court; listening, with a cool and steady smile. Then, just as things were looking very dark for her, her mother weeping softly, Miss Bell moaning audibly, she would ask if the Bishop of Buckingham might be brought in to say a word or two concerning her actions on the evening in question. A little stir, or ripple, then ran (as she had always read it did) around the court. The Bishop was magnificent in gaiters and purple skirts. Little strings tethered the brim of his hat (which he did not remove) to the crown. . . . But she could not help thinking that he was most unlike Father Keogh. So little of a sinister nature went on at St Giles's. The Vicar was, in fact, rather stout and merry. . . . However, she was confirmed now, safely gathered in . . . the smell of the red-brick Roman Catholic church at the corner only there to alarm and seduce and try her strength.

Her great friend, Pauline Hay-Hardy, had wanted them both to drop in there to Confession one late afternoon after lax-practice. Timidly, they had hung about in what they supposed to be a Byzantine porch. Undermined by the smell of incense they had ventured a step or two into the darkness. A woman with a shopping-basket knelt before a cluster of candles. Pauline retreated a little, her hand at Betsy's elbow. She put her hat-elastic into her mouth, a nervous habit she had. With their backs to the church, they saw that blue evening had suddenly come down. They thought of fires made up especially for their return; of mothers waiting; of the last crumpet in the dish, porous, soggy with butter; sweet tea; swiss-rolls; the day beautifully shut out. "We shouldn't have known if we had to pay anything," Pauline said, when they reached the cross-roads where they parted. Always, when she was left alone, Betsy broke into a trot. Then, with a sudden urgency,

128

she wanted to be home. Especially *that* evening.

Miss Bell was a Du Maurier young lady with strongly marked eyebrows and her mouth was very near her nose. Singing hymns at prayers, one side of her neck and her jaw reddened, giving her a look rather of indignation than of humility, as if she were engaged in some terse and intellectual argument with God. Once, reading the *Antigone* to them, she had taken on the same tinge.

She taught Latin and what Elizabeth Barrett Browning called 'Ladies' Greek—without any accents'. That the girls were not to be troubled with accents seemed a slur on her sex—an advantage they might have scorned, rather like being allowed over the line at a coconut-shy. She was no feminist, but did not like to waste her capabilities, which she had not so far found less than any man's.

Betsy had made a poor start at Latin with a mistress who aroused no emotion in her; but from the first declension in Greek devotion had been her spur. Later, some drama in the language itself held her—some heightened quality which she recognised as belonging to her own life; in the very sounds of the words voices wailed, lied, vowed constancy, vowed revenge, adored immoderately, accepted defeat with stubborn scorn.

Miss Bell, her girlhood not so far behind her, recalled how she had hoisted herself up from one scholarship to another; eschewing personal relationships, at which she easily failed, possessing small natural gift, and little time to develop what she had. Having reached, at Girton, some eminence, she was now slowly climbing down again, trying to steady herself into a semblance of patience with the stumbling, glancing, sighing girls. Only Betsy seemed to reward her. 'Perhaps one in a hundred,' she thought, seeing the child's bright face. She could not know that the face was bright for her; that what she had eschewed was now turned intensely upon her, a great glare of adoration. Other people's reactions to herself claimed most of Betsy's thoughts;

129

in obtaining the reaction, she was assiduous, almost stealthy; and she gathered in as a by-product (as she now was gathering in the *Iliad*) both good and bad.

For the bunches of flowers Miss Bell (feeling they were laid at Homer's feet) took no credit.

"Everyone has to be in love with someone," said Miss Beetlestone, the English mistress, who was engaged to be married. She was arranging chrysanthemums in a vase in the staff-room. "We do to be going on with, I suppose, as there isn't anyone else. Though we needn't think ourselves so clever. I am sure I remember that Sarah Bernhardt fell in love with a goat when she was young."

"Love?" said the games-mistress, the word obviously wry in her mouth. "This atmosphere in the school . . ."

"There is always an atmosphere in a school," Miss Beetlestone, who was soon to be out of it, replied.

Miss Bell listened, but did not connect any of this with herself and certainly not with the only sensible pupil she had had.

"Let us not use words like 'love' . . ."

"But I *know* it is really the same thing," Miss Beetlestone said with authority, and from her unfair advantage. She jammed the flowers down into the vase, then tried to loosen them. When she laughed, they felt she was mocking them; but she was only happy.

Even so, Miss Bell took Betsy's flowers absent-mindedly; she held them rather on one side, her eyes on the muddy Xenophon as she sorted out the difficult construction which had been so worrying over-night. Betsy was adept in asking intelligent questions just before prayers.

"I couldn't sleep," she said. "I was still working on it at eleven o'clock."

"Yes," said Miss Bell. She forgot to admonish or console. Working till midnight was the most practical thing to do: she always had herself. She was only astonished that so few of the other girls did so.

130

Harriet's carnations, browning at the edges, were scarcely noticed.

When Betsy and then Charles had gone, there was a pause in the house, the clocks seemed to slacken their pace. Elke, the Dutch girl, went upstairs and hung her bedclothes out of the bedroom window into the damp air. Harriet took her last cup of coffee over to the fire, re-read her letters, lit her first cigarette. Beginning to recuperate after the ruffle of breakfast and other people setting out, she would usually feel at this time contentment at the morning ahead, loving the ordinary, the familiar, knowing that what she must do was well within her powers.

This morning, however, she was ruffled herself, felt that a real sequence was so broken that the punctual arrival of the milk-man, the charwoman coming in at the back door at her usual time, were small mockeries, piteous pretences, like the first meal after a beloved one's death, not even reaffirming that the world goes on as usual, that in the midst of death we are in life. A circus dog, at last retired from the ring, no doubt continues its meaningless routine, but meaningless it is.

She took her letters to her desk, wrote out Harrods' cheque, answered an invitation. In her domestic life she had grown orderly and business-like. She had tried to please Charles in such ways as she could.

In the glass over Betsy's photograph on her desk she now saw her own face faintly reflected. In some respects the two faces were the same; Betsy's eyes—large, candid—matched her own; the blonde hair hung pale against the darker; but timidity was absent from the girl's expression; she seemed more engaging, more grown-up. Yet, physically, the reflection was something in the future, a forward-going ghost, awaiting the child. The faint lines on the forehead and the less clear outline of the jaw were in the nature of a premonition.

131

Harriet looked away, out at the untidy wintry garden, with its bare mulberry-tree, the iris-roots heaving up, knotted, contorted, in the otherwise empty borders, the tracks of cats across the wet, rough grass, leaves piling up under bushes. Yet winter did not seem incapable of change as it had when she was young. As soon as the leaves fell now, she felt the possibility of shoots coming up through the hard ground; autumn was implicit in summer; no season *held*. There were no more long summers. The last was when she had played hide-and-seek with Vesey and the children. Since then the years had slipped by, each growing shorter than the one before. It had not seemed a long time, her married life. Summer and winter had run into one another. Betsy had not so much grown up as unrolled—as if she were all there at the beginning, but that each birthday unrolled more of her, made more visible, though suggesting more.

In those years Vesey had in no way threatened her. Sometimes at night, his name in her mind comforted her; but she heard little of him, nothing from him. All that Hugo had forecast was seen to have been true, though not amazingly so. He had, after all, only foretold what no one else had cared to say. For Vesey had not prospered. The little touring-company had not been a stepping-stone, or if it was, Vesey had still not moved on to the next one; and barely, if all that Deirdre implied was true, retained his hold on that, though Harriet thought that she may have spoken from the old enmity she and Joseph felt for Vesey.

At the Memorial Service to Caroline, who had died during the war, Harriet had sat behind Vesey, wedged in amongst the Women's Institute. The little village church was filled with representatives from all the departments of Caroline's public life. In the front pew, Hugo and his two children were all in uniform—Deirdre and Joseph in blue, Hugo in khaki— all with commendably high rank. They made Caroline's seem a strangely civilian death. Behind them, Vesey looked clumsy in battle-dress. His neck seemed rubbed raw by the

132

rough khaki; his short hair gave him a shorn, outraged look; his boots, Harriet saw over the top of the pew as they knelt down, were huge and studded. She could hardly bear to look at them.

Hugo, Deirdre and Joseph behaved beautifully. Pale and proud, they seemed at attention and to be relied upon. Vesey's eyes were large with tears, as Harriet's were. Once he ran a knuckle under his lashes. Turning his head and seeing Harriet as she came into the church, he had looked with desperation at the women who hemmed him in on either side. They did not quite know how to greet one another: the occasion laid a welcomed restraint upon them. They were not in Deirdre's position to be able to scatter bright smiles and be thought brave: bright smiles might have been wrongly interpreted: their stately acknowledgement was more suitable.

Hearing Caroline celebrated, they were presented with a stranger. The Vicar summed up what they had never known. To set this right they both tried to picture Caroline in some less formal light—the look of her, for instance; voices are impossible. Vague, earnest, good, she sat (for Harriet) at the breakfast-table in a dream; her spectacles slipping on her nose; the children ran in and out (for meals were made for people, and not people for meals), eating when they cared to; almost in rags, the villagers thought. But her ideas had triumphed. Standing there bravely in the front pew they were a credit to her, her children; their bearing now justified their upbringing, as their good health had always justified their vegetarianism. Hugo looked old. The last time he had been in uniform, he had been like Rupert Brooke: now he was quite grey, his manners rather irritable. Harriet suddenly recalled the book Caroline had inscribed for him when they were young. *Allons*, the road is before us! 'I was a fool to remember that!' she thought, wrenching her mind back to Caroline at the breakfast-table, which did not make her weep.

133

But it was obvious that the Vicar and most of those now present could not see Caroline as vague or informal. For them, she must always have a sheaf of papers in her hand, would speak with authority, know statistics and believe in them. She had been to prison and this (but not straight away) established her public integrity.

Harriet had wondered if her own tears were perhaps for her mother. She could not imagine whom Vesey's were for. They had neither of them deeply cared for Caroline, beyond being used to her (which amounts to a great deal more than we suppose).

This morning, sitting at her desk, with the ink dry in her pen, she knew that they had both wept nostalgically, for their own youth, of which Caroline had been very much a part, for the long summers, the last especially; paining themselves unnecessarily, and they alone of all the congregation behaving badly.

Outside, in the churchyard, they had spoken to one another. Movement, action, steadied them. Even coming out of the church was a deliverance and a relief. The sky was bitterly white above the clipped yews: daffodils all slanted one way in the wind. 'It might snow,' people said, 'though late in March.' They felt braced with paying homage and 'Fight the Good Fight'.

Deirdre, with enviable aplomb, shook hands with acquaintances: standing at the lych-gate, charmingly speeding them to their cars which were parked all down the road, she might have been giving a party.

"How are you, Harriet?" Vesey asked. His face was mauve with the cold. She wondered how he could ever stand army life.

She put up the collar of her dark red coat (for 'no mourning' was as imperative as 'no meat') against her cheek, as if she had toothache.

"Deirdre is being sensible," Vesey said. "Caroline would have liked that. We must hope it is not missed."

134

"What is it like in the army?" Harriet asked shyly, her glance swerving away from his uniform.

"I didn't go until I was invited. I have scarcely given it a chance. Hugo could tell you better."

"I mean for *you*."

"You see, I never have liked undressing with other men. Naturally I always feel meagre and pathetic. But it is really only boring and silly, living miles below the subsistence-level. Then office jobs I never cotton to much—copy lists of numbers on to ration-cards—you make mistakes because it's so easy—do a pile, and then say Oh Christ, October has only thirty days, correct them all, smudges and blots, ink to the elbows, and then, oh damn, it's November only has thirty. All this in a sort of dirty post-office place, dust, broken nibs, ink-bottles full of sludge. And stuffy."

By his mocking voice, she imagined that he had not said any of this before, and could picture his desolate patience in that odd world.

"Once," he said, as if he could not stop now that he had begun, "once they gave us Weetabix, if you please, for breakfast. I thought little babies in high-chairs had that. . . . The worst of all, though, was Christmas dinner." He looked away through the yew-trees. "You know, the officers being decent and matey"—his glance dwelt on Hugo—"and us cheery, but each his own private self. I thought 'Poor men and soldiers unable to rejoice.' Perhaps not, though. Perhaps all enjoying themselves like hell." He disavowed his vision and compassion, looked back at Harriet, suddenly asked: "Do you still cry as much as when you were a girl?"

"No, of course not." At once, the tears rushed to her eyes.

"I suppose we mustn't be the last guests to go." He began to walk slowly down the path, treading uncertainly on the narrow grass verge as if the gravelled part were only wide enough for her.

"I'm sorry. I've bored you with my long complaint. How women must hate soldiers' stories."

"I only can't bear to think of the Christmas dinner."

"Oh, I enjoyed it like mad, really."

They paced along with their heads bent, not heeding other people.

"How is your husband?" he asked politely.

"Very well, thank you." She brushed aside Charles, who was, as it happened, in bed with influenza.

"Good."

"Are you going to tea with Hugo?"

"No. I have a train to catch."

Held up now by groups of people on the path, he glanced impatiently at his watch. "I don't know what we say to them, do you?"

"It doesn't matter what we say."

"But say something we must. I never know, never manage to hit the right note. I can hardly say 'Bad luck, Hugo,' but he seems to forbid anything more. Difficult to know what they expect. They are certainly not wearing their hearts on their sleeves . . . Joseph's are so taken up with rings that there wouldn't be room anyhow. It would be nice to slip out by some back way . . ." He looked desperately round him. But the little clots of people had thinned out. They were brought—unprepared—face to face with Hugo. Vesey suddenly remembered to salute.

"It was good of you to come, Vesey," Hugo said.

Harriet kissed Deirdre uncertainly. She had felt there might be a law against kissing women officers.

Joseph was easily modest of all his attainments, the rings on his sleeves, his father's pride in him. Hearts glowed to see him. He seemed young to bear the burden of all their lives. More symbolic than anyone in the army could be, much more of an individual saviour, they felt that he went out alone to defend them. They had watched him grow up: he had scarcely had time to finish doing so.

"There is no living up to them," Vesey said to Harriet in a low voice. He was smiling.

136

She had watched him go off down the road, scrunching the gravel with his great boots; and had not seen him again until last night.

A tremor in the air, as if the air flinched with apprehension, was resolved by the telephone ringing. Harriet dipped her pen in the ink. By the time Mrs Curzon opened the door, she was busy writing.

"It's your mother-in-law, dear."

"How are you this morning, Mrs Curzon?" Harriet asked on her way to the hall.

"Chronic dear, thanks. Three o'clock this morning, I thought I'd die, and I wished I would. You know how it is, with the bed swinging one way and your stomach the other. A couple of hours earlier I hadn't a care in the world. Laugh! I fell on the rockery going up the path; there I was sitting on top of the clinkers in the rain. . . ."

Harriet waited politely, the receiver in her hand, while Mrs Curzon cheered herself up. "Yes, laugh! 'Won't some gent be so good as to kindly lift me down off of here?' I was asking. Talk about the fairy on the Christmas tree . . . terrible hiccups . . . you'd have enjoyed it, madam. . . ."

"One moment . . ." Harriet put the receiver to her ear. "Good morning, Julia."

"What is going on, Harriet? Who are all those people?"

"There are only Mrs Curzon and I."

"Well, for heaven's sake set her to work. You must feel a great deal better than I do at this hour of the morning."

"We were both at parties last night. I expect we feel worse."

"I was thinking that it would be a good day for you to come to tea. . . . Miss Bastable is going out . . . she gets on my nerves, God knows, but I sometimes wonder if it isn't worse without her . . . next door to the church-yard and all those graves . . . one begins to feel like those dretful Brontë girls . . ."

137

"But, Julia, there's not a grave in sight . . . and you could never be like any Brontë girl . . ."

"Well, it's very sweet of you to say so, darling. You always cheer me up. Tea, then. Be early because of Miss Bastable going out.".

"I can't to-day, Julia. To-morrow. . . ."

"Oh, to-morrow's no good. Miss Bastable will be in. We shouldn't be able to say a word."

"I couldn't to-day. . . ."

"But why?'

"One moment . . . I can't hear. I shall just tell Elke to switch off the Hoover." Harriet put down the receiver and went and sat on the stairs for a moment, trying to think. She could hear Julia's voice, tinny and indignant. The respite was no use. She had to return to the telephone and Julia's pettishness with nothing ready-made to say.

"Where did you go? Really, Harriet, I haven't all morning to hang on this while you go and talk to servants. Where were we before you dodged away?"

"I was saying I couldn't come to tea."

"And I was asking you 'why'?"

"I have a previous engagement," Harriet said sedately.

"You sound so mysterious. I shall think you have a lover."

"Why, of course it is that. How clever of you, Julia!"

"I don't believe a word of it. You are just being thoroughly underhand."

"It is what people are about such things."

"Well, I can't waste any more of the morning. I shall go back to my gravestones."

"I will imagine you there."

"Don't think that after this you can just drop in to meals at any time that suits your convenience, will you?"

"No, I won't Julia, dear. I promise."

"I dislike just being made use of."

"Of course you do."

"And stop soothing me. You know I hate to be soothed. There was some rhyme Charles's Nannie used to say about 'He that will not when he can, may not when he shall'. Something like that. . . ."

"It sounds reasonable. Good-bye, Julia. The Hoover's starting again."

That Julia became more contentious as she aged was pitiable. It was the course she took when she could no longer invoke adoration: if she could only summon discord from them, it was at least a reaction of some violence. She did not want to be loved for her own sake; never having known what her own sake was. When Harriet mollified her, she felt destroyed. Charles had always menaced her. Feeling them aligned against her—but indifferently, in rather loose ranks—she went back to what she called her gravestones; in reality, her bullying of poor Miss Bastable.

Miss Bastable was silly as a hen. Dividends dwindling, she had nothing to sell but her own company, which most people would have paid to avoid. Julia, afraid of ghosts, feeling herself predisposed to visions, hauntings, was glad of her about the house after dark and pleased to persecute her all day. 'I've worked hard all my life,' she thought. 'If I can't have someone to fetch my slippers for me now . . .' Miss Bastable had never worked and could not, at her age, demean herself. She thought Julia a common woman—which no doubt she was—and considered herself sufficiently sacrificed in being under her roof. "We cannot live on one per cent," she excused herself to her father's photograph when Julia had been outrageous. Her position was undefined. When she was in one room, she thought perhaps she should be in another. If Julia had visitors, she could not make up her mind whether to go or stay. She hovered, starting nervily if spoken to. Julia loved pouring out tea and Miss Bastable handed the slopped cups and saucers, hoping that the guests would notice that her own hand was steady. All of the little jobs which a companion might have done

139

without losing face, Julia liked to do herself. "Leave those bloody flowers alone!" she would thunder, "I've spent hours on them," or "Don't touch the Meissen china. I always wash that myself," or "I can sort out my own silks. I'm not blind." At the beginning, Miss Bastable had once suggested that she should read aloud to Julia, for she had heard that companions sometimes did so. She would never forget how Julia took off her spectacles and stared at her, her book lowered to her lap. After a long pause, in which Miss Bastable was expected to reflect upon the poor quality of her voice, Julia raised her book again and put on her spectacles. "I do any reading aloud that's to be done," she said augustly.

Halfway through that morning she wondered suddenly if Harriet had not been dreadfully artful in conceding a lover. She did not seem quite up to such duplicity; but Julia liked to believe her to be. It was a mystery—and a reproach—that Harriet should have borne Charles so much longer than Julia had been able to bear his father. At some point, she believed, the crack must become apparent. That it should come with Harriet in command of herself, gay—as she had sounded—and behaving trickily was not to have been expected. Julia had rather given up looking for misdemeanours. No flaw had ever been revealed. Charles had flourished. Dutifully, Harriet concealed from him—as much as could be done in these days—the workings of the house, presenting him with calm, though sometimes by the skin of her teeth. He had never had to wait for a meal: if meals ever waited for him they did not seem to have done so. Julia had thought her daughter-in-law dull and slavish. "You hover about him like a praying mantis!" she deplored. "And the milieu! That provincial band of married people. I should call them a *set*. Those dretful cocktail-parties, and going in gangs to those chichi clubs at Maidenhead. I know all about your dreary little round. How *dull* you all are nowadays, and common!"

This morning, going round the conservatory with a

watering-can, she wondered if it were all as dull as it had seemed. Did not the setting more easily conceal the forbidden, illicit? The idea deliciously beguiled her. "Miss Bastable!" she called. "Will you come and mop up these shelves?" Miss Bastable ran to fetch her rubber gloves. Julia thoughtfully sprayed a little extra water over the white-painted slats.

Harriet tidied her bedroom. Downstairs, Mrs Curzon shouted at Elke, whose English was poor. She implied that Elke had headaches merely to annoy. If she did not invent or encourage them, they were certainly her own fault.

"Perhaps you're constipated," she now accused her.

"I do not understand 'constipated'."

"Have you been upstairs this morning? I mean."

"I have not yet finished the Hoover . . ."

"I mean have you done your duty upstairs?" Mrs Curzon almost screamed with exasperation. 'England for the English' her voice seemed to proclaim.

"I have made my bed."

"What's that got to do with it? What I'm getting at is have you been to the W.C., the lavatory, the toilet?" Her voice mounted. "The House of Parliament," she threw in to add to the confusion.

Silence followed. A door shut. Even the door sounded offended, Harriet thought. She went to dust Betsy's room. Here, something seemed always to forbid her entry. The young have so many secrets. Harriet remembered her own diary and her own ways with her mother.

What could only be called a snapshot of Miss Bell had gone crooked in its Woolworth's frame. She looked, Harriet thought, a brave and rather lumpish young woman, standing on some steps, wearing a gown with white fur. From a matching frame, Robert Helpman seemed to swoon towards her. But Miss Bell looked steadily ahead, her chin up, her hands clutching a book as if for safety, and her mouth trying to smile; honest and innocent and kind, she looked. Harriet felt that Betsy, not always so stable, showed discrimination in this love. Miss Bell was better than the girl from Betsy's form, who had gone in the Christmas holidays to dance in a pantomime and always looked so cute and pert and made even her school uniform seem fashionable, and wrote such long, long letters with such long, long postscripts and even mysterious scrawls on the backs of envelopes, in coloured inks.

"That girl!" said Mrs Curzon. "She ought to have been in service in my young day. I wonder why she takes the trouble to come here?"

"It's a cheap way of learning how to speak American, I suspect," Harriet said in a disillusioned voice. She went to the window and looked down into the garden. Roofs sloped away, cowls veered on the skyline. The town, embowered in a haze of naked branches, lay below. She imagined Vesey ascending the hill in the afternoon. At lunch, she must tell Charles of this. Yet if he did not come—and she began to think now that he would not—she must incur Charles's displeasure, and his scorn, for nothing. Vesey's word was scarcely to be relied upon. She had waited for him before in vain. By now, she was so attuned to the idea of their meeting that she could not, she felt, face to-morrow and the other days of her life if he did not come.

"Try to manage," she heard herself saying.

"Manage! Of course I will, dear. It takes more than a slip of a girl to upset me."

"I knew you would help me."

"Madam, dear, what is it?" Mrs Curzon, full of concern, put her arm across Harriet's shoulders. "Don't let her haggle you. I've worked for you thirteen years and please God I'll still be here when you say Curzy dear you're in your bloody dotage so here's half-a-crown for old langs syne. You know I'd do anything for you, no question of it."

"I know. You've been my dear friend."

"*Been?* Am, you mean, dear. I *am*. It would take more than a pack of foreigners to part us two."

"She's not a pack of foreigners, you know. She's a poor bewildered girl away from home. We only puzzle her."

"Puzzle! She was saying Tuesday week she went out with a Pole. 'You look out, my girl,' I said. 'You'll get caught hopping. You'll be finding yourself taken advantage of one of these days'."

"Oh, dear, you shouldn't. She couldn't have known what you were talking about."

"That's right. 'Advantage?' she said. 'I do not understand advantage'." Mrs Curzon's voice thinned in mimicry.

"It must be dreadful for her. When she first came, she could only say 'Princess Elizabeth'."

"I'll Princess Elizabeth her. Telling me we're all dirty. 'Dirty!' I said, 'and what about that duster you're using on madam's white paint'—as black as Newgate's knocker without a word of a lie . . . and wiping over the gas-stove with the floor-cloth. She knew she'd gone a step too far. 'Oh, well,' she says, 'perhaps the French are worse.' 'That lot!' I said. 'We don't care to be mentioned in the same breath.' No, honest, madam, no disrespect, but she gets you down, no mistake."

"She's very young."

Harriet, at the window, watched the white cat in the garden below. It crept from a litter of dead leaves, walked warily through an imaginary jungle, a leopard hunting its prey, stealthy, powerful. Then suddenly the fantasy collapsed. It sat down peacefully and began to lick the pink underneath of a paw. A clock striking brought Harriet to reality too.

Beyond the Terrace, the houses abruptly stopped. They did not peter out into unmade roads, and scarred building-sites with agents' boards; but concluded neatly at the edge of a park. The town, in this direction, had no twentieth-century

143

fringe. The houses had reached the limits of the park fence in Regency days, and those pale terraces and crescents were much walked by on Sundays, on Saturday afternoons were somehow saddened by whistles blowing, the punting of balls, muffled shouts of encouragement. On weekdays in winter the park was empty. No one walked along its paths. It seemed the depths of the country. The abandoned Queen Anne house on the skyline, with its crescent of trees, was shut. (In summertime, lemonade was sold there.) No one knew what to do with it, and holes in its floors went un-repaired. Dry-rot infested the panelling: fungus stood out like brackets from the pantry walls.

At the end of Jessica Terrace, there were gateposts with stone deer and iron gates padlocked. At the side of these a turnstile kept out bicycles and ensured that no great spate of people should suddenly invade the serenity of the park. Once through this, Harriet and Vesey felt alone in the wintry afternoon.

Indoors, they had started off with an air of recrimination, desire to punish one another. She had been glad to go for her coat. Vesey had looked about him, at the crimson-papered walls, the white paint and the blood-red Venetian glass, with unabashed criticism. Harriet could not forget her lunch with Charles, during which she had not mentioned Vesey, deferring it from one mouthful to the next, until she knew her voice could not be trusted. When Charles had gone, she had flown to her bedroom and had not—perhaps because she so needed to—made the best of her face. Waiting with icy hands and wrists, trying to calm herself, she had suddenly *known*, been utterly and for ever sure, that he would never come, just at the moment when the sound of the front-door bell leapt dreadfully through the house. If Vesey could not forgive her for the beautiful and brilliant room, she could not easily forgive him for what she had endured.

All the time—when she came downstairs in her rather shabby fur coat, went for a word with Elke, finally led him

144

out into the Terrace—she was conscious of him silently *placing* her. He was building up all round her her background and her past. Now, in the park, away from her home, she felt less self-conscious, less watched. Space seemed endless; even Time. For this reason, they struck off along a path in the direction of the lake without talking.

Along these paths she had pushed Betsy in a pram, or dawdled with her as she stumbled along in gaiters. Her bored gaze had taken in this scene, winter and summer. The park was a place linked in her mind with ennui and loneliness. Lovers, on warm evenings, going off down the narrower paths, had only emphasised this. Lately, she had not come.

At the edge of the lake there were iron seats. When they sat down, some ducks came up through the reeds as if waiting to be fed. After a while, they dispersed again, diving into the water disconsolately. Vesey put his arm inside Harriet's coat and drew her close to him. Sitting with his cheek against her hair, he did not kiss her, but stared across the water of the lake. For a long while they sat peacefully together.

"Would *you* know where to begin?" he asked at last. "Or does it at all matter? Are we perhaps practically strangers? I suppose at some point my idea of you must have diverged from you yourself. In that churchyard that time I didn't find any discrepancy. In your house, I did. The photograph of your daughter, for instance. I felt quite hopeless in there. Did you?"

"Yes."

"Every bloody ornament on the mantelpiece seemed to warn me off, every chair seemed a booby-trap. I felt that Charles was hiding behind one curtain, and . . . what's-her-name? . . . Betsy . . . behind another. I was angry that you made me go there. And it all looked polished up for my benefit."

"It is always polished up," Harriet said, and she smiled, turning her brow against his cheek in sensuous bliss. "Last night, I thought I could make it seem unclandestine. I thought we could be above-board. I thought I could tell Charles."

"Oh, no," Vesey said airily. "We can't not be sordid. A little squalor does not come amiss. We should only get frightened if it were all beautiful like this."

"All? There only *can* be this."

She shifted away from him and when he took her hands she drew them at once from his.

Dusk, like a sediment, sifted down through the bluish sky. The surface of the lake was ringed over from the pebbles Vesey began to throw in, one after another, with little vicious spurts of energy.

"I want to tell you about Charles," she said, "but you distract me so."

He threw away the rest of the stones and put his hands in his pockets. There he was reminded of cigarettes and pulled out a squashed packet. She shook her head and he put them back sadly, as if she had said no for him too.

"Charles," he prompted her gloomily.

"We are happily married," she said in a distressed voice. "I could not betray him. Everybody else seems to do so."

"Some people ask for it," Vesey said roughly.

"No, he's a good man. I love him." Her voice wavered over the word. "Betsy, you see, too. She's not a child now . . . I could not . . . when one is growing up, one needs one's mother to behave."

"One does indeed," Vesey said grimly. "Mine didn't."

"What are you thinking, Vesey?"

"You didn't grow out of your stammer."

She looked aside quickly.

"My beloved Harriet," he added, almost in the same breath.

"I'm too old. We are too late."

"I see why you married him. It was sensible of you. It was the best thing you could do, after all. People do marry

146

because they are frightened. How could *I* ever have helped you? I do the reverse. I do now, and shall much more. And I never have any money . . . If you are shivering because you are cold, we could walk on a bit . . . I never think fur coats *smell* very nice, do you?" he said in a conversational voice, putting her collar up for her.

An elderly man, very much wrapped up, walked briskly towards them, his terrier running with its nose to the gravel. He eyed them sternly as he passed. After that, the path, mounting towards the desolate house, seemed lonelier than ever; the house itself in its haze of branches looked as if it were painted on silk.

"He knew about us, that man," Vesey said. "I could tell by his eye. He, I daresay, could tell by ours. Oh, he knows all that we are up to, all that we are going to do . . . secret meetings, lies, evasion, kisses—like this one . . . heavens, your cold face, darling—hundreds of forbidden kisses, waiting for one another in strange places. . . . You make me feel about seventeen. You are so shy."

She tried not to think of other women, who had not been shy. They walked on, close together, in step, thigh against thigh.

The great house, with its flaky, scabrous walls, confronted them now. Between overgrown urns, they approached the windows; but, inside, shutters were drawn crookedly across.

"Do you remember the other empty house?" she asked him. Depending so on his answer—which she had tried for years to guess, not knowing that she would ever be able to ask—she could not look at him, but leant her back, the palms of her gloved hands, against the rough wall of the house. They were high up now. The blue town lay in the hollow; lamps pricked the blurred distance. The factories, on hill-slopes which had merged into the sky, were like lighted ships.

He was watching her and he did not answer. When she

147

turned, he put out his hand. They could not be out of one another's arms for long. Walking back, dreading ever to come to the edge of the park and to other people, "What other empty house did you mean?" he asked.

The streets drew out in the dusk and faded; strung with blurred lamps, arched over by gathering darkness. Strange contrasts of vague perspectives and vivid close-ups made a film-world of it, Betsy thought, and was inclined to glide up cobbled alleyways, close to the walls, hesitating at yawning entrances, her face paper-white, she imagined, her blond hair gleaming. She regretted her school-satchel, feeling for the moment like some girl in a French film; shabby, embittered, passive, poor. Glimpsing herself in a shop-window mirror, she was surprised to see that she was only stony-faced.

She stared haughtily at what really beguiled her—old posters peeling off walls; black, alarming warehouses; the little shops with their door-bells, their indifferent lighting, their flyblown window-displays. At one house, she could see right into a room, glimpsed a clothes'-horse before a fire, a littered mantel, an old man with his waistcoat open dozing in a chair. A woman was sitting at a sewing-machine, and white material flowed away from it to the floor.

One moment she felt above all this, very powerful and free; and the next, passing a churchyard, and graves, was frozen with incredulity and a stilling horror. In the busy, lighted street, the patch of darkness checked and menaced her. Unconcernedly, bicyclists passed. Women dragged home with their cares, their shopping. Under those mossy stones, beauty had collapsed, she told herself, pausing by the railings, into an absurd collection of bones. It could not happen to me, she thought. It will, she thought. Not for years and years and years, she comforted herself. All the same, she knew that the graves, in their silence and darkness, were prepared to wait. Whatever time was to her, it was nothing to them. Black ivy, with hairy, twining branches,

148

grew everywhere as if it drew extra strength here; little pots of flowers were set about like a dolls' tea-party, wretchedly pathetic. A street-lamp flung the shadow of slanting railings across a granite slab.

"What a strange girl!" Father Keogh thought, as he passed.

Life slapped at her like some clown with a balloon, she thought. Going off at a tangent from the graveyard, she recoiled from him. Though with a scarf round his neck he looked nothing. "It is the collar," she decided, skipping along at a faster pace, death forgotten. "Without that, he seems even a bit boring."

She began to plod uphill away from the shops. Houses here lay decently back behind gardens. Schoolboys came down the hill in clusters, scuffling, tripping, snatching caps. She scorned them. When one of them whistled at her, she stared at the pavement, outraged. Then she noticed that her heart was beating. Presumably it always had, but she had not thought of it. Now she could actually hear it. She was also quite breathless from her climb. She went more slowly, worried about her health, wondering if she had angina pectoris, which she had often read about.

When she turned into Jessica Terrace, it seemed really dark. That cul-de-sac, blocked by the gates of Prospect Park, was like a silent backwater, over which houses, not trees, secretively hung.

Two people coming slowly from the other direction stopped at her gate.

Her mother, who was already putting out her hand, made a wider gesture with it to include her daughter. "This is Betsy," she said, as if the fact had some tremendously dramatic and embarrassing significance.

Betsy hitched her satchel up higher on her shoulder and shook hands. She looked up into Vesey's eyes. They seemed to search her face. He had forgotten that he was holding her hand and she did not know how to remind him.

149

Her mother lingered awkwardly at the gate. Standing on a step, she looked over Betsy's head.

"Well, good-bye, Vesey," she said brightly, as if to a child.

He looked up at once and gave Betsy back her hand. She felt rather short, standing there between them.

"Good-bye, Harriet."

The fan of light above the door fell on Betsy's bright hair. Harriet's head was bent as she raked about in her handbag for her key. Before he reached the end of the Terrace, he heard the door shut. The echo of it seemed to come down the street after him.

So at supper, Harriet was obliged to say to Charles, "Vesey called this afternoon." She almost had not had to. Trying to seem casual, barely interested, her voice was flat. Not only guilt inhibited her, but the knowledge that anything about Vesey was what Charles could not bear. The matter had not much arisen; but was acknowledged. Almost as if it were a physical irritation, an allergy, he reacted in strange, betraying ways; his jaw perceptibly moved; his eyes looked down, or aside; imperiously, as one who scorned discussion, he waited for the pain to pass.

For it was Vesey who had undermined their life together; the idea of him in both their heads. In their few disagreements, he knew to whom her thoughts flew; discouraged, he remembered her girlhood's inconsolable love, and her silence ever since. Many times, when she had thought of nothing, had simply sat and stared, he believed she thought of him. He had always known that one day he would walk back into their presence as he had done the previous evening, unexpectedly. Harriet had whitened. She had presently bent her head and looked at the floor in front of her, as if disavowing a ghost. Charles could not know that many times before she had thought Vesey coming towards her in the street; her heart leaping, she had scarcely dared to look up at the stranger who eventually went by, usually a man quite unlike Vesey. Seeing one face continually in crowds is one of the minor annoyances of being in love.

"Water, Betsy?" Charles asked, with the jug held almost threateningly above her glass.

"We went for a walk in the park," Harriet said, thinking she had not said enough.

Charles filled his own glass. He had nothing casual to say. "Flash needed some exercise," he managed at last. Flash was what could only be called "a brown dog".

Again, because of Betsy, Harriet had to say: "I forgot to take him."

That sounded strange and Charles made it stranger by not answering.

'Why *did* I forget?' Harriet wondered. 'I could so easily have taken him.'

Now even Betsy began to sense something wrong, looking from one to the other uncertainly. After supper she always stayed in the dining-room to do her homework. To-night, she felt that her mother and father both lingered, as if they were unwilling to leave her and be alone together.

When she had helped Elke to clear the table, she sat down and drew her satchel towards her. This satchel seemed so familiar as to be a part of herself, and her link between school and home. Smelling its inky, biscuity smell as she pulled out her books was a little reassuring. The light rained down peacefully over her; the clock ticked; bubbles of ink and blots came out of her pen. Yet her mind was disturbed and the evening not really like others.

She fluttered the pages of her book, sighing; drew spectacles on Julius Caesar, filled in his eye-balls with ink, signed her name several different ways on the title-page. She listened for her parents' voices; but they were silent. In the kitchen, Elke knocked plates against taps, dropped knives over the floor. Mother likes him; father doesn't, Betsy thought. As for herself, she had felt a sense of complete strangeness, of being suddenly out of her element:

151

not altogether pleasant, for it was rather like lifting a foot for a step that is not there; but exciting.

Years before, she had printed inside her satchel,

> Elizabeth Lilian Jephcott,
> 8, Jessica Terrace,
> Market Swanford,
> Buckinghamshire,
> England,
> Europe,
> The World,
> The Universe.

Going thus from the particular to the general, *she* had not seemed to dwindle. On the contrary, her importance was emphasised. It was the world, the universe, which dwindled away into nothing. Thumbing her way back through the pages, she added drop ear-rings to Caesar and an Elizabethan ruffle. Later, but absent-mindedly, a pipe and a halo. She wondered why her parents were so quiet, and could not seem to settle to her work. She took her autograph-album from the little front pocket of her satchel. Pauline Hay-Hardy had done a crinolined lady in Indian ink. Across a peach-coloured page, in her cramped and screwed-up handwriting, like a doctor's, Miss Bell had written "It is better to travel hopefully than to arrive, and the true success is to labour."

Elke had switched on the electric fire in her bedroom soon after tea, so that by nine o'clock the room was nicely warm. Harriet never invaded her privacy here: she could rely on that, which was a good thing as the cupboard was full of broken china that she was hiding. She broke a great deal of china. If she cracked a plate one day and it fell in half the next, she could always excuse herself because it was cracked: if it broke in half at the beginning, she thought it best to hide it in her room.

152

She was a large blonde girl with a complacent yet driven expression which put other people very much in the wrong. Harriet was often reminded of cows being herded along a lane, at each whack on their rumps their faces looking more wounded and yet more smugly right. Sometimes too, Elke would break into a lumbering run, which was a reproach in itself.

England bewildered and bored her. There seemed nothing for young people to do. She could not accustom herself to all the absurd contrasts—the continual bathing, and the filthy shops; women doing men's jobs, men pushing prams. The old-fashioned motor-cars made her laugh; the trains belching smoke appalled her. Conversation was especially puzzling. She thought the English were as taken up with the weather as they sounded; not knowing that it was a refuge. All experiences in the war were apparently dully unmentionable. People who told stories about air-raids were thought bores.

Sunday was a strange day. They wore, not their best, but rather shabbier clothes than on other days. In old flannels, an elbow out of his leather-patched jacket, Charles would first clean his car and then go out for a drink. When guests came for sherry before lunch, they were all shabby too. Instead of a holiday, it seemed the day for doing all the odd jobs. Harriet washed the hair-brushes and her powder-puffs. After lunch, the day seemed to peter out: streets emptied: Sunday papers made a great litter: smoke hung in a haze. Charles dozed. If people called unexpectedly before supper, they were hailed, and no wonder, as a relief to the marooned. Drinks were again brought out. Betsy went on with her homework. No one went to Church but her.

All of this, Elke tried to explain in her long letters home. To-night, after coating over her peeling nail-varnish, she settled down to continue her observations. Harriet was sometimes nervous at the thought of those long letters. She saw how vague and indecisive she must appear and was

153

ashamed, personally, of the state of the butcher's shop, where flies crawled about the bloody marble and carcases lay on sawdust on the floor.

Elke put a large sweet in her cheek and began to write. Mevrouw had gone walking all the afternoon with a strange man. Meinheer was angry. Being much older than Mevrouw, he was naturally jealous. Mevrouw had even forgotten to take the dog, who was so sweet, really the only friend she, Elke, had in the whole house; but the English do not like dogs. She was not allowed to have him in her bedroom. If she nursed him Meinheer was angry. Yet the girl, Betsy, always nursed the cat, which she, Elke, could not bring herself to touch. Mevrouw had asked another Nederlander to tea, but she had turned out to be a country girl with bad accent. It was impossible to speak to her. Apparently the English think that to have the same language is enough. They would scarcely themselves wish to mix with all classes, though certainly Mevrouw drank tea with the rough woman who came to do the scrubbing. They called one another 'dear'. When Mevrouw went away for a week, Mrs Curzon kissed her good-bye. On Mrs Curzon's birthday, they drank gin together. Mevrouw said "Many happy returns, Curzy dear." "And many more years with *you*, Madam, to be sure." Both had tears in their eyes. When the cat before this one was run over, Mevrouw cried; but when the King was ill, she remained calm. Her mother's death she had referred to once very coldly, as merely a date—"I remember it was the year mother died." When the girl, Betsy, went to a hospital to have her tonsils out, both she and her mother went off laughing. They stopped the taxi on the way and called in at a café for ice-cream as if it were just a merry jaunt. That very night a guest had been put up in Betsy's room. For Mevrouw was very cold, very callous. She asked no questions and took no interest; never inquired what was in letters, nor why people were late home. Unluckily for her, Meinheer was not so incurious. He was probably at this moment asking a great many questions down in the drawing-room.

Elke's stay in England would not turn out to be a valuable experience. She deduced little from it. Her parents were sometimes disturbed.

Down in the drawing-room, Charles and Harriet sat without speaking. The wireless usefully filled the gap. Charles read *Persuasion*—his favourite book, to which Harriet imagined he resorted when wounded. She sewed name-tapes on to Betsy's blouses, thinking of the blue, enchanted park.

Charles turned pages theatrically. He knew that Harriet had expected Vesey that afternoon, though she had not mentioned him at lunch. His mother, who had dropped into his office to ask about her investments, had worried him, letting fall hints, asking advice and not listening to his answers; above all, perhaps, asking advice. She had plainly sought to enliven her own afternoon by disquieting him. Like her grand-daughter, she preferred a painful scene to no scene at all. Her attitude towards his marriage was detached and cynical. Years ago, when they had told her of their engagement, she had patted Harriet's hand in a dismissing way, as if sending her away to play in the nursery. As an afterthought, she had said: "You won't leave us stranded, will you, dear? A second time I should look upon as a clear disgrace." Even in the vestry after the wedding she had been malicious. Wound in broken marabout, she had dominated everybody. "So you have really seen it through!" she said, praising the bride for her tenacity as if she could not for any other reason. Should he be forced into the absurd and humiliating rôle of elderly husband to straying wife, would it not be only what she had awaited, and what could give her a new lease of life?

As he read, he passed his hand over his hair, with the impatient quick gesture Harriet knew. His hair was greying

155

but, as with many fair people, without much altering his appearance. At irregular intervals, he turned pages; once or twice he glanced at the fire, but never at his wife. Harriet sat very still, and wary. Her needle plucked at the cloth. However hard she tried to concentrate on her task, the blue park with its blurred vistas rose before her, its magic engulfed her as if it were only the park she was in love with. When Charles turned a page, her eyelids lowered, her mouth tightened. She wondered if he were reading the chapter on women's constancy; for the book became a reproach all by itself.

'What a novel to choose!' Charles thought. 'Only the happy in love should ever read it. It is unbearable to have expression given to our painful solitariness, to rake up the dead leaves in our hearts, when *we* have nothing that can follow (no heaven dawning beautifully in Union Street), except in dreams, as perhaps Jane Austen herself never had but on the page she wrote.'

"What is wrong, Charles?" Harriet suddenly asked. She felt that he would never speak; that he would punish her for years and years, in silence. "What are you thinking about?"

He snapped the book together in one hand as if shutting her out from his experience there. Getting up, he walked about the room, yawning against his fist, saying: "What do you mean? Why do you ask?"

"I thought you were not really reading," she said bravely.

Everything she said, he took up and repeated, looking surprised.

She thought 'I will never see Vesey again, for I cannot bear my punishment.' As if he did not want her to suspect that he suspected her, he said: "The truth is, you know, things go on at the office which disturb me. For a long time now, they have. I begin to wonder what Tiny's up to."

He watched her nervousness flatten out, listened to her voice relaxing, as she said "But what *could* Tiny be up to?"

"No good at all. With Reggie Beckett." In a devilish way,

he half-enjoyed watching her face clear, her hands with the sewing lying loose in her lap. Yet he had often wanted to tell her of these very anxieties; had often held back, hating to burden her. Now that the worries seemed nothing in the light of worse ones, he used them to cover the truth; he bided his time with them, and he trapped his wife.

Relief ran all over her face. Her sympathy was nourished by her guilt.

"Reggie Beckett? I've seen him at Kitty's, I believe. But not for years."

"He's been away." Charles looked very sternly at his finger-nails. That meant, she knew, that he was waiting for something, measuring something. "Yes, he's been away behind the scenes. In war-time, he had other fish to fry. A pity he didn't stay and fry them where he was. I'm afraid Tiny is easily used. He likes money too much. That's Kitty's fault, of course."

"Oh, no!"

"Oh, *yes!* She's idle and extravagant. She doesn't do Tiny any good. Nor me, indirectly."

"How could she affect you?"

He was a long time answering, tapped his foot on the brass fender, watched her. "I am proud of my practice," he said after a while. "I want nothing wrong about it."

He had observed the change in her. Her reverie of doubt and love and guilt had vanished from her eyes. Now, at this minute, she was an indignant woman. On his behalf.

"Is that Vesey any good?" he asked abruptly. "As an actor, I mean?"

She picked up her sewing again and said very steadily: "I have never seen him act. You must know that."

"No, I'd forgotten. I thought you mentioned last night having met in the war . . . I didn't know when . . ."

"But I told you at the time. It was at Caroline's funeral— Memorial Service, I mean."

"Well, my dear, all right, all right. I can't remember

157

all you've said for years and years and years."

If ever she looked beautiful, it was when she was angry or embarrassed, he thought.

"You ought to go to see this *Hamlet*," he said in a patronising voice. Even *Hamlet* seemed a dubious affair.

"I am sure it would be very badly done." She smiled with confidence but did not raise her eyes from her work.

"You should take Betsy."

"But it is only on for two more days."

"You knew he was coming here this afternoon, didn't you? You arranged that last night."

"Yes. Yes, he did say that he would." She looked quickly aside.

"Why didn't you mention it?"

"I never know when he means to do what he says."

"You *never* know?"

"I mean, I *used* not to know."

"Why did you attach so much importance to it that you said nothing? And if you cry, Harriet, I shall . . . I won't have it. I really will not have it."

"I didn't think . . . oh, I was sure he wouldn't come."

"Do you stammer when you talk to *him?*"

"Why do you ask?"

"It is important to me to know."

"You know I always stammer with everyone."

"I've noticed you do especially with me. It has been something I tried not to know. Do I so confuse and frighten you?"

"No. But I won't be cross-examined. I am not one of your victims."

"And I won't have you sit there crying for Betsy to see if she should come in." He took out his cigarette-case and held it very tightly in his hand.

"Then don't upset me," she said angrily, and put her handkerchief to her mouth. 'It has never been like this between us,' she thought. 'Never, never before.' For a

158

second, she felt the elation of having nothing to lose: then the room seemed to yawn open as in a nightmare—the room which Vesey had hated, whose beauty had been a warning to him.

"Harriet darling, look at me!"

Her eyes were magnified with tears.

"Forgive me!"

The tears brimmed and fell again.

"Why didn't you tell me about him?"

"I couldn't. I know you hate him."

"I don't hate him. I don't know him."

"I tried to say, at lunch."

"But surely, if we love one another . . . we are husband and wife . . . I trust you. Of course I trust you. I want you to be happy."

"I know. I know."

"You are . . . most precious to me. All you have put into being married to me . . . this house, Betsy . . . you must know that I realise what it's meant. It hasn't been an ordinary home, but something quite *out* of the ordinary— beautiful and well-ordered. For heaven's sake, don't imagine I don't know that a woman couldn't throw away so much—all she's created—nor even put it in jeopardy. If you had had more men friends, been more independent of me, you'd know that; and know that I know it. How could your walking in the park with Vesey affect our life together in this house. . . .?" He broke off, feeling that he was mentioning the house too often, looking too much round the room, as if interior decoration decided everything.

She had stopped crying, was staring down at her lap, turning her handkerchief from corner to corner. 'She does have rather snivelling ways,' he thought aloofly, and covered the thought as suddenly as he had laid it bare.

"Forgive me, Charles."

"Forgive *me*. I am behaving abominably."

"No."

159

"You will tear your nice handkerchief."

She rolled it up in her hand, and smiled uncertainly, as if she were not sure if she were able to.

"To show you have forgiven me," he said, "will you give me some proof of it?"

She closed her burning eyes. He saw that she dreaded something, perhaps being asked never to see Vesey again. It was really that she was afraid of going back to the beginnings of their talk.

"What is it? I mean 'of course'."

"Will you take Betsy to the play? And when it is over bring Vesey back here for a drink? We will ask Tiny and Kitty in. Then it will all be comfortable and. . . . Will you do that?"

"I don't think I can," she said wearily. "I don't think I care to see him before he goes. We have had too much fuss on his account. I feel I hate his very name."

"You would rather *I* hated it? It was something I asked you to do for me."

"It would prove nothing." She imagined his eyes on them and the indignity of their position. Not to accept would be declaring their love for one another.

"Then if I must."

"Not 'must'!"

"Then, I *will*. Oh, of course I will if it is what you really want. But I expect he won't come. I couldn't *make* him come. I think he doesn't care for going out at night."

"If he won't, it doesn't matter. I want you to have asked him." It was the most that, at the moment, he could give Vesey in the way of pain. "Then I shall know that you feel yourself trusted. And your silence at lunch will seem utterly absurd. When he goes away, this scene will be forgotten and we shall have nothing dismaying between us."

She began to fold up her sewing. "Very well, I'll go. I'll ask him. And now I think I should tell Betsy to go to bed. It's late."

"I'll tell her. And you should go to bed, too, my darling. You look very tired. I've been so much more hateful to you than I could ever have thought possible. I felt so threatened, though; so cast off by you. Now it is all all right." He took her hands and drew her up from the sofa. "Now it is all all right?" he repeated in a question.

"Yes, Charles."

"Don't say it as if you were a little girl who's been put in the corner." He shook her hands until he rallied her into smiling, then kissed her. The rallying kiss strengthened until she stood stone-still, her arm crushed to her side, her knuckles white.

"Darling one, I love you. Never leave me on my own."

"Of *course* not."

"You are to have everything you want for ever and ever."

"There is nothing that I want."

"At this moment you are going to bed." He rocked with her tight in his arms, his mouth on her brow. "I wish I could carry you there; but Elke might think it strange."

"Perhaps Dutch women are always carried to bed," she said shakily. "So that it might after all seem a normal thing to her."

"Have you ever *seen* any Dutch women? Yes, well then, don't be silly. You are to go up, and I shall bring you a nice drink and tell Betsy you have a headache."

"You are very comforting."

"I kiss you better, but I remember that it was I who made you cry."

'It is the worst place to be,' she thought, 'the verge of tears.' The blue park had vanished. She felt dispirited, her emotions belaboured. 'We can't not be sordid,' Vesey had said, and that strengthened her now. If he had envisaged it to her as all beautiful, all benign, she would have felt separated from him by shame. She did not know what to think any more and, strangely, it was Charles who consoled her, with the middle-aged comforts which once she might have

161

scorned. To relax in a warm bed in a pleasant room was all she could ask—not to talk, not to think, not to dream.

At the door, she said: "I am sorry, Charles, that you have those worries about your work, and Tiny, and that wretched man."

He smiled confidently. "I can deal with them. It is the sort of thing I can manage, you know."

She went draggingly up the stairs. In the dining-room, Betsy heard her go. She put her pen down very quietly on the table, as if not to disturb her thoughts. Charles sat for a moment on the edge of the sofa, his hand across his mouth, his thumbnail clicking against his teeth. He began to wonder if he had not himself built up what he had just been seeking to break down. He lit a cigarette, then went to send Betsy up to bed.

'What a long time Laertes is in France!' Harriet thought. For, having given his excellent and embarrassing advice to Ophelia, Vesey had gone and was, it seemed, forgotten. Since then, scene after scene, shot with loveliness, thread-bare with use, had lumbered by. The Queen wrung her hands incessantly; Ophelia's gin-husky voice had an unexpected catch of beauty in it. Polonius was murdered; but not, as he so richly deserved, for forgetting his lines, Harriet whispered to Betsy. Betsy frowned. She sat forward, her hands on her knees, her wrists right out of her too-short sleeves.

This was after all, Harriet told herself, a great play—though bungled and made shabby—but she could not concentrate as Betsy was, as if her eyes had never seen the like. She found the seats hard; she was conscious of the photographs of mayors hanging round her. When someone left in the middle of a scene, she watched him all the way out of the hall with interest. You could not have heard a pin drop.

Afterwards, sighing, dazed, Betsy followed her mother to

162

the car. Blue lighting laid the streets open in a livid glare. Sitting in the car, waiting for Vesey, they watched the small crowds thin out and disperse, as if the dreadful illumination made all human life dwindle and vanish. In Harriet's heart it added to the elsewhere quality of this evening; the cruelty Charles had wreaked upon her in sending her out on such a mission, and his way of exacting such a thing from her. The play, and Vesey's part in it, was something to be got over and forgotten. How could she but feel herself and Vesey mocked by the strangeness of the situation, which neither would have chosen—the very language and costume alienating them; his leap into the grave; those absurdly restrained rapier thrusts, his being not up to such display, for he could parry nothing except with words. If she had caught a gust of amusement in the audience, she denied it, and for some of the time looked at her gloves lying in her lap. Their dance together, their walk in the park, had now for ever its grotesque and piteous other side. She watched him—when she did—with her love in abeyance, as if some harm might otherwise be done to her imagination.

Anger at Charles unsteadied her. She no longer felt guilt in herself or pity for him. Pride made her hope to retaliate; but how she could was beyond her devising. Her resources were all bent on how to manage the rest of the evening, which Charles had so unnaturally prolonged.

"He was very good, your friend," Betsy said, striking her fur-gloved hands together. "But then, they were all so good, I thought."

"It went on rather a long time," Harriet said. "It is later than I had thought it would be." She imagined Charles waiting at home, glass in hand, his eye on the clock; Kitty perhaps a little the better for drink.

"Did you know him when you were my age?" Betsy pulled her gloves away from her wrists and blew her warm breath into them.

"Vesey? Yes, I knew him as far back as I can remember."

163

Betsy had not imagined her remembering back any further than her own age. That seemed a feat in itself.

"But when did you stop knowing him?"

"I didn't stop; but when we grew up we had to be in different places . . . and the war dispersed people, I found. . . ."

"He's a great actor," Betsy said simply.

"Darling, don't bite your gloves. You're not a baby."

Vesey came out of a side door and across a yard, his face mauve in the malignant light, his collar turned up, and an untidy parcel underneath his arm. Harriet started up the engine and her hands tightened on the steering-wheel.

"I thought you were simply marvellous," Betsy said, leaning to open the door for him.

"Oh, he was simply marvellous," Betsy said to Charles.

"What will you drink?" Charles asked, over her head. "Brandy? Scotch?"

"Oh, brandy, please." Vesey now took his second look at the room. White lilac was arranged against the red damask curtains; the white kitten slept on a crimson cushion. With Charles in it, the room's splendour now seemed complete. He handed drinks almost with the assumption that they would all raise them first to toast his triumph.

Kitty sat plumply on the sofa. Harriet stooped to kiss her, drawing off her gloves and putting her cold hands into Kitty's warm ones. Over by the gramophone, Tiny peered at the names on records.

"Simply marvellous!" Betsy was going on excitedly.

"Time for bed!" Charles said sharply.

"Well . . . good luck!" Vesey said, lifting his glass.

Harriet, in her letter, had let him guess why he was here. He did not fear situations, as she did; dreading his own moods more than other people's. To help Harriet, to see her for a last time before he left, he had agreed to come. He felt, though, that it was now for Charles to find something to say,

164

to sound some note, and, going over to warm himself at the fire, thought he would bide his time and look at Harriet. She sat beside Kitty, who still clasped her hands; and she smiled up at him as if drawing him into their conversation. Under the rosy lamplight, her smooth hair had a bronze lustre; pearls were twisted round her wrists where once the silver bracelets had hung.

"So you were Harriet's little play-fellow!" Kitty said. "I imagine a Kate Greenaway picture, with hoops."

"Bed!" said Charles again to Betsy, trying to pretend that his irritation was a playful sternness.

She circled her ginger-ale in the glass, drank it down quickly. "I should like to go on the stage," she said.

"I expect Mr Macmillan would discourage you," Charles said.

"I try not to be discouraging," Vesey said, and straightened the corner of the hearthrug with his toe.

"She is going to take after her grandmother," Kitty said.

"My grandmother? Oh!" Betsy laughed. "I never think about *her* being an actress."

"You had better not tell her so," Charles said. "She was a famous one in her day, and wouldn't like to be so soon forgotten."

"Well, good-night all!" said Betsy. She wiped her mouth on her hand and her hand on her skirt. "Good-bye!" she said to Vesey. "I shall never forget how marvellous you were. And you *will* sign my programme as you go? I left it on the hall-table."

"You are making him feel like Sir Henry Irving," Charles said in a pleasant, but not pleasing voice. "I hope you are used to these school-girlish enthusiasms, Vesey?"

"No. I can never get used to kindness."

"Now you must tell us all about Harriet when she was a little girl," Kitty intervened. "Some funny things, if possible. To throw a new light. Harriet won't mind."

"How could he remember?" Harriet asked.

165

"Yes," Charles said, already attending to Vesey's glass. "I should treasure it. I have only photographs."

"Then you have more than Vesey," said Harriet. "He has only his memory, which took no impression."

"She wore silver bracelets on her wrists," Vesey said slowly, looking at his glass and then at Kitty. "I remember the sound they made."

"Oh, you must go a lot further back than that to give us what we haven't got," Charles said. "She wore silver bracelets when I first knew her, and Betsy has them now, so we are used to *those*."

Vesey struggled with his memory for Harriet's sake; but remembered only her diffidence, her stammer, a bravery he was not disposed to define for them, and that once they had quarrelled (he could not imagine why). Then he suddenly said: "My chief picture of her is walking across some fields with a bunch of flowers in her hands. She was always picking flowers."

By her face he knew that he had distressed her and made her apprehensive. Perhaps the brandy, together with his tiredness, and not having eaten, had confused him. He suddenly remembered—as if some pattern in a kaleidoscope fell into place—the rest of that evening: they had walked across the fields towards an empty house; now he groped back to it across years, recalling her question in the park, her so revealing and piteous question, which at the time he had not understood. "What empty house?" he had asked. But she had gently refused to answer, and turned the conversation away towards different things.

"She always loved flowers," Kitty said, dwelling on the great jar of forced lilac.

"I feel that I am dead," Harriet objected.

"The house where my aunt lived was always full of dogs," Vesey said in a more definite voice, more sure of himself now that he was not speaking the truth. "Once there was a terrible fight amongst them. No one really cared to intervene. We all hung back. It was Harriet who ran and separated them, unhesitatingly. With her bare hands," he added.

"It doesn't sound like Harriet," Charles said. "To have such decision. And she is rather nervous of animals." No matter how much he smiled, he could not make this sound pleasant. He replenished her glass instead.

"She must have changed," Tiny said coolly.

"Yes, she must have changed." Vesey looked at her. "But she has not changed so much that she can bear all this discussion about herself. It is someone else's turn." He glanced round him, and at last at Charles, who looked at his cigarette.

"What was the play like?" Kitty asked. It was the first, not the best, thing to come into her mind. She at once regretted it and hoped to cover the question by answering it herself. "I always find it so full of people telling other people not to let somebody out of their sight. Look to this one; wait upon that! Though I was a girl, of course, when last I saw it."

"It hasn't altered," Vesey said.

"Introspective," Tiny scoffed. "Always gets me down. Bloody unnecessary to say the least." He flushed. He hated unpleasantness and there was so much in the world. For people to make it up, to fill in the empty air with invented miseries, was what annoyed and puzzled him. It seemed an act in the worst taste, and 'unnecessary' was what he really thought. "Morbid," he presently added, and stared at the wall, rather high up, where there was nothing at all to look at.

"Oh, I don't know," said Kitty airily. "When you look round you, I think you see it all going on, though in a rather mumbling way."

"Then why make up more?"

"But Shakespeare only displayed life. Someone else is supposed to have invented it," Vesey said. "I think that his plays are going on all the time, as . . ." he had not re-

167

membered Kitty's name, and turned and smiled at her instead, "as you have just said. Some more than others, of course."

"Certainly some more than others," Charles agreed.

"We are none of us so articulate," said Kitty.

"And we say one thing and mean another," Charles said. "As if we fear what we might bring to the surface."

"And our rooms are smaller, of course," Kitty added.

"It is as well not to bring things to the surface, if they are unpleasant things," Tiny said, and he wandered across to the pile of gramophone-records. "But I never see anything so very shocking going on around *me*—not even in our job where we might expect to. Most people are perfectly nice and happy and ordinary. Just like all of us here. No better, no worse. Hatred, despair, suicide, murder, all the rest, are the rare exceptions; though from the books you read, the films you see, decency would be that."

"Perhaps evil is in the eye of the beholder," Kitty said brightly. "It must be that, since you and I, Tiny, come to such different conclusions from looking at the same things. We shall have to go, Harriet dear."

She had glanced with some relief at the clock and handed her empty glass to Harriet. Harriet, who took people too much at their word over drinks, leant to put the glass on the table, stumbled, and broke it.

"My God, you're worse than Elke," Charles said sharply.

She blushed with vexation and, not able to think of anything to say, dropped to her knees and began to gather up splintered glass from the carpet. Her distress, so feebly covered, infuriated Charles. He had not designed this evening to humiliate her, but to expose to her several truths—his own love and trust and generosity; Vesey's inadequacy, which he did not doubt; and her position in his—Charles's—world. The sight of her gathering up glass from the carpet made him see that anything she suffered only served to separate them.

"For God's sake, leave it, leave it!" he said impatiently. "I'll get you a new glass, Kitty. You must have one for the road."

"One for by-byes," Tiny agreed.

Kitty began to demur, but thought better of it, and her second thoughts this evening were all better than her first.

Only Vesey noticed that Harriet's wrist was bleeding. He put her in a chair and took the little folded, scented handkerchief out of her cuff and wrapped her hand in it. "Darling, where's a bandage?" he asked, for the handkerchief was seen to be quite inadequate.

Kitty and Tiny looked in terror at the door. It was not so much the word 'darling' as his voice which frightened them. "I'll get one," Kitty said, almost running out of the room.

"Like a brandy, old dear?" Tiny asked, anxious to follow his wife.

"I am so dreadfully clumsy," Harriet stammered. Vesey lit a cigarette and put it between her lips.

"Here we are!" Kitty said breathlessly. Charles was behind her, bringing her clean glass.

Vesey took the bandage and kneeling beside Harriet began to bind her hand.

"What have you done *now*?" Charles asked. "Really, my dear girl, you have a genius for agitating your guests. I shall never forget—shall you, Kitty?—the time she broke the bottle of brandy?"

"Certainly to-night is nothing if we measure it against that," Tiny said, trying to see a joke where no joke was.

"I dropped a dish of mashed potatoes once," Kitty said unhelpfully. It was obvious that she was throwing in the dish of potatoes and herself as well to try to rescue her friend.

Imperturbably, Vesey unrolled the bandage over Harriet's hand and the blood starting through it was soon covered, as her nervousness was by his sympathy. She watched his bent head, his expressionless face. He had the power to cut her

169

off from the rest of the room, so that Kitty's rushes of kindness were scarcely heard, and Charles's words no longer mortified her. His silent attention so enisled her that it was as if he bandaged her heart as well as her hand. He heeded nothing else in the room, but what he was doing. His very lack of words upheld her, steadied, even, her love for him, to which this terrible evening, so otherwise devised, had quite committed her.

"Well, cheers, then!" Kitty said, smiling at Charles. She did not know whom to comfort. Her impulsive movements seemed in all directions.

"Let us pour whisky on the troubled waters," said Tiny, raising his glass, meaning less than he said.

When Vesey had finished, he looked briefly at Harriet, then away.

"Thank you," said Charles. "It was a mercy you were here with your first-aid. If her hand is so bad as that, we should all have been helpless."

Charles's behaviour began to be inexplicable, to himself, and even to other people. His attitude to his mother was part of the change. Now he talked of her a great deal—as she had been as an actress, and strove to remember some of those successes which at the time he had resented. He seemed all of a sudden to know a great deal about the stage without ever having gone much to the theatre. A photograph of Julia as Cleopatra, with hair low on her brow, looped and strung about with pearls and looking bad-tempered, was discovered among some old letters and left propped-up on his desk. He often spoke of her precarious and arduous life, although she had been, as he said, at the very top of her profession. 'So God help those who aren't,' he seemed to imply.

His attitude to Tiny also changed and relaxed. Those suspicions were lulled as others took their place. He went to the Smoking Room at The Bull when he left the office and had a few drinks with Tiny and Reggie Beckett. He was comforted by that solid, men's world.

As his relations with other people improved, his life with Harriet deteriorated. 'I shall default first,' he seemed to declare. 'Nothing can be taken from me that I any longer desire.' He defaulted with sarcasm. He withheld from comment on the clumsiness, which he had engendered in her, in a positive, underlining way. Under his scrutiny, cups seemed to fall to pieces, rugs arched up to trip, buttons dropped off clothes.

Betsy changed, too. She began to read Shakespeare aloud in the bathroom, where a slight echo gave, she thought, a haunting quality to her voice. Elke could only suppose that the whole nation was strange, perhaps crazed by the late war. It was the Englishness in them, she decided. Her letters home grew longer and longer, her expression more closed. She became sick for home. 'She is like Ruth amidst the alien cornflakes,' Betsy thought one breakfast-time. Her best jokes were unrepeatable, though she repeated that one to Pauline Hay-Hardy. They nearly died of laughing. Pauline said: "Oh, my *dear!* You'll be the death of me." "She picks at her boiled egg with little red, chipped nails," Betsy said. "Oh, *don't!*" Pauline gasped. "I shall *heave.*"

Elke wrote: "She shuts herself into the bathroom and shouts at the top of her voice. She wipes her mouth on her hand. She is more like a child with her knees showing. She is allowed to talk at mealtimes." The first part sounded very amusing in Dutch. Her parents worried over these letters. They hoped that Elke would not try to speak at the table when she returned.

Betsy's ideas of Miss Bell also began to shift round. She descended one level from that on which Vesey now left no room for her, and, descending, she could not help but come nearer to Betsy herself, who felt in her presence rather more ease and confidence than before, since there was less to lose. Miss Bell had seen *Hamlet*, too. It had been an uneven

171

performance, she said: not liking to say that she thought it had been even. Hamlet had conveyed, sustained, the suggestion of great suffering, though chiefly that caused by stage-fright, she was bound to say. "And what did you think of Laertes?" Betsy asked. Cautioned by the light in the girl's eyes, Miss Bell tried to recollect anything about Laertes. "He was a friend of my mother's," Betsy said, alarmed suddenly of adverse criticism. "I thought he seemed a very nice person," Miss Bell replied. "Oh, he *is*," Betsy said fervently. "I wondered at the time," Miss Bell, added, as if she were speaking of long ago, "if he might not have made a better Hamlet than . . . than the one who did." "I *agree*," Betsy agreed. "*I* thought so at the time, too. I am sure he will be a very great actor. One day."

To depose one adored one in order to confide in her about the latest, was an exquisite pleasure. She found she *liked* Miss Bell more than before. "But she is only human," she thought recklessly. . . . "I can say anything to her." It is dangerous to think people human, who once have been divine.

Julia found a new lease of life in her concern for her son. 'Ah, the meek inherit the earth!' she thought of Harriet, convinced of some shadiness. She was determined to confirm that women are all sisters under the skin. Light, light, was her touch. Her innuendo could scarcely have been taken up but by the most attuned and guilty ear. Everyone else became tiresome.

"Go and grapple with Miss Bastable's soul," she told the Vicar when he came to call. "I have domestic problems to sort out."

At least he knew how to treat a woman of the world; was smooth, urbane, though suggesting, to be on the safe side, that this was how he was proof against evil.

"I would rather talk to you. Besides, I should stand no chance against your influence."

172

"But she is lapsing; falling from grace," Julia said, anxious to be rid of him. "She played Patience on Sunday instead of going to Evensong or whatever you call it."

He leaned forward and picked a chocolate out of the box which she had once, with indifference, offered and had now forgotten.

"Once I was in a room," he said, wishing to talk about himself, "when, suddenly, and for no reason, I felt an evil presence."

She laughed carelessly and glanced over her shoulder.

"It was ten o'clock in the morning," he said, as if this confirmed what he had said, which she felt it did.

He picked out a coffee-cream and dropped it into his mouth, brushing his finger-tips on a paisley handkerchief. "Perhaps," he said, with his mouth full of chocolate, "in the light of her life here with you, Miss Bastable thinks that she can be good without religion. A greatly-shaking deception. She is up against what she thinks of as your goodness."

"I think I am good, too," Julia said.

He picked out a caramel.

"Don't *you* think I am good?" she asked.

He leant back and chewed and smiled and said, with his eyes shut: "I think you are presumptuous." He would not open his eyes.

"That means 'taking liberties'," she cried. And at last he opened his eyes. "I was using theological terminology." His look rested upon her.

She seemed appeased.

"Where is Betsy off to, looking so starry-eyed?" Kitty asked, as Harriet opened the door. "I saw her going off down the Terrace as if she were on her way to heaven . . . an exciting sort of heaven, I mean. When I called out, she gave a violent start. I often notice that when people smile, they look less happy than they did a second before. It can be rather saddening. I thought *her* smile . . . Betsy's . . .

173

quite spoiled her happy look. I hope she got it back again."
She stripped off her gloves and, standing before the hall
mirror, ran her fingers up through her hair, seeming to move
in, to take possession of the house; led the way into the
drawing-room and brushed some scattered lilac petals off a
table into her hand as she passed.

"It's a great occasion. She is going for a walk with Miss
Bell."

"Will she go from one adoration to another, I wonder?
A sort of emotional progress? Who could be sure, when they
are terribly susceptible to other personalities, that it would
all end after marriage? Once begun, it must surely go on a
lifetime? Each one seeming in turn *the* one . . that Natalie
Slapdash or whatever her name was, whom Betsy so adored
last year . . . do you remember? . . . one might find that
one's husband was, after all, only taking his turn. Not that I
wish to worry you . . ."

"There's nothing I can do."

"I know. Playing a lot of games and having what people
call a lot of interests can't help, because one is always capable
of doing two things at the same time . . . especially if one
of them is *feeling* . . . I have never really been like that
. . . perhaps I am too self-centred . . . but someone once
told me about loving . . ." she glanced aside . . . "said
that whatever she did, no matter how hard she worked, with
every step she took and breath she breathed she thought of
it and felt it and remembered. How is your hand?"

Harriet, for no reason, put it behind her back. "Oh,
better."

"Were *you* like that, as a child? Always having to have
somebody . . . those extravagant passions?"

"No. I didn't enough get the hang of other people . . .
the mistresses at school merely alarmed me."

"I so agree. And then they always had moustaches or spat
when they talked. Though they scared the daylight out of
me, I contempted them." Kitty smiled comfortably; put her

174

feet up on a stool and brought a cushion down behind her head.

"But you loved Tiny . . .?" Harriet said doubtfully. No one could pretend that Kitty did still, but once, surely . . .?

"Everybody has to get married," Kitty said authoritatively. "And then, I am, as I said, a selfish person. Even children . . . even Ricky . . . I love with a sort of anguish, which is more to do with me than with him. I'm glad your hand is better. I was quite worried."

"There was nothing to worry about."

"I think when I was young I was flirtatious rather than passionate," Kitty said, as if the previous conversation had justified, even demanded, this confession. "Therefore it is difficult for me to imagine that one person is all that much more important than another. If I was *fond* of someone, I had reached the heights. My heights rather. No one could hope for more. Can other people be so much more wonderful than I am myself, I used to ask. And one knows how very unwonderful one is oneself. Did you ever meet anyone who seemed more wonderful than yourself?"

"Many people."

"You are being modest."

"I have nothing to be modest about."

"It is true modesty to believe that. One might even call it humility," Kitty said disdainfully. "You have too low an estimate of yourself. So low that one begins to think you are dissembling. Would you be lit up, transported, at the idea of another person's company . . . as your daughter is?"

Harriet, standing before the fire, her hands clasped behind her back, looked gravely ahead, knowing it was useless to answer. Kitty twisted her pearls, brought them up over her chin, but kept her eyes cast down.

"Why are you doing this to me, Kitty?" Harriet asked in a tired voice.

"Because I love you . . . am fond of you, I mean."

"What is it you want to know?"

175

"Nothing. I know it all already."

"Then . . .?"

"I only want to say 'no one is worth anything'. We are all the same. One is as good as another. It will pass." She spoke rapidly and as if one thought cancelled another and all of it was nonsense. "You've been married to Charles fifteen? . . . sixteen? years. And you were quite happy. About other people you have to ask yourself, 'Could the same have been true with them? How would those sixteen years have passed?' How can marriage be exciting that lasts so long? And don't we love for ever the one we didn't marry? Requited love is just as good as the other kind, and *that* may be requited in the end, leaving you no better off than you were before. Match sixteen years against the newest love, or imagine it after sixteen years. Isn't the result calculable? I am sorry my commonsense is so common, but I have to be cruel to be kind. You don't mind my taking my shoes off, do you, darling, for they're giving me merry hell. Suède *draws* so."

She kicked her shoes across the floor and stretched her toes. A ladder ran up her stocking and she tried to stop it with a blob of spit. She was growing negligent and untidy. She smoked in the bedroom, dropping ash into the hand-basin; her brushes were fringed with hair: she used her crushed-up scented handkerchiefs to mark her place in novels; in her kitchen, the cats drank milk out of Rockingham saucers.

"Those magazines in hairdressers'," she went on. "Those letters readers write in about their problems. 'Is this love? Am I in love?' As if love were a special kind of fish one catches in one's net . . . sorting through a handful of weeds, wondering 'Is this the right thing? Is this what I am after?' But how can you catch what is only a mood, or a reflection of yourself? Forbidden fruit would be just as boring as the other kind if we ate it all the time."

"Fruit! Fish! Reflections!" Harriet said restlessly,

176

turning to face the fire, her hands on the chimney-piece.

"Then let us come to Vesey. Let us call everything by its proper name. I shall be very harsh, I warn you. I shall use words like 'infatuation'."

"Everything I feel is beyond words, so none can affect me."

"You are letting yourself drift into difficulties."

"Yes, I know that."

"Very difficult difficulties."

"What does 'infatuation' mean? Or any words like it? I loved him when I was a child, I know . . ."

"And the *idea* of him ever since. . . . Our feelings about people change as we grow up: but if we are left with an idea instead of a person, perhaps that never changes. After every mistake Charles made, I expect you thought: 'Vesey wouldn't have done that.' But an idea can't ever make mistakes. He led a perfect life in your brain. When he turned up again, the climate was right for him, tempered by your imagination. But his climate isn't right for you."

'His climate!' Harriet thought, staring down at the fire until her eyes smarted. The word expressed something of her feelings at being with him: how she had loved, when she was young, merely to stand close to him. When he had drawn away, he took something miraculous from her.

"I won't remind you of your child," Kitty said.

"And I won't mention the fact that I find this conversation painful."

'Always laughing at nothing, those two!' Elke thought passing in the hall.

"But painful or not," Kitty said, "I must say, darling, do be clear; don't drift. Think of consequences. Remember Madame Bovary. No, I'm sorry, I don't mean to be offensive, only—well, Charles snapping and snarling, everything uncomfortable, storms in the air; glasses crashing to the ground; blood flowing . . . because someone's face, or voice, obsesses you. When really everybody is the same."

177

"No," Harriet protested. "All that makes life worth living is that we are completely different from one another and then—and it is always wonderful when it happens—see little likenesses; find some quickening, some response; some common ground."

She spoke quietly. When a coal dropped on to the hearth, she started dreadfully. She seemed, Kitty thought, to be in a state of dazed convalescence, weakly remote, yet irritated by trifles.

"Why don't you have a good cry?" she suggested. "Sooner or later, you must."

"Years fly by: at first, I couldn't believe I would ever be middle-aged, as my mother was: now I can't believe that I am. It has all melted away and meant nothing. Anything that comes now is much too late."

"Exactly!" Kitty said comfortably. "So don't jeopardise what you *have* got. Lovely word 'jeopardy'. I always adored it. Since I was a child."

"I must see him again."

"Why not leave it as it is?"

"It *isn't*. Nothing *is*. I know nothing. The other night was only confusing . . . dreadful for him . . . I couldn't tell him how sorry I was . . ."

"Write it."

"We have only one life."

"The other night . . . if you left it there . . . it wouldn't be too bad to remember, surely? Charles behaving intolerably, no doubt, but only because he loves you. Vesey's love and sympathy was somehow conveyed in spite of us. I am sorry I am so full of good advice. Perhaps I am only trying to stop you having what I have never had myself."

"Whatever your motive, it could never be that."

"But I do love you. People I love I like to see nice and cosy and within my ken. I can't bear them to be ranging about, and having sorrows and adventures, and endangering themselves, and being in jeopardy."

178

"You have always been wonderful to me," Harriet said, in a light, bright voice. But she did feel remote and convalescent. Kitty was almost unreal. Isolated, she could see only blurred people moving about her, hear only muffled sounds; was, though approached, really unapproachable.

"It's funny," Kitty was saying. "We seem much more the same age now we're older. Though, of course, that's really for you to say, not me."

Kitty had gone when Betsy returned. The lilac petals fell unheeded. The drawing-room fire was somehow between-times; its beautiful afternoon crispness and energy gone, and the logs which had been put on for after supper hissing steadily. Although Harriet had plumped-up the cushions and straightened the rug, the room still in some way looked awry; a window was widely opened to let out cigarette smoke, and the curtains shifted along their rods.

It was lucky, Betsy felt, that she did not need to be welcomed home or to be cheered. Standing with her back to the smoky fire, she suddenly put her finger-tips to each side of her brow, drew her hair back from the temples, and with a look of vacant stage-inanity, a hollow pathos, surveyed a chair which stood crookedly against the wall, then dropped a mad, lopsided curtsey. When Charles opened the door, she was hastily tying her shoe.

"Well!" he said, hitting his leg with the rolled-up evening paper. This was his traditional entrance.

"Hallo, father."

"What are you doing down there?"

"Tying my shoe-lace."

"You always do the simplest thing as if you were up to some mischief. Where's your mother?"

"I haven't seen her. Upstairs, I expect."

"How've you been getting on?"

"Oh, very well, thank you."

Charles lifted glasses from a tray and held them to the

179

light—two smeared with lipstick, the others clean. For an instant, before he was relieved, he felt a sensation of disappointment, almost as if he were cross at being baulked in his pursuit of pain, at being deprived of a beloved suspicion. He poured himself a drink and took it upstairs.

Harriet was sitting before her mirror.

"You're doing your hair a different way." He held his glass for her to take a sip as she usually did. This evening, she hesitated before she drank. "Aren't you?" he asked.

"I was only parting it a little higher, but it doesn't suit me. I thought perhaps I should have a fringe."

"Then please think again," he said coldly, as if she had outlined some immoral plan.

"Kitty came," she said.

"You had a nice afternoon's chat about your hair-styles, then." He liked that—to picture, when he was at work, the womenfolk gathered cosily by the fire eating pretty cakes, talking about trivialities. It gave him a feeling of safety.

"I am going to do my nails," Harriet warned him.

"Yes, I'll go. I can't bear that smell. But come down soon, darling, come down soon. There's a lovely murder in the paper." He thought that she had all day to do her manicure.

Betsy was not so upset by the smell of nail-varnish. She even unscrewed bottles and sniffed.

"Darling, I hate being hung over," Harriet complained.

"I had a lovely afternoon."

"I'm very glad. Where did you go?"

"To the heronry. Miss Bell knows everything about birds. I wouldn't have thought them possibly interesting, would you?"

"Perhaps a lot depends on who explains them to you."

"Yes. It must be that. When you can't tell one from another, I never think anything is interesting."

"If you knew enough, you could tell all kinds from one another."

180

"I mean, ones of the same kind. I mean, all herons look alike unless they are deformed, which isn't a very nice way of distinguishing them. Another thing I'm bad at is racial prejudice. I don't mean to . . . but I feel I have it awfully badly . . . and I struggle with myself because I naturally know it's wrong. The thing I always think is I couldn't fall in love with a Negro, or a Chinaman, or an Eskimo . . I absolutely couldn't . . . I try and try . . . but, you see, they just wouldn't be real . . . I mean, not all that much more real to me that people you love ought to be. They would just seem exactly like all the others . . . I should feel so ridiculous. . . ."

"It isn't necessary for you to fall in love with them, my dear. No one expects that of you. Nor indeed with anybody else, for years and years. If you are going to start putting yourself to the test about all the people you don't care to fall in love with, you'll have a wretched, wretched time. There'll be so many more of the one than the other. Do you know that, every night for at least ten years, I've told you to stop playing with those ear-rings? Do put them back into the case carefully. You *should* try, Betsy dear, to think of other people not just in terms of *you* and your emotions about them. . . ."

"I expect you treasure this?" Betsy picked up Lilian's old prison-gate badge and peered at it.

"Why?"

"I should treasure anything of yours."

"Well, dear, yes, of course, but for heaven's sake don't cry." Cut out that agony! she willed her daughter, remembering her feelings towards her own mother.

"Especially if you had been in prison."

"Would you have liked me to have been in prison?" Harriet asked in a surprised voice, as she carefully painted her nails.

"Well, I'd have been proud, I mean."

"Would you?"

How things can swing right across the heads of one generation, Harriet thought.

181

"They looked so lovely," Betsy said. "In those funny old-time costumes." Poor Lilian seemed quite cast away into a romantic past, into the dressing-up box. She seemed many, many years back now and a part of history.

"In those photograph-albums of hers are there none of you and Vesey as children?" Betsy asked.

"Of Vesey and me? No, I am sure not. Why?"

"Oh, you've gone over the edge. I wish I could do your nails for you. I'm sure I could. It would be practice for me —though of course I shan't do it myself when I'm older," she added, thinking of Miss Bell.

"What put photographs into your head?"

"I love photographs . . . ones of old people when they were young . . . those of you in swim-suits down to the knees and with little sleeves."

"Darling, they were bathing-costumes. Short sleeves, yes; but surely not down to the knees?" Harriet laughed, thinking: 'I never let my mother know I thought her old.'

". . . and funny bathing-hats like helmets—Pallas Athene. Are you sure you haven't got just one of Vesey?"

"No, dear, no."

"Oh, well . . . a pity."

"But why?"

"I adore him," Betsy said simply. "I can scarcely think of anyone else."

"You don't know him."

"Yes, the funny thing is that I feel I do."

"Betsy . . .!"

"Yes, mother?"

"It does seem the slightest bit odd to me sometimes . . . I mean, the way you speak of people; of adoring them, for instance." She stood up and made a great business of waving her hands about to dry her nails, but her face was flushed. "*Wouldn't* people think it odd . . . do girls talk like that . . . at your age? Vesey is . . ."

'. . . old enough to be my father,' Betsy thought She was

182

sure her mother had almost said that, and for some reason stopped.

"I know your father would be quite annoyed to hear you speaking so extravagantly."

She was walking about the room. When she turned, Betsy was sitting on the dressing-table stool, looking steadily into the mirror with a look of engaging innocence, her hands clasped loosely in her lap as if arranged there by a photographer.

After supper, Charles, throwing the white cat, who had been sick, out into the garden, reported a red glow in the sky.

"Across the park towards the farm."

"You did throw the poor little thing viciously. Imagine feeling sick oneself and being hurled out into the unknown like that."

"*Because* it was sick I threw it. This house is like . . ."

"The cat-house at the Zoo," Harriet agreed.

Charles sighed. "It seems whatever I do is wrong."

"It does seem that."

Harriet was desperate, for Vesey seemed to have vanished again; had neither telephoned nor written. 'If he had always been either less cruel or less kind!' she suddenly thought. "I'm sorry, Charles. I was really not thinking what I said."

"Shall we stroll round the park and see what it is?"

"See what what is?"

"All this red in the sky."

"If you would like to."

"Oh, can I, too? Can I? I'd love to," Betsy cried.

"No, you do your homework and then go up to bed," said Charles.

Harriet folded her sewing. "I'll wash up the coffee-cups first. I think Elke has broken enough for one day."

"I wish I could go," Betsy said.

Charles waited for Harriet impatiently. When she came back, he could not even let her fetch her coat, but threw over

183

her shoulders one of his own. He imagined the fire crackling away without him, something immense, obviously—a church, or, better still, the Park Hotel. He could quite picture the tiny figures in grotesque attitudes, black against the flames, as they jumped into outstretched blankets, women in nightgowns moaning on the lawns, frantic activity with ladders, and then, just before he arrived, the great building leaning, bowing, collapsing. By the time he got there, the ambulances would have gone, the spectators thinned, someone would turn and say to him: "You should have seen it go down."

"Charles, I can't keep up at this pace!"

He slackened for a moment, but the sound of a fire-engine not far away, set him off again. He could definitely smell burning in the air.

"The weight of this coat!" Harriet said.

Betsy felt very little like work. The beautiful afternoon had unsettled her. It had been weird and solitary out there— the strange birds and the great trees clotted with nests. There had been a fight with some rooks. The sky, the empty marshland had echoed with harsh cries.

Miss Bell had talked of her own schooldays, and her days at Girton. Once or twice she mentioned the name of a rather famous writer she had met. It was rather dragged in, this name, Betsy thought; but the idea immediately horrified her. She quickly brushed away this little speck of disloyalty.

Miss Bell had invited her back to her bed-sitting-room for tea, had drawn the dark blue curtains and lit the gas fire. Betsy had not been there before and could scarcely believe that she now was. Sitting in front of the fire with a piece of bread wobbling on a fork and refusing to change colour, she looked carefully round the room. It was a nice mixture of pagan and Christian. A highly-coloured triptych of the Holy Family had one place beside the clock, a yellowing plaster copy of the Winged Victory, with rather more broken off

184

than should have been, had the other. Dusty crosses from Palm Sundays were stuck behind photographs of the pediments of the Parthenon. Examination-papers, half-corrected, lay about, weighted down—though nothing would fly away in this dead room—with lumps of stone from the Excavations at Cnossus. Betsy admired it all very much, imagined Miss Bell sitting by the fire, in the blue dressing-gown which hung on the door, drinking her bedtime cocoa. Bulbs came shinily up out of bowls on the window-sill; the kettle sang on the gas-ring. But the toast went black before ever having been brown.

Miss Bell made her room serve an educational purpose. She explained about the Excavations, and pieces of stone lay about on the hearthrug for Betsy to look at as she ate. On the bureau, she could see a photograph of what she supposed was the famous author—an elderly woman, with a pen held to a piece of paper; rows of books behind. She was glancing up as if she heard heavenly music. The photographer had caught her in the nick of time, thought Betsy, who hated other people's affectations; a moment later and inspiration might have spoilt it all, the head bending, the pen ruining the nice sheet of paper. She was a little jealous of the famous author for having her photograph in Miss Bell's room. As soon as she could, she began to talk about Vesey. She needed no more encouragement than silence. When she went home, she left a very worried young woman, sitting over her gas fire staring at the pieces of stone but thinking of other, livelier things.

But Betsy herself was stimulated beyond any settling down to work. The thought of the fire, of the glow in the sky, had finally unsettled her. To get a better view she went up to her mother's bedroom and drew aside the curtains. Branches stood very picturesquely against the stained and lightened clouds. It must be at the side of the park.

Below her, a wedge of light widened and Elke stepped out of the front door. The white cat took the opportunity to

185

slip in. Her hands making a shelter on her forehead, Elke surveyed the scene. Perhaps another war was beginning (and water lay between her and home, as well as between her and the enemy. With characteristic phlegm and stupidity, the English had scarcely moved away from their wireless-sets). Or was it another strange festival, like the one in November, whose origins they had tried to explain? The more they had explained them, the less reason she saw for firework-displays or any sort of rejoicing. She went indoors again. Betsy dropped the curtain.

Before she went to bed, she thought she would try on a few of her mother's things. Sitting before the mirror, she fixed Harriet's pearls in a loop on her brow and a bunch of violets behind one ear. They could not be back for ages, she knew. If Elke said anything, she could always drive her into silence with some remark like "What about Thursday evening?"

Busily clipping on ear-rings, lifting the trays of the little jewel-case, she came upon a sealed envelope, rather rubbed and faded with age, but with no writing on it. What do people conceal at the bottom of jewel-boxes? she wondered. Instructions in the event of death, perhaps (in which case she would love to read them); or a love-letter (in which case she would dearly love to read it). She imagined the first rather than the second, and with the bunch of violets still tangled in her hair, held the envelope against the light, but it was too opaque. Then, for her curiosity was too great by now to brook even a slight delay, she took a nail-file and ran it along under the flap as neatly as she could.

She drew out an old photograph and a folded piece of paper. On the paper was written "Dear Harriet, I am sorry. Love Vesey." The photograph was rather a yellowed one of three children sitting in a row on the grass. The middle one was undoubtedly Vesey as a boy. An hour or more ago, her mother had denied ever possessing such a photograph. Trembling now, Betsy ran to her own room to glue down the envelope. She could not make it look as it had been, but was fearful of her mother's return. She hid it again at the bottom of the case. In the next tray she dropped the ear-rings and the pearls.

"What you do?" Elke asked at the doorway, in her slow and gutteral voice.

"Just trying a few things." But the violets caught at her silky hair. She sat there pulling the blonde strands out of the flowers, willing Elke to go away.

"I think your Mamma do not like you to go in here . . ."

"What about last Sunday?" Betsy asked in a threatening voice, but her hands were frozen. She longed to be alone.

After all, it was only a hay-rick on fire at the edge of the park, by the farm. First of all through the empty streets they had tracked it down. When they met anyone, Charles stopped to enquire. It was a wholesale newsagents', gutted completely: it was the Nurses' Home by the Hospital: or cow-sheds, perhaps; for someone had heard cows lowing.

"Cow-sheds!" said Charles scornfully. He had not come so far merely to see cows being rescued. But the cow-sheds were untouched, and the rick blazed undisturbed now; the firemen for some reason had let it go. They watched it; standing by the beautiful fire-engine. Water ran all over the road, plaited its way down the hill in wandering streams.

"What a good job," Harriet said, "that it was no one's house!"

"Well, of course," Charles agreed irritably.

They had bickered all the way there, until their hearts were tired: now the flames lulled them. They stood in silence watching—Harriet, in the big coat with its turned-up collar, her hands in her pockets. Charmed and transfixed by the flames, held back to a certain point by the heat of them, their voices useless against the crackling and the steady roar, they watched for a while and then, as if by mutual consent, turned away, stepping over the rivulets of water and walking, with heads bent, back along the road.

187

"We could go perhaps to Italy," Charles said. "I could get away in a week or two."

His voice now was conciliatory.

"Italy?" Harriet felt that her troubles were already too many, without Italy being thrown in to worsen the confusion.

"We need a change. We haven't been getting on well together lately."

How they were to get on better entirely on their own, thrown together by a foreign country, day in, day out, Harriet could not see. She felt that he was putting too much faith altogether in guide-books and sightseeing and the boredom and annoyances of travel.

"Well, Charles . . . who could look after Betsy?"

"She could go to stay with my mother."

"They don't get on well, those two."

"I think they're so exactly alike . . . let them fight it out between them . . . fun for both."

"And Elke? She's too young to stay in the house alone."

"She could go, too. And fight it out with Miss Bastable."

"Poor Elke! You mean shut up the house? In which case, what about the cat?"

"The cat," Charles said, nodding patiently.

Then after all, she said: "I don't think I want to go."

"You always said you would love to go to Florence."

"Did I? Oh, you know how things are nice to talk about, but such a very great effort when it comes to putting them into practice."

Italy began to worry her dreadfully. She thought of the two of them sitting opposite one another in trains and in restaurants, wandering together in strange streets or, catalogue in hand, along the walls of art galleries. She felt a panic as if someone she had never met before had asked her to go away. I should be less frightened with a stranger, she realised. I should fear less the things that he might say.

As if she were recovering from a serious illness, Charles took her arm and, walking at half the pace of their outward

188

journey, held before her what he thought were tempting little pictures of the future—the sun, the sea, flowers, Florence, Rome. Miserably embarrassed, she listened; ungraciously, she replied.

When they reached home, standing on the steps while Charles unlocked the door, she looked back over the park. The sky was quite dark now, black branches sawed across it. No one walked in the empty streets; but in one house she could hear a piano being played.

"This cat's indoors again," Charles said. "How did it get in?"

"Perhaps someone came," Harriet said, glancing at the telephone-pad. The house was very quiet; Betsy and Elke both in bed.

"Mr Birdcat—it looks like—belled-up for Meinheer," she read. "I love 'belled-up'."

"Birdcat?" Charles paused at the front door, the kitten tucked into his overcoat. "I suppose it was 'Beckett'." Very gently this time, he put the cat down on the top step.

'Since she took the trouble to seal it and hide it, she could not have forgotten it,' Betsy lay and thought in bed. 'That wouldn't happen.'

She hugged her scalding-hot water-bottle. Her stomach and the inside of her arms were almost permanently mottled with scorch-marks. It was heaven to be in bed. Often she lay and made up scenes in which, for instance, she rescued the detested science mistress from a ledge of rock and coolly left her in the middle of a spate of uncharacteristic gratitude; or nursed Miss Bell through an illness of such an unsavoury nature that no one else would approach her.

She rarely drew these scenes to their conclusion: sleep overtook her. To-night, it overtook her, too; but thoughts of Vesey and of her mother tumbled about in her dreams as they had done in her waking mind. Romance, passion, seemed out of her mother's orbit. The revelation was not

189

disenchanting, but the shock of it placed her mother in a different light. It was a shock which brought her out of her sleep again and again, to lie and wonder. Harriet had concealed the truth, then kept it hidden by a lie. She had talked very little about her girlhood. Betsy had few pictures of her, few stories. When questioned, nothing seemed to have been remembered. She did not say "When I was a child" or talk about the past. Once she had laughed in a puzzled way, saying that her own mother's stories of childhood had bored her. "But didn't she tell you of the olden days?" Betsy persisted. "It didn't seem 'olden days' to her," Harriet tried to explain, "and my childhood doesn't to me." "Then you should remember it all the more." "One remembers," Harriet said, "such silly things, nothing worth telling; no stories, certainly." "But didn't your mother tell you about going to prison and marching in Emily Davidson's funeral procession?" Harriet said. "I tried not to listen, I hated it so." "I wish I had known her," Betsy said. "When I have children, I shall tell them all about the war—having evacuees here, and the bomb that fell in Prospect Park. I shall say 'I'll never forget that night' and things like that."

It was as if her mother had deliberately built up an unmemorable past. Vesey had been covered-over: she had kept him in hiding. And had treasured things about him. One walk in the park with him had somehow illuminated her—as Betsy now saw, remembering their return that twilight. Her own love for Vesey suffered nothing. She felt no anguish or resentment for Harriet. She was too young—in spite of all her romantic and dramatic ideas—to feel for him anything but a fixedness of attention. If he and her mother once were lovers—as she, on no evidence, supposed—then he was only brought nearer to her by the fact. Her feeling—on sight of him—had been so strong that she began, in the early hours, to wonder if there were not some distinct affinity. Life, as she had so far known it, heeled over, her vision slanted,

190

some assumptions were submerged, others were exposed to the strange, disturbing element of air. She began—with some passion—to exchange the idea of Charles for that of Vesey. With the intensity she would one day turn to selecting a lover, she now selected a father. Charles appeared at once remoter and nobler. She loved him no less because she adhered to Vesey. He had always seemed old and rather negative to her. She was the sort of girl who occasionally turned over in her mind thoughts of her own illegitimacy, not with repugnance but a sense of importance. She was self-infatuated enough to repudiate ordinary origins. Her mother—apparently—could not be doubted. Her father—Greek literature confirmed it—could. She did not fly as high as royal personages, but few middle-aged actors of any looks or presence had escaped her conjectures. Even a poet-laureate was not, in her opinion, beyond suspicion. That life was so unlike Greek literature had been the worse for life, to her mind. To-night it came—on the strength of a cryptic note, a faded photograph—magnificently near to it.

In the morning, she began a bombardment of casual and oblique questions—about Harriet's early life, betrothal, marriage. Harriet herself barely noticed. It was a thick, foggy morning. When she came down, there was a letter from Vesey. At first, she had not known his writing. Then, suddenly sure, she slipped it, unopened, inside a book. Now she waited feverishly for them to be gone. "You look tired, Betsy," she forced herself to say.

Betsy hoped to exploit this look, for she had not done her Greek homework.

"Why didn't you wear white when you were married?" she asked in an offhand way.

"For one reason, my mother was too recently dead."

"What was the other reason?"

"I should have felt absurd, I suppose."

"But why?"

191

"Darling, do eat your breakfast. I daresay I just hate dressing-up."

"What a funny thing to hate."

Harriet turned on Elke her including look and speaking more loudly, said: "You wear white in Holland for weddings?" as if the Dutch were a little-known tribe.

"Always," Elke said uncompromisingly.

"What *did* you wear?" Betsy asked.

"I've told you before—a grey suit."

"Grey!" said Betsy. "I don't know how you could've."

The fog lay close to the windows. The train seemed to be grovelling its way towards London, but the banks on either side were obscured. Harriet wondered if they were passing open fields or the backs of factories, and she cleaned a space on the window with her glove, but all she could see reflected were her own frightened eyes.

Although it was only late afternoon, the cotton-wool fog had been discoloured into darkness, and the people in the carriage seemed tired already; lulled with boredom, they sat with their arms folded, and stared at pictures of Lincoln Cathedral, or old houses at Norwich, untempted ever to travel there; and yawned.

Heat rose steadily round their ankles. The evening papers were all discarded. The train was not yet late enough to make an excuse for conversation. Harriet wondered if perhaps the English, great talkers though they are, long for a crisis to unlock their tongues, which fear of rebuff imprisons. 'Perhaps that is why we talk so much about the weather,' she thought. 'So much more than we care.'

They sat and wondered about one another. Harriet was the woman in the corner who kept combing her hair, and chafing her hands in her muff. She had tried to stop doing that, for her hands were not really cold.

"Half-an-hour late," the man opposite at last complained. "A frost on top of this will be a treat."

192

"No fear of frost," said another. So they began to talk about barometers and weather-forecasts. Then they paused, staring at one another's feet. Presently, they decided to continue; but gradually, sloping away through dahlias, chrysanthemums, potato-crops, towards the Government ("This lot we've got now"). Soon, one was saying: "I'm a fairly ordinary chap, but it strikes me . . ."

'How untrue!' thought Harriet. 'I can never believe that anyone thinks himself ordinary. I never think that I am an ordinary woman.' She glanced again at her reflection in the steamy window. 'There is no one else like me,' she told herself. 'I represent no one. I am typical of no one. No one else thinks my thoughts or understands my hopes or shares my guilt. I am both better and worse than I would admit to other people.'

"But why should the train be late?" a large girl rather like Elke was asking. She smiled round the carriage. She looked the soul of goodness, Harriet thought, the salt of the earth; her face was honest and unadorned. She spoke English with contemptuous ease, invoking hostility from all sides. It was felt that, though it is necessary for foreigners to speak English, to do so easily is an affront. "In Switzerland," she said, "the trains are punctual, and not so dirty."

After a brief silence in which the others all came together and sank their differences as if they were in an air-raid shelter, not a railway-carriage, the obvious spokesman said: "The fog, of course. On account of the fog he can't see the signals."

Yes, that perfectly explained, they all felt. As for the dirty train, it was theirs; they enhanced it by being its possessors. The dear train. The beloved fog.

"In Switzerland, we do not have such fog," she said simply.

'What hope is there for world peace if people travel about from one country to another?' Harriet wondered.

Now the more experienced travellers began to predict the

193

end of the journey. They took out their tickets and sat a little more on the edge of the seats as if that might hasten matters. When at last blurred lights ran up to meet them, Harriet's heart lurched with pain.

Stepping out on the platform, she suddenly felt that Vesey would not be there, and could not look at the people waiting by the barrier. 'He must claim *me*,' she thought. But it would be too difficult. Her own difficulties had been so very great, and if his matched them how could they ever manage such a marvel as to find themselves at last in the same place at the same time? So she walked quickly, as if she had some destination; but if he were not there, she had none. She was afraid that it was despair she was walking towards and she pressed her hands together in her muff and her look was not nonchalant, as she would have had it, but anxious. She made little plans to cover her humiliation, which now seemed certain—a brandy when the bar opened and then home by the next train. Charles would never know about the excursion. She would be, in a way, saved. If her will had not ensured her good behaviour, circumstances would have done so. ("In Switzerland we do not commit adultery," she seemed to hear that forthright voice explaining.)

"Why are you smiling?"

Vesey took her by the elbow and they went through the barrier. Under the broken arched glass, the station was like a scene in hell. Sulphurous mist thickened the air, slime covered the platforms, figures disentangled themselves and scurried away, all to some evil end, one felt; but they moved within a greater stillness and though they seemed free to come and go, they were all enclosed.

Outside, the fog was a smoke breathed out by some foul mouth. Obscurely, it enfolded them. It was a night to have chosen, they said: part of their general helplessness.

A beautiful woman hurried past, and disappeared, and a rose, falling out of her furs as she ran, dropped at Vesey's feet. He picked it up. The sound of the woman's

194

heels clicked away from them and was lost in silence.

He walked beside her with the rose hanging from his hand. The taste of the fog was at the back of their throats. They could see only the shape of one another and, when they spoke, so private, so safe did they feel that they neither paused nor dissembled. In this blurred world, words were more beautiful and they used them more truthfully than at other times.

He stripped himself of his despair about his work; she shed her anxieties and her fears.

"When I was young," she said, "I stole from Caroline a photograph of you. I had nothing. That, and the note you left for me when my mother died I put into an envelope and sealed it down and always kept it."

He was unbearably moved and afraid to speak.

"The other day, I saw that it had been unsealed and stuck together again. I never opened it myself. It was enough knowing it was there. I felt cold with fear when I saw, not so much at its being discovered, as at myself discovering such an action in Charles. Wastes of horror and misunderstanding lie between us now."

"Keep nothing, my dear one. Don't be a sentimental woman. Have now. This evening. All the rest is a dust laden with threats."

"I can't. Suppose I were left with nothing!"

"If scraps of paper are all you have, you have nothing. Besides, Charles might want to fight me."

They came to a small tea-shop in a mean street. In the furred darkness it was a dim oasis. A card saying OPEN hung crookedly against the door, and in the window a plate of cakes lay in a strange light, like fossilised cakes in a museum. They looked so permanent. They could no more moulder away, they felt, than could shells or pieces of stone.

"They would hardly melt in the mouth," he said.

They stopped and looked in the window, his arm through hers.

195

"I love you stealing my photograph," he said. "I will for ever cherish you. Which would you have of those cakes if you could choose?"

"Perhaps the Chelsea bun."

"Or that cornucopia broken off some garden statue . . ."

"Fantastic, unappetising cakes!"

"Let's go in and eat some. Let's have that very plate out of the window!"

But what began as a joke threatened to sadden them and when the cakes lay between them and the bewildered waitress had withdrawn, the joke crumbled and panic swept through them. They could not glance at one another. To discard so affected a piece of playfulness was difficult and the Chelsea bun was uneatable, especially as a joke.

"A second-hand flower," he said, laying the rose beside her plate.

She picked it up, but would not look at him.

"Charles," he said, bravely beginning to unwind *his* Chelsea bun, "would take you to a lovely place at once— with music and forced lilac and something nice to eat. It is tempting Providence for us to go out together."

"Because we are alike in some ways, there must be disadvantages, as well as benefits."

He broke off bits of the bun and began to eat.

He is hungry, she thought. She resented his hunger, deplored his letting her know about it. Very sedately she poured tea, her glove over the handle of the pot.

The shop was empty. The waitress, having thrown coke all over the fire, so annulling it and chilling the room, disappeared through some curtains. They could hear some over-confident voices and some over-confident dish-washing; and all the time, the phlegmy fog thickened the darkness beyond the windows and enisled them there.

With a great effort, he tried to wrench their evening away from disaster, and leaning forward, pushing aside his plate, said: "Forgive this horrible place!"

196

She looked round at the filmed mirrors with advertisements on them, at the green-tiled tables, the antlered hatstand, the vase of pampas-grass like plumes which had been dipped in the fog.

"It doesn't matter where we are," she said, and knew this to be true.

"Do you remember when I made Joseph and Deirdre eat chops?"

"Yes."

"I suddenly remembered that the other day. I can't think why."

Harriet had never forgotten. She saw him now—the thin, white youth he had been—leaning over to cut Joseph's meat, remembered the exhaustion of her desire.

While he was talking, he stretched his hand down beside his chair, curling his fingers to attract a little white cat, like Harriet's Blanchie, which came sidling to him. Very delicately, she sprang upon his knees and began to thrust her claws into him as if she were stitching his clothes. She was pink and white. The light shone rosily through her ears; the little pads of her feet were covered in pink silk. They both watched her as they talked. She reminded Harriet of home. Trying to forget, she said: "Tell me about your lodgings."

Stroking the cat until her fur crackled, he said: "I took down the picture over the bed. Psyche at the Pool. One foot in the water, one hand on the bosom. The landlady thought I did it from moral indignation, but it was only indignation. There's a large oblong now, with the pattern of the wallpaper very bright. The window is over a yard with dustbins and ferns, and by the window there is a marble-topped washstand that I use for a desk—very cold to the wrists. The bath has a green stain running down under the geyser and . . . am I depressing you? It is rather like George Gissing perhaps . . . I eat my meals at the washstand, too, and rather nasty they are, and I wrote those letters to you sitting there. Your letters I keep wrapped up in a paper bag in the top right-hand drawer of the chest. I thought you would like to know. My books are in cardboard boxes underneath the bed."

She built up his life in her mind. It was like reading a novel written by someone one loves: allusive, intimate, between-the-lines reading.

The waitress came through the curtains and turned the card on the door, so that now it said CLOSED. She watched it swinging to and fro. He put the cat on the floor and brushed white hairs off his clothes. He took a handful of money from his pocket and paid the bill, and soon they were out in the street again and another scene, another little coloured picture was left behind.

The street was silent. They walked closely together in the deserted city; sometimes his shoulder brushed her cheek, once he took her hand inside her muff. They could see nothing; only sometimes, as they passed under a lamp, dead leaves stuck to the pavement. The fog beaded their hair and their eyelashes; her muff was stary with it; their coats had a bloom of moisture on them.

In all London there seemed to be no other people; yet when they entered a pub in a mews they found that it was full, and blue with smoke. But the crowd made an island of them, too, like the fog. They sat down unnoticed in a corner. The scene was teeming and Hogarthian. Between the close-packed legs, a dog ran round, nosing at the slopped beer on the floor; voices were too vibrant, and every laugh was like a peacock's scream.

"When we were young," Vesey said, "I never did know what you were thinking. I had the burden of taking all the risks, initiating everything. Once I purposely brushed against you as we went in to lunch—a little experiment. You blushed, but it might have been in anger. When you sat down next to me, you touched the knives and forks nervously, as if you hesitated. Yes, like a child waiting to say its Grace.

"I was feeling that all the happiness in me had broken out into blossom; but doubt soon began. Soon I was sure it was all an accident, you seemed so indifferent again."

She looked defiantly at a man standing by, who turned his head, overhearing her words. "There was a pink azalea in the room," she went on. "I sat and stared at it and at first it seemed that my happiness was like that; a great flight of blossom, a great running up the scale."

"Nowadays,' she thought, 'perhaps always, happiness has to be isolated. Only when we blot out all that surrounds it, can we have it perfect, as we so often have perfect grief.' She felt that she must not grope backwards over her conscience, or forwards over her desires, but keep her contentment in this different climate while she could.

They stayed in the pub a long while and when they came out into the cobbled mews, they walked along slowly, close to the garage doors.

"What will happen to us?" she asked.

"Don't worry now," he said. "Don't relate this particular evening to any of the rest of our lives."

The fog had enfolded their hours together, as if they were jewels in a box. He would go back to his room with the marble washstand, the faded walls. She would sit in the slow dirty train, watching her reflection in the window, no longer combing her hair, no longer chafing her hands in her muff. When Charles came home much later from his Old Boys' Reunion, she would be lying on her side feigning sleep.

Vesey stopped between the dark buildings and kissed her, drew her inside his opened coat. His hands gripped her thin shoulders.

"At night, I take you to bed with me. You lie down in my arms underneath the square patch where Psyche used to hang. Without you I am quite alone. My life is one long sordid squabble with other people. You were always my beloved, though I didn't know what way to behave. With you in my arms, though, I am always at peace. In my most

199

desperate longing for you, I am still at peace. I lie and remember things—like that time we went in to lunch—and imagine other things. You justify everything, hallow everything. It doesn't any longer matter if I cannot pay the rent."

She felt, even in the soles of her feet, the palms of her hands, her striving for him, against all matters of time and place, so that she could not loosen her arms from him and believed that her nerves could not endure their separation. She was beset by him, as she had been as a young girl.

"You will come again?"

"There are so few chances."

"Does it make you feel furtive and unlovely?"

"No. It is beyond any of that."

"To tell lies, I mean."

"If I use the lies to get to you, they don't matter to me."

"I wish I were rich," he said carelessly, glancing away over her shoulder, down the mews. "I wish you hadn't that Betsy. I wish we were eighteen again. Talking eases me, breaks up the concentration of my body. I am not saying anything that means anything. I also have to know that you and Charles are together in the night. I am glad you are saved that pain. I mean, of thinking in that way of me. You see how unselfish I am? I take the worst part willingly. Never think of me on those occasions, will you? I beg your pardon for mentioning it. But if you could possibly banish me . . ."

"I can only bring you near me when I am alone . . ."

When they walked on again, the rose that he had tucked into her coat, fell down on to the greasy cobbles. They stooped to look for it, but couldn't find it. Each time he struck a match to help them to see, the little splutter of light seemed to drive the beautiful fog back into his face.

2

Aт the beginning of the spring, Hugo fell ill. It was uncertain weather: a queasy sunshine alternated with a glowering violet sky; a choppy wind set all the bushes jigging.

Hugo's illness was Harriet's only way of seeing Vesey. They sat on either side of his bed staring at one another. Then at times, she would feel whipped up into excitement. She moved consciously, with his eyes on her: what she said to Hugo was always for Vesey's benefit. Hugo found her good and gentle. Although shy in her dealings with him, she was more soothing than Deirdre. He was not such a fool that he thought Vesey good to be there, but the loveliness in the room invigorated him, he felt part of the exquisite tension and drew strength from it. Sunlight came in with them. He suddenly saw that life is short and happiness a good thing, to be made much of. He lay there, feeling washed up and discarded, saw that they made use of his illness. There they could be together without blame. His death would remove their chaperon, and send Vesey back to lying and scheming. He did not think that Harriet would lie or scheme, not knowing that they acted in unison and that one could not be separated from the behaviour of the other.

Although he brought them together, he was a brake upon their love; he kept it a matter of glances, of sudden downward looks, of hands accidentally brushing together. He wondered what would happen to them. His wondering took him from one day to another. Feeling no pity for them, not judging them nor abetting them. They might have been characters in a play, though less interesting

201

H

since it was a play whose conclusion he would not see.

In the end, they were not there. He died in Deirdre's arms; his son standing at the foot of the bed. They had been a happy, loyal family. He thought, in his last hours, and when he was able to think at all, that something had been accomplished. Perhaps Harriet and Vesey had no place there.

The next time they met, the blinds were drawn. Joseph and Deirdre were once more polite, composed and well-behaved.

"I always remember," Harriet said, as she and Vesey walked in the tangled garden, "how he helped me when my mother died. I had never been to a cremation before. He made me sit down and listen to all that would happen, so that nothing could shock me. When the coffin began to slide away, he said I should think of a liner on a slipway, beginning its voyage, a sad and yet a noble occasion. He spared me nothing, but when the time came I was all right. I was grateful to him. He was kind, and didn't jib at difficult things."

"He didn't cotton to me much," Vesey said. "He always made me feel tricky and emotionally disorderly."

A half-blind spaniel waddled at their heels. When Vesey threw a stick, trying to make the dog run, it only turned a watery and indifferent eye.

In the dell, Deirdre's old swing was caught up on the branch of an apple tree. There were the remains of a house Joseph had begun to build in an oak many years ago.

Vesey unhooked the swing and Harriet sat on it. It was sheltered there; the first warmth of the spring seemed breathed up from the earth. The newly-unfolded leaves of wild daffodils and lords-and-ladies looked varnished and brilliantly green among dead leaves and broken twigs.

"This is the last day then," Harriet said, swinging a little, but with her toes dragging on the ground.

"We shall have to meet in London," Vesey replied. He leant back against the trunk of the tree, the palms of his hands pressed into the rough bark.

202

"The other day, when I went there shopping, I was dreadfully questioned. . . ."

"We could make up some lies, invent some places for you to go to, to have been to."

"We are making a monster of Charles, which he really is not."

"Is. Is not. It couldn't matter less. We need not waste time discussing him. Doesn't he ever go away anywhere?"

"Not without me." She did not tell him how she had been evading Italy for the last month or two.

"I thought all husbands went off sometimes to conferences and so on. I've seen jokes about it in *Punch*."

"The point is—Charles doesn't."

"If he did, would you come away with me?"

She felt terror at the idea. She gripped the ropes of the swing, trembling. Hating danger, she could foretell the difficulties and embarrassments, the perhaps disastrous consequences.

He caught at one of the ropes and steadied her drew her back against him, his hands over her breast.

"Then that is settled," he said. "We need only await the opportunity. Alas, no one's love-making ever was so long-deferred as ours!"

He pulled her away from the swing and lay down with her in the fine grass among the budding daffodils. The warm sweetness in the earth seemed magnetic, dragged at their limbs, silenced them. She lay with her head on his outflung arm. His hand reaching at last the bareness of her breast lay so tenderly upon her that she felt a pause in herself, her blood seemed, she fancied, to make a deep curtsey. Held up, checked, she breathed a long breath to bring her bosom closer to his hand, gathered his head against her shoulder. In his eyes, she saw her own face reflected and above them, beyond the trees, a wall of the house and windows, and all the curtains drawn across.

.   .   .   .   .

203

"So you've cut yourself a fringe?" Julia said in a patronising voice. "It makes you look all eyes."

"But Mrs Jephcott has such beautifully expressive eyes," Miss Bastable said.

"Beautiful, perhaps: expressive, no. Expressive eyes, my dear Miss B., have to express something. Harriet's remind me of that fairy story—what is it? Bluebeard—'I see nothing but the sun making a dust and the grass looking green'."

She lifted her ruined face, her voice rang ominously. Her hands—a little contorted with rheumatism—looked too big for her slight wrists; her sleeves fell away from her now shrunken, blue-veined arms. Her gestures were less impetuous, more tragic, perhaps more beautiful. Her eyes had a waiting emptiness, which was her imitation of Harriet.

"What *could* you express, darling? What have you suffered in your sheltered life? Married out of the schoolroom . . .?"

"I was working in a shop at the time," Harriet said, laughing.

Julia glanced at Miss Bastable, who quickly took up her embroidery.

"All sunny," Julia intoned. "All sunny. Your husband's loving care. He spoilt you. He was afraid you'd run off like the other one."

"Behave yourself, Julia!"

"Perhaps, Miss B., you'd be good enough to put the kettle on for tea, if you can tear yourself away from your tatting."

"You're a cantankerous old woman," Harriet said, when Miss Bastable had quickly rolled up her work and fled. She was either snatching it up in confusion, or tucking it away from sight. "Cruel to that poor woman," Harriet continued.

"Poor?" Julia echoed. "She lives here in the lap of luxury, as they say. She will see out her days in gentle pastimes. Nothing 'poor' about her."

"She is a pathetic character."

"Don't *mumble* at me. You either mutter or stammer. I

204

see nothing pathetic about her. She has her fancy-work. She has her famous gentility and her memories of her late papa, as she calls him. I think she is rather more to be envied than I am. She has more life to live, for one thing; and I love life and hate the thought of death. Age improves her, I do believe. She is certainly more handsome now that her moustache is grey, don't you think? *Much* more distinguished. Why, I wonder—since we are talking of improved appearances, or changed appearances—why all this furbishing and renovating and hair-trimming you are going in for yourself?"

"I felt a dreadful weariness and distaste one day when I looked into a mirror. Although I didn't feel like that inside, it was clear that was how I looked—frayed at the edges. What I wanted was never to see that again, to be as different as I could and in any way I could. . . ."

"False, betraying hearts!" Julia said, staring at her own crooked hands. "To leave us schoolgirls inside, and to destroy us from without in so many dreadful ways; stiff joints, knotted veins, cushions of fat, ruined bosoms, uncertain teeth . . . darling, I do know what one feels and with what appalling suddenness it is too late. One moment one is scorning lovesick young men; the next, and everything has suddenly gone, young men are lovesick for other women, one is alone, a figure of fun, perhaps. You must take what is offered at the time. I never think infidelity is a thing one ever regrets. . . ."

"I merely complained about my shabby looks," Harriet protested.

"You think I want to enliven my old age by dwelling on your affairs?"

"I do not. What a horrible idea! And I have no affairs."

"I know otherwise. Although I ask no confidences of you . . ." She paused and looked about the room, as if it were somewhere strange to her. "No, I really don't care to know," she said, when Harriet remained silent. "So

205

depressing! Modern love-affairs seem such sordid, morbid little concerns. Drinking gin in bars, cars parked at road-sides—imagine making love in a car! It is beyond me to think how such a thing could be done. The gears, as I believe they are called . . ."

"Believe? You know perfectly well."

"And once I saw a film . . . a middle-aged couple in raincoats, and it all took place on a railway station . . . can you believe me? In my day, we should never have cared for that . . . we did such things at home, in the proper place . . . when our husbands were out. . . ."

"You conjure up such a lovely picture of salmon-pink satin boudoirs and lace négligées. What if the husband should come back in the middle?"

"The middle? The middle of what?" Julia sounded aghast. Miss Bastable was bringing in the tray. "We will discuss this when we are alone." Her voice became loud and toneless.

"We will do nothing of the kind," Harriet said. "We will leave it there, in the pink boudoir, if you please."

Harriet thought of the drinking in bars, lingering in tea-shops, railway-stations, benches in parks; in streets under a dark building, in the darkest place between two lamps. The course of unlawful love never does run smooth; or with dignity; or with romance.

Julia was now—affectedly laborious—discussing the lengthening daylight, as if to imply to Miss Bastable that nothing more intimate could be mentioned in her presence. "That little spell after tea before we light the lamps, so very welcome," she said in a high-pitched social voice. "And one is so grateful for it in the early mornings. The birds singing," she added vaguely. "Soon it will be summer. That's another thing, you'll notice," she said in a lowered voice to Harriet, "the way the seasons go flying by."

All through Lent, Betsy went to church a great deal. Miss

Bell noticed her there, with misgivings which she could not clearly specify. Although religious herself, Betsy's own devotions seemed to her in line with a general agitation she manifested, and with a falling-off in her Greek. Work undone, yawnings, stupidity, were in Miss Bell's mind whenever she glanced at the pale girl with the pale gold hair and the beret set straight on the top of her head. She sat always in the same place, by a pillar, as if she hid there. When she knelt down to pray, she kept her eyes ahead, her long hands on either side of her face, her pathetically red wrists thrust out of her too-short sleeves.

She had, these days, a vacant, a distracted air. She did not sleep well. She sat sometimes on the edge of her bed, in a state of suspended consciousness, feeling only the slightest ruffling on her spirit of time passing by: once was so disembodied that it seemed she need only lift her arms to drift away, to float, to fly. She lifted her arms, but remained bound by such heavy roots, her imagination was so confounded, that tears came into her eyes.

Once, passing through the school hall which smelt of furniture-polish, was hung with brass-rubbings and shields, and in whose parquet, grand-piano, mirrors, the bitterly white sky outside was reflected, Miss Bell found Betsy rather mopish, standing beneath the green baize notice-board, her hands on a radiator. From all the rooms near-by came the authoritative, raised voices of women teaching.

"Why do you palely loiter?" Miss Bell asked, in the schoolmistressy, quoting voice which sometimes dismayed her.

"I was sent out of Scripture."

Miss Bell hoisted her books up her arm. It was not the girl's defiance which checked further questions, but the rule that she would not enquire into her colleagues' reasons or methods.

"You will have to pull yourself together," she said curtly;

her neck reddened as she went off down the hall.

Through her misted eyes, Betsy read again all the little notices and lists pinned to the board. Her hands patted the too-hot radiator. She was so deeply into trouble now that she was sure she could never right anything. She prayed for catastrophe, for a break of great violence after which she might be permitted to begin again. She felt that if she complained of pains in her side her mother might send her at once to hospital. Her grandmother had died of appendicitis. They would be unlikely to delay an operation. Afterwards, frailer, thinner, she would return to school and find her slate wiped clean. Or she would indulge herself in a nervous-breakdown up to the very verge of madness. Like Hamlet she would voice many opinions which she now repressed, creating special circumstances, spreading alarm.

One of the prefects, eyeing her aloofly, came into the hall, took up a great brass bell and swung it to and fro. In the classrooms, desk-lids banged, the authoritative voices were raised above scuffling confusion, then one door after another was thrown open; polite murmurings accompanied the mistresses out of the rooms, noise mounting when they had gone. Soon, girls came out, eating biscuits out of paper bags. They strolled in the hall and perched about in clusters on the window-seats. It was too cold to go out. A bitter wind raked the shrubbery. They were all in quarantine for mumps, feeling their necks expectantly from time to time, fancying little symptoms.

"You *are* a fool," Pauline Hay-Hardy said. "You'll be sent to Miss Anstruther in the end."

Betsy smiled faintly; but she felt singled-out and victimised, in a position of solitary danger.

"And it puts her in such a hell of a bate with us," Pauline complained.

"You must look after yourselves."

"Well, there's no need to be rude. Have a ginger-nut. They're quite nice and soft."

"I like them hard," said Betsy.

"You always want to be different to other people."

"Different *from*," said Betsy. "Anyhow, I *don't* want to be different. If ginger-nuts were meant to be soft, they'd make them soft in the first place."

"Look what you said about Saint Paul."

"I meant it."

"No one pleases you these days. Vanessa said she wouldn't ask you to her party; you'd only turn your nose up."

Betsy had watched the invitations handed round, her heart as still as a stone.

"I probably should," she agreed. "Look how boring it was last year. All those girl-guides' games, and forfeits. Postman's Knock, too; of all things."

"You and Ricky Vincent kept cheating so that you went out together."

"Ricky Vincent!" Betsy said in a withering voice. "We were practically in our prams together. I'm so used to him, I wouldn't cross the road to say hallo. Besides, he's conceited. And he calls his mother 'Mummy'. I would cheat *not* to go out with *him*."

"That's right! Fly into a bate. Someone else you don't like." Pauline screwed up her biscuit bag and took a slide across the parquet to the waste-paper-basket. Betsy's heart turned over when the prefect took up the bell again. Mademoiselle appeared promptly, while they were still herding into the form-room. Betsy sat down and clasped her hands under her desk; her verbs unlearnt; her reading unprepared.

Harriet sat on a seat in Regent's Park waiting for Vesey. Only the faintest breeze wrinkled the lake. Flecks of dazzling colour, the tiny new leaves dotting the trees, the broken sunlight, gave a painted look to the scene. The bushes sprang apart, then closed, as birds burst out of them.

Pale, flaking houses enclosed the tender greenness. People with coats swinging open, walked on the paths, admiring the tulips which still, though it was early evening, were flat open in the sun. A middle-aged woman sitting near Harriet seemed flat open in the sun, too; lying back, relaxed, indifferent, sleeping like a cat. When she stood up suddenly and clapped on a red hat without a glance in a mirror, she became a different woman, guarded and suspicious. Harriet smiled, watching her assembling herself and striding away towards the gates.

Beside her on the seat a man and a girl held an uneasy conversation in lowered voices. "Surely you have *something* to say for yourself after all this time."

The girl smoothed her gloves.

"Ah, now, I see what's wrong, what's different, I mean," her companion said. "You've been plucking your eyebrows. Trying to look sophisticated, eh?"

The girl turned an ugly red. She had hoped to have improved herself, had taken trouble over this dreadful meeting.

"Suppose it were like that between Vesey and me!" Harriet thought, glancing away in the direction he would come.

"Seen any of the old crowd?" the man asked the girl.

"Only Phil."

"Oh, yes, I remember."

"Have you?"

"I?"

"Seen any of them?"

"Not a glimpse. You know how it is. One loses touch. Other places, other people. And then after a while, well . . . quite frankly . . ." he, not quite frankly, laughed . . . "one loses the urge, you know."

"Yes."

'Yes,' thought Harriet, 'he has disposed of the Old Crowd all right, in his mind, and in hers.'

A hand on her shoulder was Vesey's. She looked up, not startled, and smiled.

"I'm sorry I was late," he said.

"No, I was early."

"*Not* husband and wife," the man on the seat said, staring vaguely after them as they began to walk away. The girl looked wistful. "Even if married people ever did meet one another in a Park," he added.

"I had this rehearsal which went on and on," Vesey said. They walked slowly along the path.

"You look tired."

"Yes, I'm tired. But seeing you winds me up again, like having a drink. Let's have a drink."

Crossing the road, he held her arm close against his ribs. She had the beautiful sensation of being cherished, felt, as she walked down the street with him, a girlish triumph in his love, as if she said to the passers-by "*He* is the one I always wanted."

They turned through swing-doors into coolness. Dimpled glass was rosy in the evening sun; a parrot squawked across the empty bar. Harriet sat down at a table and watched Vesey as he brought the drinks. He looked ill, though he had never been robust. His shoes were worn away sharply at the heels, a tuft of thread hung from his coat instead of a button.

To be daring and open in public places now stimulated them. When he came to sit down, he put his hand over hers on the table, engaged her with his glance; and, when he drank, first pledged her.

"And this evening," he asked, "where are you supposed to be? Obviously not sitting here in a pub in Baker Street with me."

"No. A Miss Lazenby . . . I never got to Christian names with her . . . but I knew her when we were in that shop . . . now she works in London, and, although Charles scarcely approves—she has lax morals, he says,

211

and I suppose he's right, though I'm not able to say that of anyone myself . . ."

"Darling!"

"Sometimes I see her . . . I was in a way fond of her . . . at least, I followed her adventures with interest . . . they were like a wonderful serial story, you know. I go there to buy gloves and get the latest instalment, and occasionally we lunch together. Oh, rather rarely . . . but this evening the friendship has suddenly blossomed or ripened and we are at the cinema together."

"Would that be probable?"

"I had no other way of catching the last train."

"You can't have to account for every hour."

"I expect people who aren't to be trusted must be prepared for that."

She looked briefly at the door as it swung open for someone to come in.

"I don't like it for you. I wish we were not so cheap. Tell me about Miss Lazenby's adventures."

"For one thing they dovetail so beautifully. As she emerges from one, another is always waiting for her. Sometimes she emerges with a fox-cape or one of those dear little fancy wrist-watches that don't work. She certainly does have nice things and it's far better for her in London . . . she meets a much nastier type of man. But she's not young any more . . . I wonder what can happen."

"You are always wondering what will happen to people."

"It is odd and sad how some girls slip into the habit of not marrying."

"You panicked into it too soon," he said coolly.

"I know it was wrong, especially to Charles, but how can one know there is anything else to wait for?"

"At twenty?"

"And at thirty," she said quietly. "And after that."

"You can never forgive me, can you?"

"And you will never understand about Charles."

212

"I do understand."

"There was another girl I worked with . . . a Miss Lovelace . . . a warm-hearted, a tragic person. She hadn't much money . . . we none of us had a halfpenny by Thursday each week. What she had, she spent on clothes. She didn't eat enough, and was lonely. Her adventures didn't dovetail. There were gaps. In one of these gaps, feeling weak and wretched after 'flu, she simply lay down on the floor with her head on a cushion right inside the gas-oven. . . ."

"But, Harriet darling, it is our lovely evening out together," Vesey protested. "Stop remembering such dreadful things!"

"It wasn't all sad. There were four of us in that shop. I think we loved one another, or were used to one another. One becomes very close to people one works with—in a distinctive, a particular way, don't you think?"

"Sometimes," he said guardedly.

"Even ill-assorted people. When I was married, I felt lonely, and missed them. I asked them to tea once on an early-closing day; but it was quite a failure. They were stiff and cautious and polite. They admired everything exhaustively. It was so uncasual. Handing cups to them, I suddenly thought it was a dolls' tea-party. I felt like a little girl playing at keeping house. Miss Lazenby looked round her all the time and didn't swear, which she usually never stops doing. Charles came home before they left . . . in fact, I thought they never would leave . . . for my sake—I suppose he sensed what a failure it all had been—he tried to rally them. But they would scarcely respond. Miss Brimpton, the eldest, gave a refined titter or so, but the others deliberately held off . . . they had strong moral codes about not encroaching on another woman's interests. I knew it could never be the same again, that the next morning they would discuss it all, liven up, become homely, racy, unselfconscious, but that I'd not be there to hear it, or share in it."

"If you had stayed there . . . not begun playing house . . . you'd have withered and withered. One day, I'd have walked in for a yard-and-a-half of elastic . . ."

"It was a gown shop; not a draper's."

". . . I'd have walked in for a gown . . . I never know when a frock becomes a gown . . . I would have leant across the counter . . ."

"We didn't have counters."

". . . and said 'Dear Miss Claridge, will you marry me?' And in your poverty you'd have been glad enough to. Shall I go and grovel to my father? If you will sacrifice Betsy, I will sacrifice my pride. I will even swallow it, which is worse than just throwing it aside, don't you think? More painful. I will give up my brilliant career as an actor, and go to work in an office, starting at the bottom, as sons do—like going up in a lift . . . get out at each floor and take a look round . . . 'Hallo, you chaps, nice to see you. Sorry I can't stay' . . . right to the top. A desk in the next room to my father's— not quite so large, and two telephones, instead of three— 'Take this file to Mr Vesey.' 'Young Mr Vesey,' I think they'll call me. In a few years, my father will retire, knowing the reins are safe in my hands. I shall move into the next room and sign cheques and go to conferences. The secretary will be ringing up for reservations, putting documents into my brief-case. 'New York on the phone, Mr Vesey.' Can you imagine this?"

"No."

"I can *imagine* it. My mother might plead for me, though she doesn't cut much ice, which one must do to reach my father's heart. I wonder how has my life been so much worse than *that* sort of life—office-life. Neither seems very estimable to me. If one worked in a coal-mine or a vineyard, it would be different; but my father and I seem much on a par. I did no more harm than he—except to you. Who— except you—is poorer on my account? Many people are poorer on his. In fact, I suppose he earns his living by

214

making them poorer. Whereas I, at least, have made *him* richer, by being cut off without a shilling, I mean. I could sometimes have done with that shilling. It has been on my mind. It proved that he could not even be an unnatural father naturally. 'Well, you've had enough warning,' he told me. 'No one to blame but yourself,' and so on. I shuffled about, waiting, but he made no offer. I thought perhaps he would send a postal-order, but he never did. My mother sent me some loose pound notes in a mauve envelope— seven; a funny number, I thought—and a box of marrons-glacés. 'I remember you adore these,' she wrote. I didn't know which she referred to."

All the time he was talking, he was breaking up dead matches into little bits, arranging and rearranging them. She watched him gravely. When she raised her eyes to his, their seriousness did not match the words which had been spoken.

"I have nowhere to take you," he said. "There is nowhere for us to go."

"Vesey, I think you are ill."

"I was born fagged-out. But I never have illnesses."

"Does that woman give you enough to eat?"

"More than enough. A glimpse of it is that. Her cooking is a sort of curse she brings down on the food. Only weird incantations and endlessly patient malevolence could wreak such harm. I can scarcely complain, of course. Cynthia and I hardly ever pay our rent . . . we honestly can't afford to. She said we were like fishes sucking at the hull of a ship—a lively piece of imagery, I thought."

"Cynthia?"

"That girl who came to the dance with me."

"Oh, yes."

"She stays there, too."

Harriet smiled faintly.

"Darling?"

"Yes?"

"What is wrong?"

215

"How could anything be wrong?"

"I wondered that. Well, let us have another drink."

'Of course,' Harriet thought, 'he has the other life, of landladies, and lodgings, learning parts, rehearsing, making up. He goes home late at night. He knows other women.' But she had not wanted to imagine it. They had been alone in the world, surrounded by strangers, anonymous and safe. Blurred voices formed their background; covered their words to one another. No one turned to them, or spoke to them. The incurious crowd had kept their secret.

The streets about the railway-station were deserted. As they passed beneath lamps, their shadows swung round and lengthened before them. Draughts swirled under the dark arches, bits of dirty newspaper lisped along, grit was in the air. In the empty space below the high glassed roof they felt dimunitive, a symbolic man and woman, dwarfed, helpless, as in some film about the future.

All the kiosks were shuttered, the symbolic train waited, the clock's hand jerked from minute to minute.

The hour was so late to Harriet and she felt that she had been so long from home, that Miss Lazenby and the cinema seemed the most absurd excuse, devised recklessly. She began to fear her return.

"Do you wonder what will happen to us?" Vesey asked. "Since you wonder so much about other people."

They were walking down the length of the train.

"Nothing *can* happen to us. All of the obstacles are insurmountable."

"Poverty; Betsy . . ." he began to enumerate.

"And Charles, too. Apart from Betsy, I could not deal a blow like that. Marriage is an institution. One fails it again and again, but I expect one mustn't begin to question it, or the world falls to pieces. . . . Please don't hold my hand, Vesey. There may be people I know on this train. . . ."

"There *are* no people on this train. It is so empty it seems

216

sinister. I don't like having you get on it. There is no knowing where it might not take you. Do you mean," he said, opening a door, "that we are to go on like this, for years and years?"

The compartment smelt stale and was dirty. They sat down, opposite one another, and he leant forward and took her hand again.

"Those evenings in the loft when we were young, playing hide-and-seek with Joseph and Deirdre. . . . I was remembering it all the other night."

"Yes."

"How we wasted our time! Darling, you're shivering."

Her smile was stiff over her chattering teeth.

"I do apologise," Vesey said, "for this cold night and this dirty train. Someone has turned the heater off."

"What time is it?"

"We have two minutes."

"Don't get carried away." She at once flushed at her ambiguous remark.

A fat man wrenched open the door and brushed past them. They resented him so bitterly, thinking of all the rest of the empty train, that they looked steadily away from him, and seemed to congeal a disapproving silence about them.

'Now anything that hasn't been said, can't be,' she thought.

Vesey was staring at her. Sometimes he nodded to himself, as if he were learning her features by heart, committing her face to his memory. She turned to the window, uneasy under his scrutiny, too conscious of her faults; then, when she could no longer keep her eyes away, looked quickly up and flashed a nervous and meaningless smile at him, her hands twisting in her muff.

He stroked the muff, as if it were a cat on her lap. "You're tired," he said aloud and then whispered, with a sideways glance at the fat man in the corner, "You know how to pull the communication-cord?"

Suddenly, the train began to move. She flung open the

door with such suddenness that she hurt her shoulder. Both lost their heads. "Ah, careful, love!" she cried as he leapt out on the platform.

The train now tore them apart. She saw him lift his arm in farewell, his hand disappeared, and then the windows were blank with darkness.

"Cutting it a bit fine," said the man in the corner.

His accent was painfully impressive.

"Cold in here," he added; for she was shivering still.

"We put the heater on," she said. 'We!' she thought in a panic, and took up an evening-paper Vesey had pulled from his overcoat pocket.

"Cigarette?" The man offered a large gold case.

"No, thank you."

"You look tired."

Surprised, she glanced at him.

"Been to a show?"

"No."

She began to read her paper, making a great business of it, rustling and refolding and really settling to it.

"London's changed," he continued. "Very quiet round the pubs. I and a friend were in one or two to-night. No one speaks to you. Drinking in pairs, frightened to enlarge a round, so little money about. Not very sociable. Not unless one joins a club and then you pay through the nose. Been to the flicks?"

"No."

Harriet thought: 'If he moves, I shall pull the communication-cord.' She put such vehemence into her reading—without seeing one word of it—that he was silenced. Gradually, she relaxed. She began to go back over the evening—her waiting in Regent's Park, that dazzling scene with the brilliant water, movement, the flowers in the evening sun; the parrot in the sunlit bar; the restaurant with the seedy, shuffling waiters; the slow walk to the station; their clumsy farewell.

218

"How's old Charles?" the man in the corner suddenly asked.

Surprised, frightened, she looked at him again—a dressy man with beautifully polished shoes; full brown eyes and a little trimmed moustache; his features too small, too much in the middle of his round face with its heavy folds of flesh. So many men like him.

"Do I know you?" she asked in a vexed voice.

He crossed one knee over the other, brushed at his trousers with a careless hand. "Yes, dear." He stared at his swaying foot, smiling; enjoying this train-journey more than he had hoped. "Yes, we have met."

"I am bad at remembering people," she said aloofly.

"Perfectly okay. For my part, I never forget a face. Beckett's the name. Reggie Beckett."

"Oh, yes."

He took his hat from the rack. "I get out at the Golf Club," he explained. He came and stood by the door, close to her. "I must leave you with your memories." He opened the door and stood ready to jump down as the train slowed. "Don't worry, old dear," he said just before he slammed the door.

"Worry?"

"Not a word to Charles."

He winked gaily and nodded and disappeared.

"Well, there's one thing I am not and never have been, that's a charwoman," Mrs Curzon said firmly. "I said to her 'I'm a lady cleaner. That's what we call it in England, and that's how madam herself always thinks of me'."

"But, Curzy dear, I don't," Harriet protested. "I just think of you yourself."

"No, but in conversation to anyone you'd refer to me as 'Mrs Curzon, my lady cleaner'."

Harriet looked doubtful. "The truth is, I never know what anyone is." (When she had once referred to herself as

219

a shopgirl, Miss Brimpton had corrected her with 'sales-lady'.)

"Elke, for instance," said Mrs Curzon, "is a mother's help. That's what they call all them foreign girls. Now, what the devil are you up to, madam dear?"

"I was going to polish the mirrors."

"And can't I be asked to do it? What am I here for?"

"I asked Elke to do them yesterday when I was in London. I expect she forgot."

"Yes, I expect she conveniently forgot," Mrs Curzon said, breathing sarcastically upon a mirror. "I expect she eased it out of mind. When it comes to dodging things, she's as wide as Regent Street, no denial."

"I wonder if you should use a chamois-leather," Harriet said doubtfully.

"Oh, yes, finish it off with the shammy, of course," Mrs Curzon said promptly. She did not like to be told; 'but credit where credit's due,' she thought, 'she seldom interferes.'

"Did you have a nice time in London, madam?"

"Yes, very nice."

"Anything much in the shops?" Mrs Curzon asked condescendingly.

"Oh, I thought so."

"Things are coming back. I'm not Labour myself, madam, though Fred is, well before I met him I was, naturally, but you know what it is with his sort—jaw, jaw—'That's right, I said, we'll move out the chiffonier and stand a soap-box in its place' . . . 'the Union this, the Union that' . . . it gets you down, madam, straight. But I like to speak fairly and, no disrespect, things do begin to brighten up. Grumble, grumble, they do on the bus, mornings. 'What d'you expect with this lot in?' they say, the slightest thing goes wrong, like the bus late or the conductor giving them a bit of lip, which richly some of them deserves. I said the other morning 'Did the other lot give you so much as a bottle of cough-cure, let alone a set of teeth and such-like?' No, God judge me, madam, I like things set out fair, and when you see things coming back into the shops you must draw your own conclusions. Now what's worrying you, dear?"

"Nothing, Curzy. I shall polish these desk-handles while I'm in the mood. It's a fidgety job."

"And couldn't I do it for you?"

"You're doing the mirrors," Harriet said without irony. "And I must, after all, do something."

"You do too much. I said to Fred the other evening: 'Madam does far too much.' "

"And what did Fred say?" Harriet asked.

"He said: 'So you always say, Florrie. I'm sure she does,' he said. 'Not many like her from all I hear,' " Mrs Curzon improvised easily. " 'There's some,' he said, 'regards theirselves a cut above it, but not your madam apparently'— because I always speak as I find. You know that. I don't say anything I wouldn't say to your face. Well, you know me. Better just fetch the shammy now and give it the final."

Harriet, tidying her desk, tucked away papers neatly. Vesey's few letters she found, not where she had left them, not as she had left them, hidden and enfolded; but lying loosely upon some other papers and her first sight when she opened the drawer.

She sat quite still, hoping by her stillness to catch some memory unawares—a moment when she herself had left her letters where she now found them. But no such recollection overtook her. She felt that the discovery cancelled Charles's easy, reassuring behaviour on the night before. He was still up when she returned. She heard him, as she put the key in the lock, playing Schumann. With beautiful serenity, the sounds came flowing through the house to meet her. As she stood at the drawing-room door, he smiled and nodded as he played, as if he could not stop, or were playing for her benefit. Above the music, in a sleep-talking monotone, he asked: "Did you enjoy yourself?"

'I must,' she had thought, 'go over and put my hands on his shoulders.' His very playing asked her to do this. Still at the door, she said: "Yes, thank you."

A scream seemed to struggle up through her silence. Her lungs, withholding it, ached. Then he stopped playing and shut down the piano. He was cheerfully busy about the room. He poured a drink for her. Calm, bland, he asked no questions; made no enquiries after, for instance, Miss Lazenby. He lulled her to bed and there made love to her.

Now, she saw in this, not so much her own distress, as her knowledge of having been duped; one betrayal unfolded to reveal another. All of her treacheries, her husband had cynically observed. He watched her—until she seemed in her own eyes both deluded and delusive; fallacious; trumpery. No *woman*, she felt, could have bided her time, as he had.

She began to regard herself as an enormity, an outcast. She remembered Kitty's words; how she had thrown Madame Bovary in to prove her point. Certain that she wreaked ill on all who came near her, and would ruin her husband and her child, she seemed to herself to infect, to contaminate society, whose rules she had never before been tempted to break; which, with the extra spur of her natural inadequacy, she had, in fact, strengthened and maintained.

When she married Charles, she had seemed to wed also a social order. A convert to it, and to provincial life, and keeping-house, she had pursued it fanatically and as if she feared censure. No one had entertained more methodically, or better bolstered up social interplay. She had been indefatigible in writing letters of condolence, telegrams of congratulation; remembered birthdays and anniversaries; remembered bread-and-butter letters and telephone-messages after parties. She had tried to do everything right for her daughter; had never missed a speech-day or an end-of-term concert; had talked to form-mistresses and shown interest, as they themselves put it.

But now she flouted what she had helped to create—an

illusion of society; an oiling of wheels which went round but not forwards; conventions which could only exist so long as emotion was in abeyance.

'But I am not the first, or last, woman, to fall in love with someone not her husband,' she thought despairingly. She wanted not to feel monstrous, or abnormal. But there was no safety in numbers. She could only think of women who, in the name of love, brought down great harm on others and died in poverty and solitude or even—such was her anxiety— on the gallows. But ordinary women, the women who sat in tea-shops drinking coffee in the mornings, these kept their lives within bounds. They did not let loose suspicion and deceit in their homes. 'But I do not know where to turn,' she suddenly thought, and put her hands over her eyes and brow.

"Madame ducky, what's up?" Mrs Curzon asked. She dropped the chamois-leather and put her arm about Harriet.

'I cannot be so *bad*,' Harriet thought, 'not so through-and-through bad; for Curzy loves me and she is a good woman. Unless I delude her, too.'

"What is it, lovie?"

"I have a headache."

"Go and have a lay-down and I'll bring you up something. London never suits me, either. My daughter up there—well Hammersmith—she gave one of those cocktail-parties. I wish you'd seen it—port, brandy, lovely ham-sandwiches. Well, next thing, I'm sitting on the lavatory singing. No, I felt bad, straight. Never again. Fred was wild. 'If there's one thing gives me the creeps,' he said, 'it's a woman had a drop too much.' How I come to work next morning I don't know. I kept thinking 'No more London for you, Florrie!' I like a nice drink with the rest, but I like it steady. When we go up to The Jockey darts' nights I always reckon to enjoy myself; but steady. A nice laugh, only no one out of hand. I always think if you stick to gin-and-french . . . you ought to do that, madam, you won't go far wrong.

Then, of course, a Guinness is nice shopping. . . ."

"Curzy, if you will let me get a word in, I will say that my headache is nothing to do with getting drunk. . . ."

"All the same, dear, you want to lie down. I'm sure the master would say the same."

"I'm better now."

"Shall I make a cup of tea?" Mrs Curzon asked hopefully.

"Yes, yes, do that."

When she was alone, she tore the letters across and dropped them on the fire. "Keep nothing," Vesey had said. "If that is all you have, you have nothing."

Betsy, from a turret window, watched the other girls going home. She could hear their bicycle-wheels on the loose gravel and car doors slamming. When at last they were all gone, out-of-sight beyond the budding trees in the avenue, the school seemed an echoing shaft at the foot of which the caretaker tramped the stone passages, bucket-handles clanked and sharp voices rose from the kitchen. The rosy sunset was absorbed by the rosy brick school building, castellated, machicolated, in the Edwardian style. Mullioned windows flashed ruby. Glossy poplars shimmered.

The turret was one corner of the Science Room. All round, on windowsills, tadpoles darted in weedy tanks, frog-spawn floated, bleached shoots edged out of splitting chest-nuts. Against the walls were what Betsy thought of as merely curious contraptions—tubes of glass and rubber and flasks of coloured liquids. Nothing here touched her imagination. She had spent tedious and unprofitable hours sitting before a balance with tweezers and paper-thin weights. She could not bear to be so accurate that a thumb-print or a fleck of dust might affect, as she was warned, her calculations.

She loved the personal, the particular, to adore and to be herself adored. But here, in this room, she was the protagonist of no drama. The cold compiling of facts had so little emotional appeal. The search for truth was the

224

bleakest pursuit. At one end of the scale were the over-large personalities, the clash of wills, which she read about in Greek. Even at her faltering stage of learning she grasped, and was quickened by, the thrust and colour of this drama. Her inaccuracy was but a racing-on. At the other end of the scale were this neat room; and precision; the tadpoles, all alike; and the book full of figures and diagrams which she now sat down to study.

She bowed her head over the book, but was not learning. It seemed beyond her now to bend her mind to anything but thoughts of Vesey and her mother. The figure of Vesey himself, she exploited in her imagination; she tracked him down and fastened to him. She pursued him in any way she could, ransacking her mother's desk for letters, importuning her with oblique questions, sifting evidence.

At some moments she felt shocked and afraid at the way her thoughts ran on; at other moments, only bitterly excluded. But at all times Vesey obsessed her. When she read them, she felt that his letters—attenuated, allusive as they were—by-passed her mother and were meant for her.

She was separated from her family and friends by the very enormity of the thoughts which haunted and burdened her. She had forgotten her life before she had such thoughts and she did not want to be deprived of them; she could not return to the days in which there had only been Miss Bell, and she believed that with her new love and knowledge she would play some momentous rôle.

In the light of this idea, her lessons seemed trivial; but the punishments which fell upon her isolated her more. Shut in after school, as the day faded and familiar sounds receded, she felt a solitariness more profound than she had imagined possible. 'For make no mistake,' she warned herself, 'we are all alone. There is no one going along beside us.' This seemed a horrifying discovery to have made; as horrifying as to see for the first time that there is not always justice in the world. Lately, she had been made, by her companions, to

225

feel beyond the pale. Even Pauline had fallen from dark comments into silence. There were limits to rebellion, she said, as there were limits to compliance. One can be as embarrassing or irritating as the other. And Betsy had made too swift a descent. "No one's perfect, I'm not myself," Pauline had said generously; but she was tired, she implied, of championing her friend. Altogether tired. "I can't understand you," she despaired: and Betsy could believe that no one would. What now went on in her head was so different from other things which they had shared—religion, for instance (they had been confirmed together), and literature. Both had fallen in love with Lord Nelson. Then, later, with Edgar Allan Poe. Later still, with Robert Helpman. Pauline had not shared the enthusiasm for Miss Bell, as she leaned herself more towards adoration of Miss Beetlestone; but both had agreed that the feelings they experienced were different from, and more serious than, the absurd deliriums of other girls.

Her eyes were on the page while she thought. When she shut them, she could see white diagrams printed on darkness. She had looked so hard, and seen nothing. 'I shall never learn it,' she thought. Each time she made an effort to bend her mind to the lesson, her mind, like a threatened creature, wrenched itself free. She wondered what climax could put an end to it; imagined running away, lowering herself out of the turret-window on a string of dust-sheets. She fidgeted with a gas-tap at the edge of the bench, leaned down and breathed the gas. 'The only time when we aren't lonely is when we're dead,' she suddenly thought. 'Then we can't be.' The gas made a hissing sound. She was just going to turn it off when Miss Bell opened the door.

Meaning only to open the door, to give her message and go, Miss Bell leant into the room, with her arms, as usual, full of books.

"What are you doing, Betsy?"

She came in and shut the door. "Turn off that gas at

226

once. Surely you mayn't touch those things?" She spoke, from the Classical side, with an aloof contempt. "What are you supposed to be doing?"

"Returned work," Betsy said flatly.

"Yes, I had a message from Miss Smythe, that you may go home now. It distresses me that you should be here at all."

"Oh, I am always in trouble," Betsy said lightly.

" 'Always' is not an excuse," Miss Bell said, leaning against the door. " 'Always' makes matters worse; not better, as you imply."

Betsy thought, bowing her head over the bench, swinging her legs from the high stool: 'Surely, when matters become so bad, one cannot any longer be held responsible?'

"You cannot take refuge in 'always' and 'worse-and-worse'. It is all in yourself, of course; nothing from outside. And if you were not staying in for Miss Smythe, you would certainly be staying in for me. The work you handed in this morning was an insult, I thought. An insult to both of us. Perhaps you intended it to be."

"No."

"It was third-rate work; and you are not a third-rate person."

The figures in the book slanted away and tears ached in her eyes. She put her hand up at the side of her face to hide them.

"You had better go home," Miss Bell said coldly. But Betsy could not stir, nor take away her hand. "Or your mother will be anxious."

At that, Miss Bell could see the tears rolling down the girl's wrist, into her rather grubby cuff. The things she did for other people's good always dismayed her. Because it was not her instinct to be harsh, she was harsher than ever. The means, she believed, justified the ends; but that is a doctrine in which our instincts are often terribly defied. Her impulse now was to take the girl in her arms; but her training would not allow it, and her arms were, in any case, full of

227

books. She did, however, hand over a clean handkerchief;
for Betsy was struggling to manage with her sleeve.

The handkerchief finally defeated her. She put her head
down on her arms and tears soaked into her blouse and all
over her chemistry book. Her hair parted untidily at the
nape of her neck and dropped forwards; her shoulder-blades
stuck out like wings. Miss Bell put down her books at last
and laid her hand on Betsy's arm.

"What has happened?" she asked. "I have to be harsh
with you, although it is the worst part of being a school-
mistress. Unless you take yourself in hand, you will never
pass your exam. I had great hopes for you, you see. I hadn't
for anybody else. If you could only tell me what is
wrong . . ."

"But I couldn't."

"Perhaps you are in trouble at home?" 'She is certainly in
trouble here,' Miss Bell thought, wondering how trouble
elsewhere could explain or simplify matters.

The real *trouble* with Betsy, at her age, was that nothing was
explicable, even to herself. When she wept, it was from
confusion. Her ravelled emotions fatigued her. She was
overwrought from uncertainty, more than from any specific
cause.

Dragging confidences from those who wish in the end—but
in the end—to tell, requires patience. Miss Bell sat down on
a stool and wound her wrist-watch, while she thought of
questions she could ask.

"Have you quarrelled with your friends?"

"I have no friends," Betsy said reprovingly.

"You and Pauline, I thought . . ."

"Pauline *loathes* me."

"Well, you and I were good friends, I always believed.
And I think you should talk to me. . . ."

"Yes, only I don't know what to say."

"Whatever comes into your head . . . it could be sorted
out later, if necessary."

228

"Yes, only I don't know where to start."

"Start at the last thing you can remember and go backwards. I will try my hardest to follow. If you could just be not too long. I think your mother may begin to worry for you. . . ."

"Oh, she won't do that. Nor care." At the moment, Betsy believed it to be true.

Miss Bell cast warily about for something to say.

"She only thinks of Vesey. . . ."

"Vesey?"

"I told you about him . . . you remember, in *Hamlet* that time. . . ."

"Oh, yes."

"My mother goes to London, to see him."

"Yes, you told me they were old friends."

"I think of him all the time." Betsy glanced down at the Chemistry book, as if that would prove the truth of her words. She brushed tears from the page. "When he came to the house, I was sent to bed. I leant over the banisters and watched him go. It didn't seem to matter at the time; but, later, I realised how sad I'd been. When I look back on it, I realise how I felt. I never seem to know things at the time, because then I only feel excited."

"Do stop fidgeting with that gas-tap, Betsy."

"I'm sorry."

"What are you going to do with your life if you are to be at the beck and call of your emotions in this way? If you are like this at fifteen . . . sixteen . . . whichever you may be —what will twenty-five and thirty be like?"

"Thirty?" Betsy said, dismayed.

"You must learn now, before it is too late. Hard work is a great stand-by. You throw it to one side, instead of making use of it."

She had always found her own support in work—not for the turning aside of obsessions (she never was obsessed); but in saving her pride and covering her loneliness. Betsy's state

229

of mind alarmed her. She was anxious for her present and her future. She could not pass off these revelations with Miss Anstruther's easy formulae—"one doesn't," "one is not," "one mayn't". From fondness of the girl, she would have liked to protect her from those conventional phrases; but she suffered from a strange caution fostered by her failure at human-relationships and a reluctance to be shocked or jolted from the neat life she had planned for herself. She was not often at a loss to know how to behave rightly. She had found convention not often at war with her conscience and was brave enough to act according to her conscience if it were. This afternoon, the issue seemed more confused. Her heart and head did not run in unison; her conscience was silent. She felt that she should listen to all the girl had to say; yet was at the same time unwilling for her even to have out her cry, lest the door should open upon Miss Anstruther with her "one was rather surprised" look. It would seem— for Betsy's confidence would be respected and concealed— that she was comforting the victim of another mistress's detention.

Now, checked and dry-eyed, though tear-stained, Betsy stared before her. Her forsaken look was pitiable.

"I will wash this handkerchief," she said quietly. "Thank you for lending it to me." She spoke as if there were nothing more to be gained by words, with the touch of pride of one who has been offered help and then rejected.

"Don't you understand," Miss Bell said desperately, "that no one in the world can really help you, but you yourself? You must not be such a slave to your feelings. They're more than strong enough for you to manage, without all this extra embroidery. You said yourself, that it was *afterwards*, not at the time, that you were so overcome, that you felt so . . . bereft," she concluded, a little surprised at the word, which she had used before only in translating Greek. Andromache, Hecuba; but scarcely Betsy Jephcott.

"That was before I knew."

230

"Knew what?"

"That he is really my father."

Betsy gave her a terrified half-glance. 'It is out,' she thought. 'It is settled now.' Once it was in words there could be no more uncertainty.

Miss Bell was lost in the strange landscape which unrolled before her eyes. All of Miss Anstruther's phrases came into her mind, and she could see the use of them. They drew decent veils, they warned away reality.

"You do realise what you are saying——?"

"Yes, of course."

"Don't cry again."

"I am so alone. I don't know what I am supposed to do, or be, or what will happen to me. . . ."

"What reason have you for saying such a thing? I mean, I suppose you *have* a reason?"

"I read some letters."

"You should never read other people's letters," Miss Bell said mechanically. "It is a grave thing to say. I think you have been mistaken."

Betsy was sure now. She believed wholly what had been a vague conjecture. She was at peace.

Miss Bell had been brought up in poor respectability. Miss Anstruther's girls were brought up in well-to-do respectability. Harriet had been the one mother above others on whom Miss Bell had pinned faith, the one who had listened, discussed, encouraged. Betsy's work had reflected the solid worth of her environment. If the environment fell to pieces, then her work must also. The flesh, the devil, came close to Miss Bell; nudged her. Loneliness she understood: fear she understood. She did not expect others to be as brave as she had had to be herself. Pity over-rode her. She took Betsy in her arms; as Harriet never did. She comforted her; as Harriet would not have dared. Her eyes felt congested with tears.

"You must never tell anyone what you have told me," she

231

said in her clipped, authoritative voice. "That will be the consequence of learning things you were not meant to know. But I will always help you, if I can. And I shall be thinking of you, though you may sometimes doubt it—for I must always be impartial. When you need me, I am here." She smoothed Betsy's tangled hair. "And if you try, if you work, and overcome your . . . difficulties, I shall know. You will know that I secretly applaud."

Betsy, with one of her grandmother's gestures, which, if Miss Bell could have recognised it, would have cancelled out all that had been said, put her wrist against her throbbing brow.

That looks are inherited none dispute. Character goes down the years. Temperament is handed on. Genius skips from one generation to another, crops up strangely. That gestures should do so is strangest of all. More strangely betraying, they are also more miraculous: they hold the significance and the wonder of human personality. The way in which a hand is lifted in farewell, may have been learnt, determined, unfolded, in the womb.

3

In the summer, Vesey went to the seaside in a play. Far from Harriet, he could only write to her. She hid the letters about for a day or two and then destroyed them when they were learnt by heart.

In the heat, Vesey flagged. The large resort seemed to exhaust itself with its own noise—the military-band on the promenade playing 'The Two Pigeons'; the sea behind; the peevish gulls above; and, against the reedy trills, the clashing pom-poms, people's inextricable voices running on and the slow, slow scuffle of their feet along the hot asphalt; and children crying. The streets were congested; even the shops flowed out on to the pavement with bunches of wooden spades and canvas shoes; piles of buckets; revolving stands of picture post-cards.

He stayed in one of the boarding-houses which went off at right-angles to the promenade. In the bay-window a table could be seen set out with engraved tumblers and napkins folded like fleurs-de-lys. The hydrangea by the front door faded through innumerable shades of blue. Between the outer door and the glass hall-door sometimes crabs languished in buckets. Children forgot their vague purpose in bringing them there and, when next they needed the buckets, found the poor creatures dead in an inch or two of cloudy, rusty water. "What a horrid smell!" their mothers said.

On Saturdays the fresh intake arrived. Vesey would watch gloomily. The nice silence, the whispering first meal would soon be exchanged, he knew, for what could only be called larking about. The young men in blazers would soon

233

be making apple-pie beds and suggestive remarks. Catch-words from the wireless were the common coinage of their talk. Precocious children joined in these exchanges and were exhibited. Mothers grew tireder as the holiday went on and thought of the piles of dirty clothes in the trunk upstairs.

Vesey did not wholly escape the exuberance. For him, it was the background of the entire summer, not only a fortnight. People, thinking him lonely, drew him into their conversation. Sometimes girls tried to coax him out on the front steps for a photograph. When cheery men hit him across the shoulders as they came into the dining-room, he tried not to cough. He wondered how all their spirits were kept up at such a level. They behaved as if they were drunk, he thought; but drink did not enter into their lives. Only once or twice in the summer two husbands might chum up and slip out for a light ale while their wives were tidying the children for lunch. The strangeness of this could be judged from the wives' level looks above the children's heads as they bent to tie on bibs or cut their food. A chill was on the air.

The younger ones mystified Vesey. He did not know how people could behave so badly unless in the last stages of inebriation. "I love only the gaiety of those who can be grave," he wrote to Harriet. "The other side to this is just low spirits. You would pour cool scorn, holding your lovely head high."

In an arcade, echoing, crowded, smelling of old newspapers and the damp sand that was trodden in, he bought a box stuck all over with little yellow shells like grains of maize. On his way home, he saw that he could never send it to her and he felt foolish and baffled. His joke became pathetic, as had other jokes between them.

He began to realise that neglect lay deep in him, too deeply to be eradicated now—neglect of his friends (for he had not made the social effort), his life, his love, his body. It was not his nature to be sorry for himself; but he wondered how he had come to make such a wry thing of his life. At school, masters had criticised what they called his attitude. Casting round for an attitude, though, he had found only blankness. 'Of course, my mother was a bad lot,' he thought, 'but I can't blame her. She was always very nice to me.'

In the afternoons, he sat slackly on one of the iron seats which seemed to have grown laboriously out of the asphalt of the promenade, as the shrubs grew out of the baked earth of the ornamental gardens behind him. He felt invalidish and apart, watching the people on the sands below him. All afternoon the light would turn slowly round, making small alterations to the appearance of the scene. He became fascinated by the reddened, blistered youths and the strapping girls who sparred about and slapped at one another; the physical repartee entranced him; the unavailing struggle. "Oh, you *are!*" the girls would cry, victorious in their defeat, sprawled out and spattered with sand. Near-by, a nun with her thin face bowed under a complicated coif waited while the orphanage boys, wearing too many clothes, walked at the sea's-edge, their boots dangling over their shoulders. Children built sand-castles, each his own separate castle, sitting back-to-back, talking in busy, rapid sentences, bickering as they patted the sand with little spades. Alone, away from them, a baby sat, making jerky, aimless movements with his arms. He raised his fists and sand flew away out of his closed hands. At tea-time, food came out of baskets, paste-sandwiches, greengages with broken skins, shrimps; even parcels of fish-and-chips, cooling, and dripping vinegar. Little boys would begin to grizzle, holding themselves tightly between their legs. "You *would!*" mother would grumble. Father would look in-differently at the sea.

Sometimes, depressed almost to nausea, he rejected it all: at other times, his heart was unbearably touched. In the evenings, as he walked to the theatre, the trodden sands, the empty deck-chairs at different angles, some in pairs, turned towards one another, set a scene for a ghostly conversation-

235

piece. He became conscious again of the sea turning over.
When he left the theatre it was dark; then the sound of the
sea muffled all others: it dragged without mercy at the sand
and shingle: a long way up the coast a lighthouse ticked off
the seconds. He thought of Harriet as he walked home. He
seemed to have wasted their lives.

In the morning, the rowdy young people, the whining
children, the so persistently funny men, would infuriate him,
so that life seemed a mean and gibbering charade; but then at
night or in the evening his mood would soften. Somehow
linked with Harriet were the empty chairs. The attendant
who folded and stacked them seemed a symbolic figure,
shadowy, Lethean; he erased the day and all remembrance of
it.

In a café one afternoon, he saw a little girl who reminded
him of Harriet as a child. Her long hair straggled over her
shoulders, her thin arms were covered by a tight jersey. She
sat at a table with her father and two younger children.
When the tea was brought, her father nodded at her with a
casual and flattering gesture. Colour rode up in her cheeks.
She stood up and lifted the tea-pot with two hands. Vesey
could see that the father, so apparently relaxed, was ready to
spring to her rescue. The wobbly stream of tea descended
into his cup. He took it from her with careless thanks. She
smiled. She shone with relief. "This is my first time," she
said, "of pouring out." Vesey looked away. He felt a
personal guilt towards the grave, successful and beloved little
girl, besides a tardy guilt towards Harriet. 'Love is not
difficult,' he thought. In the child's father it had seemed the
simplest thing, as was the expression of it. He began to hope
that the mother was merely resting for the afternoon, and not
dead. But having seen so much happiness, he desired more.
He imagined the mother at home in child-birth. "I will take
the children out to tea," the husband had said. When they
returned, he would run upstairs. He would be excited, not
anxious, over his fourth child. He would call to his daughter

236

to come and see. Going sedately upstairs, with her self-conscious little smile, she would imagine a wonderful future, not just pouring out tea, but of pushing prams, of straightening the baby every yard or so and plumping up his pillow, so that he would be a credit to her. 'But perhaps after all the mother is dead,' he thought, as he paid his bill. 'Perhaps it is their first holiday without her. He is trying hard: and succeeding much better than those who think they have no need to try.'

Through the summer, Harriet lived at peace without Vesey, and could have lived a long time thus, she thought, serene in her indecisiveness, freed from the machinery of deceit. His letters flurried her, so that each morning when there was none—and sometimes weeks passed without—her relief was stronger than her disappointment. The future was a foreign country.

She found, though, that love was a disorganising element. Dropped into their midst, it had the power of upsetting other relationships, so that she felt emphasis shifted all about her, as if her world had slipped; as if a general subsidence had taken place. No one was the same. Charles was polite, evasive, Betsy moody and uncontrolled.

Harriet began to hope that the change was only in herself, that she had become morbidly attuned to the inclinations of other people. She hoped that Kitty's anxious—and Julia's malicious—watchfulness were quite imaginary. Tiny, even, behaved differently. She had often heard and read that to be loved has some infection in it; but it was repulsive to her that this should account for all his new attentions. His suddenly intimate manner worried her and she could only fancy that Reggie Beckett had told his story well. At times, her anxieties would seem an hallucination—when, for instance, she entered the tea-shop where her friends gathered for their morning coffee and thought that a silence fell, and at Betsy's Speech Day, when Miss Bell seemed so palpably to avoid

237

her, and reddened as she met her glance. 'It is a sort of mania,' she told herself, 'to hear whisperings, to feel oneself the centre of conjecture, and persecuted.' But in such ways provincial life cracks and collapses about the individual. She had seen it happen to others, and was afraid. She felt, too, that she was at the mercy of those who were worse than herself, who merited ostracism, as she did not; but there was no comfort in defiance and she found that, in practice, she tended to propitiate. When she and the other women discussed recipes, children's ailments, clothes, she entered in, and offered up, with forced enthusiasm. "It is all my world!" she seemed to declare. "To make a really spongy sponge-cake my whole ambition!" When she reached home, she would despise herself, and idly wondered if any of the others were playing the same game.

Betsy's strained manner persisted after she had brilliantly passed her exam. Her rebellious attitude towards Charles, her sulkiness, had been accounted for—successively—by over-work, late nights, anxiety, too much excitement, too little fun, re-action, growing too fast, and perhaps a deficiency in iron. But success and praise, even an iron-tonic, wrought no change. Her manner was put down, at last, as a passing phase. Harriet would have discussed the problem with Miss Bell, if Miss Bell had not been always walking in a different direction.

'It is true,' she reflected, 'that we are all members one of another. When one man falls, he takes others down in his arms.'

"If Tiny goes west, we do, too," Charles said. "Whatever silliness he may be up to will have its repercussions on our livelihood."

Harriet thought: 'Men say "livelihood". Women say "lives".' "Livelihood" was only half-threatening, she felt. It seemed only to mean that they would be poorer. The strictest economy. No *bought* flowers. She said good-bye to

238

Mrs Curzon in tears, but Mrs Curzon would not go. "It isn't the money, madam dear," she wept. "It was for better or worse between us two right from the word go."

"Harriet, dear, there is no need to cry! It is at the moment only the dreariest suspicion."

"Oh, it isn't that. You know how I am. I was thinking of Mrs Curzon."

Charles put one knee on the piano-stool and struck an arpeggio or two, as if limbering his patience as well as his fingers.

"Please tell me!" Harriet pleaded.

"What is the use, when you scarcely listen? Young though you may be compared with me, you are still too old to be this exasperating child-wife you sometimes affect. You make me feel like Carlyle."

"My thoughts run on too quickly. Mrs Curzon was really connected with our ruin. . . ."

"Ruin? Oh, Harriet!"

He played the scale of C Major, his eyes shut, his head bowed. Then a chord. Then he shut the piano.

"Ruin? You see how you romanticise! There's no ruin. There's perhaps a loss of pride, a falling-off of confidence, so consequently a falling-off of income. Mean little economics, such as I despise. Perhaps sell the piano," he added, with impressive nobility—for he was the only one who ever played it. Harriet thought: 'Very well! I was only saying good-bye to Mrs Curzon, as you are to the piano.'

"But what makes you suspect Tiny?" she asked dutifully.

"You know I think that he and Reggie Beckett make schemes. . . ."

Her mind swerved at the name. "Yes, I remember you said so."

"When I go into Tiny's office, Reggie is always sprawling there on a chair. . . . 'Just popped in for a cuppa,' he says—he has all those mannerisms of speech . . . or they are talking about racing . . . the place blue with smoke . . .

239

how any work gets done. . . . Once or twice I've seen clients I always dealt with myself by-passing my office and disappearing into Tiny's. Just dropped in for a cuppa too, I suppose. I might as well pack up and open a café. If I question Tiny, he becomes so painfully evasive that I find myself embarrassed too. I have half a mind to tackle Reggie himself before it is too late, if it isn't too late already. I feel like taking him by the scruff of the neck and dropping him out into the street."

"I don't think I should," Harriet said quickly. The less Charles confronted Reggie, the better. To do so in anger might loosen his tongue dangerously.

"Can you imagine me? But whether Tiny likes it or not, I shall tell him to spend less time with us . . . difficult to be really unpleasant, though, I suppose. . . . I meet him in a bar and he insists on buying me a drink. I can't refuse, and then I have to buy him one back . . . always these awkwardnesses in a little town. It isn't easy to be ruthless, and having enemies is embarrassing for everybody. If only Tiny didn't so want to get rich quickly . . . to get rich, I mean. Kitty gets greedier as she grows older. And lazier. It takes some living up to on an ordinary income . . . if she is never to do a hand's-turn in the house . . sit about eating Turkish-delight all day and reading *Vogue* . . . and her grand schemes for Ricky. . . . He's as bad . . . utterly spoilt. In many ways I am sorry for Tiny, saddled with them both."

"Kitty thinks Betsy is spoilt."

"All children are spoilt," Charles said impatiently, not to be side-tracked by *that* argument.

Miss Bell had nowhere to go in the holidays. She stayed on in her bed-sitting-room and saved her money. Next year, she hoped to go on a tour of Greece, which she scarcely apprehended as geographical; but rather as some shifting image in the air, to which the Hellenic Society would magically convey her. Since Miss Anstruther had given her a term's notice, however, the image had receded. She had never really believed that she would go.

The holidays seemed long to her. She made little treats for herself—a day's walking, bus-rides, lunch in a café. She wondered if the girls at the library despised her for changing her book so often. Sometimes she saw Betsy at church.

"You should ask her to tea," Harriet said.

"Oh, she wouldn't come."

"Why not?"

"She said once that she hates going out to tea."

"To have sherry with us before supper then. . . ."

"Oh, no, she doesn't drink."

"You seem to have all her habits by heart."

Harriet felt the poor young woman's loneliness. She had seen her sitting alone in the café, though Miss Bell would not catch her eye.

One Sunday evening, Betsy walked home from church with her. It had been a heavy and colourless day. Winter never has such a darkness as this day had had with its obliterating leaves. The pavements were gritty and hedges dusty. Winged seeds lay in the gutters under the sycamore trees. Women sat at upstairs windows, slackly watching the passers-by. The air seemed caught up with the suspense of waiting for rain, and nothing could allay Miss Bell's ennui and depression. She had tried all the afternoon to walk it off but it trotted along at her side like some unwanted dog. All she could hope for now was to begin a better day to-morrow. Even conversation with Betsy was an effort.

"I daresay they were pleased with you at home about your examination?"

"Oh, they were pleased enough," Betsy said grudgingly.

"Well, I was very pleased. I was pleased with your work, and that you had the character to do it."

To this, Betsy could find no answer. She made an ungracious, scoffing sound.

Miss Bell said, in an off-hand way: "I am leaving at the

241

end of next term. The other girls won't know for a time. Perhaps you'd keep it to yourself until they do."

Betsy whitened and then frowned. "You can't," she suddenly said.

"I am afraid it is rather disappointing."

"How *could* you? What can I do? What will happen to me?"

"You'll be all right now."

"I won't be. I'm not. I can't ever be left on my own like that. Why? Why must you?"

"I think I should make a change."

"Where are you going then?"

Miss Bell stared ahead of her at the long, deserted street which appeared as dull as her own future.

"I don't know."

Betsy walked on in a stubborn silence.

"I know I can trust you," Miss Bell said. "None of the others must know. . . . I have no choice, you see. Miss Anstruther has asked me to—to make a change."

"Why should she?"

"Learning and teaching are two different things. I could learn, but I cannot teach; so there is nothing I can do with what I know."

"You taught me everything."

"But the others learnt nothing, and you would have done as well, or better, with someone else . . . the results were bad and discipline worse . . . you know yourself how noisy the classes have sometimes been. . . ."

"But I didn't guess . . . if we had known . . . I wish I had made them stop . . . but sometimes I was as bad myself. How can you forgive us?"

"Easily. There is scarcely anything to forgive. You only took advantage of a fault that was in me. Girls don't respect learning. It was all I had."

She would not say that Miss Anstruther had complained of Betsy's high marks—"not that one is never satisfied . . .

242

but a better *average* result . . . one doesn't care to see favourites made . . . and it has been bad for the girl's nerves. Never concentrate on one child to the exclusion of the others. . . ."

One afternoon Betsy was seen leaving school late, red-eyed: Miss Bell soon after. Miss Anstruther liked to have her girls going about the school safely in droves and was annoyed that one should be seen in the town with a swollen face and wearing the school hat-band.

"But if you aren't good at teaching here, why should you be better at it somewhere else?" Betsy asked, brutal in her dismay.

Miss Bell gave a faint, prim smile. "I must put more into it next time, I can see that." 'And will never grow fond of any of them,' she thought.

4

At the sight of the room, Harriet felt a dismay so private, so profound that she could scarcely breathe: it was a fit culmination to such a journey; a destiny, as well as a destination.

An ancient gas-fire stood in front of a coal-grate, without concealing the litter of match-sticks and cigarette-ends behind. She found a shilling for the slot and put a match between the broken ribs, but she felt that for all the blue, roaring light that shot upwards the room would never warm.

She knelt on the mangy rug and shivered, certain that not Vesey or anybody else would ever be able to stop her doing so.

The meeting with him after so many months had been a pain in itself; the first shock of non-recognition, and his altered looks. She had thrown her suitcase into the back of his borrowed car with a shamed self-consciousness. "It is all so awkward and premeditated," she apologised.

"It certainly could not have been *more* premeditated," Vesey said. "Or not, at least, by me."

He was a bad driver. She began to wonder how often he had done it before, he so quickened his pace at corners as if to get round them quickly. She held to the side of the car and thought how sad and humiliating it would be for Charles if she were killed in such circumstances. "I haven't much petrol," Vesey said. "In which direction have you fewest friends? Berkshire? Oxfordshire?"

"All my relations live in Oxfordshire, and Charles has friends in Reading."

"Surrey?"

"Surrey would be lovely. There is only Aunt Ethel at Camberley, and she is bed-ridden."

It had begun to rain. When they stopped for a drink, he ordered large ones as if in despair. She noticed his shortness of breath, his fagged look. Worry seemed to lie down in her like a tired animal.

"Well, Harriet, cheer up. Surely with such wickedness in mind, you should be gayer?"

"I think you look ill, Vesey."

"Yes, I had 'flu."

"How long ago?"

"I think it was about yesterday," he said carelessly.

A drizzling rain veiled the countryside. As they drove on, the architecture grew more depressing, thrusting out gables and turrets amongst monkey-puzzle trees and laurels.

A great insistence on private-property spread about a rash of white notices. In every copse, trespassers were warned; every bank of rhododendrons was protected; little patches of grass were enclosed with posts and swinging chains; public-houses united in an onslaught of hostility to charabancs. Little teashops called 'Pantries' or 'Kitchens' abounded. It could not have been more disenchanting. Vesey was nervous for her: she, for Vesey. Both dreaded the other's depression.

Crouching over the gas-fire, she was near to tears, and felt that soon she would be nearer. To steady herself, she began to walk about the room. At every step she took, the great wardrobe creaked. She could see herself in its filmed mirror; anxious; tense; her hands clasping her elbows tightly; her shoulders hunched up. She saw so clearly that her youth was gone. Her body had bloomed and had faded. She brought to Vesey all the signs of middle-age, the blurred outlines and the dullness of the flesh. She thought of undressing at night, her waist pinched, her sides creased and reddened from her corset; the brightness of girlhood softened, dimmed.

245

When Vesey came in, she could not glance at him, but kept her eyes on the fire and her hands spread out before it. She was afraid lest he should mention signing the hotel register or discuss plans. She was conscious of a curious dichotomy, and felt that one half of her must shield the more sensitive: her mind spoke with both a brutal voice and with pleading.

Vesey sat in one of the uncurling wicker-chairs and stared at her.

"It is a funny place," he said. "Or I hope it is funny. If you could see the funny side of it, Harriet, it would be a great help to both of us. That long laurel drive tempted us here. We thought we should be hidden and safe here, just because it lay well back from the road."

Harriet began to walk about the room.

"We are behaving with infinite absurdity," Vesey said. "Why?"

"We are frightened of one another."

"If Charles telephones, I shall say I was at Kitty's. . . ."

She pushed open a window and looked down into the garden. Rain fell loudly on the laurels. Below were some wet bushes with soft white fruit like camphor-balls all over them. She could hear cars swishing past on the main road. It was a dead part of the day and seemed to be no time at all.

"How different when we were young," Vesey said. "We never had weather like this . . ."

"I walked past Caroline's house in the summer. There were new people there. They had painted it outside and mended the fence. Different curtains seemed strange . . . it was all somehow snubbing and upsetting . . . people always seem bumptious and inconsiderate when they move into someone else's house . . . I mean, a house where someone else has lived a long time."

"Every lick of paint is a reproach," Vesey agreed. "Darling, I am going to take you home again."

She turned away from the window and stared at him.

246

"You don't really want to stay, do you?" he asked.

"I'm sorry, Vesey. Oh, I am only nervy. It has been so difficult to arrange. I kept thinking that at the last moment Charles wouldn't go: Betsy would come back too early; or Elke. There were so many things that could go wrong. . . ."

"There still are, you think."

She sat on the edge of the bed, and looked so disconsolate that he went over and sat beside her.

"If only we were young again!" she said in a tired voice. "And might have a second chance."

"I think perhaps this is supposed to be it," he said doubtfully.

"There aren't second chances; except by ruining other people. . . ."

"Someone has to be ruined."

"I can't choose that it shall be someone else."

"I hate self-sacrifice. Of all things, I suspect it most."

"That's just the sort of thing people say."

"This pink, sooty bedroom doesn't help us," he tried to comfort her. "All the same, I won't allow you to stay. I don't know how I ever thought I could. I just wanted to have you till the last moment."

"I don't know what you mean by 'the last moment'. "

"Dear Harriet, I'm going away. My father is sending me to South Africa."

"To South Africa!"

"You may well be amazed. I used to say it would be the last place I would go to; I do hope that's not so. My father, of course, is naturally inclined to such a business-man's paradise and to those squalid politics. When I see other people treated badly, I shall begin to be glad that he was not much worse to me than he was."

"This isn't true!"

"Yes."

"Then why tell me only now?"

"This week-end is too great a risk to run, for someone who

247

must go away so soon. Even I find I cannot allow you to throw away so much, for nothing."

"I didn't know you'd seen your father. Are you so ill?"

"The part I thought I might get, I didn't get. Yes, I am rather ill. I hope I seem pathetic to you. I hope I arouse your maternal instincts. . . ."

"You see, you don't wear enough clothes." Trying to convince them both that his negligence alone was the cause of his illness, she laid her hands against his thin shirt and could feel his warm chest through it. "October, and you have no vest! How could you, Vesey? And you are always catching cold. You worry me so very much. But I simply can't believe that you will go away."

"Suppose Charles telephoned to-night and you were not there; and returned home, and you were not there. What would happen to you then? If he found out about us being here in this horrid room?"

"Don't frighten me!"

"When I have to go away, and have nothing to offer, and cannot look after you, I mustn't endanger what little you have. That would have been clear long ago to an honourable person. And now even I have caught the idea. . . ."

"Please stop saying 'even I'. Both you and I decide things . . . decided this. . . ."

"I have nothing to lose."

"We shall never be together then?"

"Have you ever been happy when we were?"

"Sometimes when we were children: when we danced: the night in the fog in London. . . ."

He put his hands under her arms and drew her down to lie beside him, on the bed. The rain hit the windows like rice; the fire roared hollowly; the autumn afternoon discoloured into darkness. She shut her eyes and tried to go back to her girlhood and the empty house, with sun coming into the dusty room. Vesey had said: "I wish the bed were still here. We could draw the curtains round, and lie down side by side."

They lay side by side and Vesey stroked her hair away from her temples. When they kissed, she could imagine, in the darkness under her eyelids, the evening sun, the empty air. Perhaps from below, in the tangled garden little Joseph would begin to call them. "Vesey! Harriet!" She saw him running on the rough lawns, his hands cupped at his mouth, calling "Coo-ee! Coo-ee!" as they did when they had played hide-and-seek.

"What are you thinking?" Vesey asked. He took her wrist and shook it gently.

When Charles had gone, Kitty said: "I didn't understand one word of all that. I could only gather that he is rather angry with you."

She insulated herself with boredom.

"He has, I suppose, every reason to be."

"What will you do?"

"If only we could have had a little longer. Do? I don't know. I'm as deeply in as Reggie Beckett."

"How did Charles find out?"

"One of his clients . . . when nothing in the way of dividends was forthcoming, he threatened to go to Charles. Things promised no better; so he did."

"Poor Charles!" Kitty said easily.

"I didn't mean any of this to happen. It seemed foolproof. A great shock to him, of course. . . ."

"Where has he gone now? I thought he was off somewhere for the week-end. A conference, was it?"

"I think he went home instead."

Kitty thought: 'Well, I hope he won't get another shock there.' She said nothing. While they awaited catastrophe, she thought she would varnish her nails. She looked a picture of perfect calm; but she was inwardly disturbed by all the questions that she would not deign to ask. She thought: 'I married Tiny for better, for worse; but I thought "worse" was just Tiny himself; not any added

249

calamity. It will be too bad if I am to be poor, or disgraced as well.'

Charles had not looked forward to telling Harriet the bad news; but when he found that he could not, he was quite frustrated. Very rarely had he been in the house when it was empty. He discovered that his steps on the polished boards had a different sound and that a closed smell pervaded the rooms.

Threads of rain appeared on the windows. He could not understand why the fires were built in the grates, but were unlit, and wondered where Harriet was. He opened the engagement-book on her desk, but the week-end was a blank.

When he found the cat shut in a shed with plates of food and her basket, he began to feel alarm. He went up to their bedroom and began to open drawers and look into the cupboards. Nothing seemed to be missing. Her pearls lay in their case; her diamond earrings in their box; her slippers by the fire. She had gone out, but perhaps only for a little while. As she was not at Kitty's, he telephoned his mother, whose insinuations tormented him.

He looked at the clock. He could not have a drink even, because it was not quite opening-time, and it would have seemed utterly debauched to him to begin before six o'clock. But as soon as the clock struck the hour, he poured himself a large glassful of gin and put it at one end of the piano and sat down to play. He played, he thought, with marked brilliance, although there were so many interruptions. He had to get up to draw the curtains and put a match to the fire, and fill his glass. At seven, his mother telephoned to ask if Harriet had returned. "You *are* a fool, Charles," she told him. "I'll ring again in an hour."

"But why?"

"To find out if she's come back; but she won't have."

"Well, please don't. I'm busy."

250

As he walked away from the telephone, he thought: 'I don't want to wait here; but there is nowhere I can go.' He imagined himself ostracised at the golf-club or in the Saloon Bar at the Bull; his erstwhile companions turning their backs as he entered, avoiding his greeting.

Drinking seemed to agglomerate all his feelings, so that self-pity and indignation lay side by side with pride and scorn. His lips moved as he played. He argued continuously with himself; explained to Harriet; inveighed against Tiny and Reggie Beckett. After a while, his hands dropped on to his knees. He knew his real bitterness was with Harriet.

He stood up rather shakily and poured himself another drink. "You are not fit to be the mother of my child," he suddenly said, loudly and dramatically; but then the absurdity hit him. His mood crumpled; he felt that everything had been taken from him in one day.

At half-past eight, he began to fear the sound of the telephone and his mother's cruel questioning. He knew, by the strangeness of the room, that he had been drinking too much. The chairs held out their arms imploringly and had a waiting look; the stillness of things seemed only temporary and some objects, for no reason, detached themselves from their background and came very close to him. "Too much gin," he explained to himself, "and I must go on like this until closing-time."

But the sound of a key in the front-door sobered him. He heard footsteps in the hall, and the telephone ringing. The footsteps paused and then retreated. He heard Harriet's light, tired voice. "What do you want, Julia? . . . I've been out all day with friends . . . oh, please don't make mysteries . . . of course, I've come back."

Charles braced himself to hear this over again, but Harriet put down the receiver and went upstairs.

'Mother didn't get the truth,' he thought. He wondered what Harriet would say to him, and which friends she would choose to have been with. 'If that were really

251

true, it would be wonderful,' he thought.

When she came in, he felt that there was no chance of escaping her lies. 'She will be cool and rude and rebuking,' he thought, 'because she is so desperately defensive.' He saw no way out for either of them. She would not tell him the truth and he could not endure her deceit.

"Hello, Charles."

She stood behind a chair, with her hands laid nervously on the top of it. They were blue with the cold. He supposed that she did not express surprise at his presence lest he should retaliate with questions about her absence. He could imagine her falsely haughty replies.

"You look cold. Would you like a drink?"

"Yes, please."

"Whisky? Gin?"

When he handed it to her, he touched her cold fingers. She went back behind her chair.

"Better?" he asked, watching her sip.

"Yes. Thank you. Your mother telephoned as I came in. She wanted to know where I was."

"Oh, yes."

Harriet shut her eyes and drained her glass.

"I didn't tell her the truth."

"Indeed, why should you?"

"I said I had been to see some friends; but I was really with Vesey."

Embarrassment stiffened her mouth. She said the name clumsily.

He took her glass and filled it. Now that he had the truth from her, he had no knowledge of how to behave. 'How sad that we can't speak to one another without a drink to help us along!' he thought. 'Is shyness the only feeling we are ever to share?'

"I'm glad you told me."

"I was not afraid; but deeply embarrassed."

"I know. Either means you don't love me."

252

"One *can* be embarrassed—hopelessly embarrassed—with people one loves."

"Perfect love casteth out awkwardness," he said solemnly.

She glanced at him in doubt. It was plain that he had been drinking too much; but was perhaps masquerading as worse than he was.

"It was kind of you to come back," he went on.

"Not *kind*."

"Why did you?"

"I meant not to . . ."

"But with the best will in the world you found you must."

He veered uncertainly from one mood to another: words were more like prevailing winds than any expression of his course, or destination. 'In this way, we shall come to grief,' she thought, but felt too tired to be so careful.

"You thought of your husband and child," Charles suggested. "And of the little cat shut up in the shed. Have some more gin?"

"Not for a moment. Why are you here, Charles?"

"I had some bad news before I could leave this morning and after that I couldn't leave."

"What was it?"

"It has all been rather a day." He put his hand over his eyes for a moment as if he could not sort out his thoughts. "Reggie Beckett has disappeared, leaving Tiny to clear up the sort of mess that never can be cleared up."

Harriet came cautiously from behind her chair, and held her hands out over the fire. "Yes?"

"Oh, you wouldn't understand. Kitty, for instance, finds it all terribly tedious."

"Explain, though!"

"Reggie wanted some capital for a company he had floated . . . oh, this was some time ago. All he needed was a patent from some man . . . quite up in the air, but Tiny saw himself making a fortune, and he put in money. Then, of course, he was in a good position to find other people to do the same . . . Reggie offered him five per cent on all he could get invested . . . they were all our clients, of course . . . used to coming to us for advice, easily persuaded. I wish you would have another drink."

"In a moment."

"Their trouble was that the patent was sold to someone quite different, who has, put the thing into production, and it is they who will make the fortune, not Tiny, or Reggie. They have all thrown their money down a deep, deep well. First, restlessness set in; then suspicion. This morning, it was all made clear. I blame myself; I shut my eyes to a good many things."

"Charles, I am so sorry."

"Kitty's first words were 'Are we going to be poor?' You emerge from the test better."

"I wonder what will happen?"

"Perhaps we can rise above it," Charles said grandly.

"Don't have another drink."

"Oh, Harriet, darling, why did you come home? I am afraid that you just thought that I might be here."

"No."

"Then why?"

She rested her arms on the chimney-piece and her head on her arms. "I will be different. You shall never be worried again. If you could forgive me . . ." She made a fence of little phrases, which seemed a treachery to herself.

Waiting in terror as he came across the room towards her, she felt his shadow fall over her and wondered how she could bear the moment when he touched her. Instead, he put out his hand and took up the cigarette-box.

"I won't ever ask you why you came back, or what happened. I'm jealous of Vesey, but I don't want you to love me in that way. Marriage seems serious to me. I despise people who give in. And I like the idea of you as my wife, and the authority, the position, we have together. Patience

254

is needed to make a marriage—a pity to throw it away. And now that I'm in deep water, this house, and you in it, means more. If you had really gone—and on this particular night—you'd have taken my pride and courage with you. As long as you're here, it's all merely a challenge to me. The sort of thing I can manage—dealing with people, and earning our living."

Then, feeling that more confidence was returning to him than was justified, he quickly lit a cigarette and began to walk about the room.

"I think I should like another drink now," Harriet said. She watched him as he poured it out, and then before she lifted the glass, said: "I hope I can help you. I will try. And won't worry you in other ways."

"My dear girl, don't cry, don't cry! It would be the last straw."

She smiled. "Then I won't." But, choking a little over her gin, she felt the tears began to fall. She turned her back to him, and wiped them quickly away.

"Of course, Italy's out of the question now," Charles said.

5

AT the end of the assembly hall, across the great lake of parquet, Miss Bell was decorating the Christmas tree for what Miss Anstruther called 'the Poor Children's Party'. The next day, her girls would distribute its presents and hand round gaudy jellies. The children would call them 'miss'. Some of the nicer girls would feel foolish and false; others would glow with their good work. Miss Bell, hanging up frosty bells and coloured balls, merely carried out orders.

Outside, the light thickened into darkness; the hall with its smell of yew and floor-polish looked mysterious and exciting to Betsy. She took a little slide towards the Christmas-tree and walked round it admiringly.

"You are here late," Miss Bell said.

"I had a talking-to. About my essay on Rossetti. She said it was morbid."

"She?"

"Miss Matherson-Smith. I thought she meant just anything about Rossetti, and I wrote about him digging up his wife's body to get at the poems he'd buried with her . . . nice and gruesome . . . her hair came away with the poems . . . madly decomposed, of course."

"My dear Betsy, please!"

"Well, it *ought* to have been about 'The Blessed Damozel'. . . . Can I put some of the stars on?"

"If you are careful. They have to last from year to year."

"Yes, they were here when I first came."

A sadness fell over them. Miss Bell switched on one of the lights. It shone down over the tree and a brass-rubbing of a crusader on the wall behind.

"You *will* give me your address?"

"Yes, of course, Betsy."

Miss Bell could foresee the carefully chosen Christmas-card; the letters, growing shorter; and by next Christmas, no card at all.

"I think perhaps you ought to be getting home," she said.

"Just let me hang up a few more. The tinsel's dreadfully tarnished. I love Christmas . . . everything about it. . . ."

"Are you happy now?"

"If only you weren't going. I wish you would tell me where it is."

"A school in London, to teach Latin."

"And Greek?"

"Latin," Miss Bell said flatly.

"Miss Bell . . ."

"Yes?"

Betsy plunged her hands right into the prickly branches to hang up a frosted ball; she felt the sharp needles on her wrists and suffered them as if they were a punishment. She wanted to say: "I sometimes said things without knowing if they were true." But she could not. She was obliged to let Miss Bell go with whatever vision of her mother she had in her mind.

"What is it, Betsy?"

"Nothing. I am sorry you aren't going to teach Greek as well."

"Yes, it is a pity."

Miss Bell took out from its tissue-paper a rather dis-coloured wax fairy doll, and mounted the steps to tie it to the topmost branch.

Vesey said: "Mother, please not to pry. Just throw all the papers into the suitcase."

He sat down suddenly on the edge of the bed, feeling dizzy, frozen round the mouth.

257

"I'm not prying: but other people's things are so intriguing. Whose photograph is it in the paper-bag?"

"Harriet's."

"I do think it is touching of you to love your childhood's playmate still."

"Why is it so much against people to have known them a long time?"

"It does work that way. The further one looks back, the duller and duller one's friends seem to have been."

"You are a strange sight, mother, in this shoddy room."

She could not resist glancing in the mirror. Dressed in pale grey, her only touch of colour was her lavender hair.

"Well, dear, there it is: it need never have happened."

Vesey swung his legs up on to the bed and lay back with his eyes shut.

"When Harriet comes, there is a fiction I want you to support. I'm going home with you, you understand, only for the time-being; then I am off to South Africa. Father is sending me."

"And he would, my love, if it is what you want. It has all been nonsense between the two of you . . . both so self-willed."

"It is only what I have told Harriet. She is coming to say good-bye to me before sailing. Even her husband feels I am a poor challenge to him now."

"Well, I do wish she would hurry. Stanley's coming for us in the car at five."

"And who is Stanley?"

"Surely you remember? He's an old friend of the family."

Vesey smiled at her new euphemism.

"One of those dull ones from the old days?"

Barbara took some bronze chrysanthemums out of some bronze-coloured water, and stood there while slime dripped from the stalks. "Where can I put these? God, what a stench!"

"In the waste-paper-basket by the chest-of-drawers," Vesey said tiredly.

"Doesn't that woman ever clean your room? Everything is so filthy. And your shoes, Vesey! They have great holes in the bottoms. No wonder you are always having influenza."

She opened drawers and bundled his clothes into the suitcase. In the middle of doing so, she suddenly sat down on a chair and began to cry.

Vesey turned his head weakly, irritably, towards her and asked: "What is it? Please don't!"

"No, I mustn't, because of Stanley coming. Yet I can't stop. I didn't ever mean it to be like this. When you were a little boy, I always imagined we'd have fun when you grew up . . . go out together. I can't think how it has all happened so differently . . . finding you in this terrible slum, this dirty room, and your shirts an absolute disgrace. . . . I suppose that, as usual, I am to blame."

Vesey lay with his hands clasped above his head. He tried to remember his father's flat: the blonde satin; the pale furniture; the jardinière with strange ferns; the lacquer cabinet full of bottles. But he expected that it would all be changed—a different fashion now; perhaps Victoriana, with wax fruit and plush curtains.

Barbara dried her eyes carefully, restored her face and continued to pack. She had insisted on doing this while Vesey rested, partly from real alarm at his fatigue and partly as if to atone for a lifetime's neglect with half-an-hour's attention.

'I shall go to bed,' Vesey thought peacefully. 'I shall lie in a cool, smooth bed. When my father comes in, I shall pretend to be gravely ill, so that he will not rake up the past.'

"I can't think why you didn't send for me months ago," his mother said. "Look at these socks!"

But he did not look. He wondered how he would ever walk to the car when Stanley came; felt in a dream of weakness.

Barbara, with the packing finished, waited impatiently at the window.

"Would that ghastly woman bring us a cup of tea?"

"Perhaps; if you asked her nicely."

He knew that she would. She would perch on a corner of the table in that littered kitchen and give of her best, very woman-to-woman, falsely motherly, her condescension barely descernible.

Whenever he heard a car in the street, he wondered if it would be Harriet, or Stanley. He pictured Stanley as a music-hall bounder with a grey bowler and brown buttoned boots. He would call Barbara 'old girl'; but Vesey's position would bring out the best in him, as it could not in Vesey himself. He hoped that Harriet would come first, that his mother would leave them. He had nothing to say; but would like to see her sitting beside the bed, drinking tea, smiling awkwardly.

Although his eyes ached, he forced them open. When he closed them, he seemed to be floating; the bed dissolved under him.

In the kitchen, he could hear his mother talking about his influenza and a clatter of cups being set out. He heard a car slow and stop outside the house. A door was slammed. The footsteps across the pavement were light and quick. He raised himself and slid his feet down to the floor. The sound of the door-knocker seemed to be banging in his own heart. 'She is coming,' he thought, and he looked up through a shifting mist and saw her face. She put her bunch of flowers down on a chair and said his name and took him in her arms.

THE END